THE
DESCENT

BOOK THREE OF THE TAKER TRILOGY

ALMA KATSU

SAGA PRESS

LONDON SYDNEY **NEW YORK** TORONTO NEW DELHI

SAGA PRESS

AN IMPRINT OF SIMON & SCHUSTER, INC.

1230 AVENUE OF THE AMERICAS, NEW YORK, NEW YORK 10020

This Saga Press trade paperback edition January 2022

SAGA PRESS and colophon are trademarks of Simon & Schuster, Inc.

For information about special discounts for bulk purchases, please contact Simon & Schuster Special Sales at 1-866-506-1949 or business@simonandschuster.com.

The Simon & Schuster Speakers Bureau can bring authors to your live event. For more information or to book an event, contact the Simon & Schuster Speakers Bureau at 1-866-248-3049 or visit our website at www.simonspeakers.com.

Interior design by Jill Putorti

Manufactured in the United States of America

1 3 5 7 9 10 8 6 4 2

Library of Congress Cataloging-in-Publication Data is available.

ISBN 978-1-9821-6571-0
ISBN 978-1-4516-5185-0 (ebook)

PRAISE FOR ALMA KATSU
AND THE TAKER TRILOGY

"I was fascinated by the story—what a story!"

—Charlaine Harris, #1 *New York Times* bestselling author

"Katsu shows an acute understanding of human nature. . . . [She] is at her best when she forces her readers to stare at the almost unimaginable meeting of ordinary people and extraordinary desperation, using her sharp, haunting language."

—*USA Today*

"Alma Katsu's searing tale of otherworldly lovers and eternal obsession will seduce you from page one. . . . As irresistible as the hauntingly beautiful, pleasure-seeking immortals who scorch its pages. You have to experience it for yourself!"

—Kresley Cole, #1 *New York Times* bestselling author

"A rare and addictive treat."

—Danielle Trussoni, *New York Times* bestselling author

"Beautiful, mesmerizing."

—*Library Journal*

"This is a great book. And by great, I mean devastatingly so, like reading *The Scarlet Letter* while riding a roller coaster, on acid. Seductive, daring, soaring, and ultimately gut-wrenching."

—Jamie Ford, *New York Times* bestselling author of
Hotel on the Corner of Bitter and Sweet

"More than a wee bit dark, and super sexy."

—*Cosmopolitan*

"A dark, gothic epic that moves effortlessly from the tempestuous past to the frightening present."

—M. J. Rose, internationally bestselling author of
The Witch of Painted Sorrows

ALSO BY ALMA KATSU

For my husband, Bruce.
Thanks for keeping things from falling apart.

Hell is empty and all the devils are here.

—William Shakespeare, *The Tempest*

PROLOGUE

The dreams came almost every night.

At first, I almost didn't take notice of them. When they started, Luke had been gone only a few months and I was in that black fog that follows the death of a loved one. During the day, grief would fall on me suddenly. I'd look at the clock to find that an hour had passed and yet I couldn't account for the time. Evenings were worse; I'd lie alone in the bed Luke and I had shared waiting for the night to inch by. Evening meant long hours of insomnia, listlessness, fitful snatches of sleep, and the pale lavender-gray of dawn coming too soon. The occasional nightmare could do little to impress me compared to that slow hell.

I first realized I was having nightmares when bits would suddenly bob to the surface of my consciousness: a flash of pale pink flesh, soft ochre candlelight, a streak of crimson blood.

It was only by the end of the fourth month, when I started to have something resembling rest again, that the nightmares bled through, and I couldn't fail to take notice of them then.

What made them especially unsettling was that they were not about Luke but about Jonathan. I hadn't thought about Jonathan in a long time, certainly not after Luke and I settled on the upper peninsula of Michigan, in that lovely cottage where we lived together for four years. It would've been logical for Luke to be the one haunting my subconscious considering what we'd gone through at the end: his long, lingering illness; months shuttling him through rounds of treatments that all turned out to be for naught; weeks in the ICU; and the final stretch in the hospice, where he waited to die. That living nightmare had consumed my days for our last nine months together, and I couldn't see any reason why it shouldn't consume my sleeping hours as well.

I remember quite vividly the dream that made me realize something unusual was going on. It started up like the beginning of a movie I'd seen before, and sensing that I was about to have the same nightmare I'd by then been having nightly, I tried to wake myself up. But that never works in dreams, does it? No matter how hard you try, you can't make yourself wake up. Instead, it's like you're Houdini trussed up in a straitjacket and chains and submerged in a dread that's numbing and deadly, like ice-cold water. There's nothing you can do but struggle against the restraints in the hope of freeing yourself or just keep going until, by the mercy of God, you're released from the dream's stifling clutches.

The dreams always took place somewhere that was both familiar and yet unknown to me, in the peculiar way that the subconscious works. Sometimes it was in a dark, shaggy forest that could almost be the Great North Woods that had surrounded my childhood home of St. Andrew, but was not; or a crumbling castle that I might've visited during my never-ending travels, but had not; or a dilapidated mansion with broken plaster walls and ruined woodwork that could've been one of the houses I'd lived in during my long, circuitous life, but was not. Strangely familiar, familiarly strange, these settings that tried to embrace me and push me away at the same time.

The dream that struck me as too strange to be simply the normal functioning of the unconscious mind started abruptly in a new setting, a dark, narrow passage whose walls were made of huge stone blocks. Those walls gave the impression that I was in a solidly made old fortress. From the cold dampness of the stone and the tang of mildew in the air, I assumed the passage was underground. It went on and on, turning and turning again, twisting in on itself like a maze. What's more, the passage was disconcertingly narrow: a normal-size person wouldn't have been able to fit, and small as I am I could barely squeeze through. I hurried along as quickly as I could, desperate to get out of the claustrophobic space.

Finally, I came to a door. It seemed to be as broad as it was tall and somewhat crudely made, its heavy wooden planks held together with metal straps. The wood stain had yellowed with time and almost glowed beckoningly in the darkness, but up close, the lovely patina gave way to a frenzy of scratches, as though the door had been attacked by frantic clawed animals.

Although this subterranean room was likely used for storage or perhaps as a wine cellar, the knot in my stomach told me that probably wasn't the case. I knew from other dreams on other nights what I would find behind the door; something bad awaited me and I didn't want to go on. I wanted to wake up, to break the dream's horrible spell, but once I'd entered the dream world, I was locked in, doomed to play out the dream to its end.

I opened the door. Air rushed at me, damp and foul, the way air smells and feels when it has been shut up underground. There was very little light and I could see only a few feet in front of me. I sensed movement in the darkness ahead and went toward it. You might even say that I went toward it *because* of what was waiting for me, something I was helpless to resist under any circumstances.

The first thing I saw were his hands: a man's hands wearing heavy iron manacles. Then I saw his arms, drawn overhead by a chain attached to the manacles. There were nights in my dreams when the man had been forced to dangle at the end of his chain, and let me tell you, that was a horrible sight, tendons strained to the snapping point, his arms wrenched from their sockets. Tonight, he had been allowed to stand, though his feet could barely touch the ground. Even though I couldn't see the man's face, I knew who it was; I could tell by the broad shoulders and the long torso, the elegant natural arch to the small of his back. All I could see of his face was a cheekbone and part of his jaw, visible through a tangle of disheveled black hair, but that, too, was enough.

It was Jonathan, stripped naked and bound in chains. Every one of the dreams, regardless of where it was set or how it started, always ended the same way, with Jonathan being tortured and punished by someone I couldn't see, for reasons I wasn't told. As he hung from his manacles, he reminded me of Saint Sebastian, his flesh pale and his head tilted sideways as though nobly resigned to his fate, ready to endure whatever punishment awaited him. There were bruises on his otherwise perfect body: a bloom of red and purple on one hip, a darker, larger one running the length of his right flank. His upper back bore crosshatched scrapes. He gleamed from head to toe with sweat and was flecked with grime. Needless to say, seeing him like this was a punch to the gut and made me violently ill. It also repulsed me to realize that despite his brutalized condition, I still found him beautiful—because it was impossible for him *not* to be.

I called his name but he couldn't hear me. It was as though we were in two separate rooms and I was looking at him through soundproof glass. It was then that I realized his wounds weren't healing instantly as they had when he was immortal, the same as I, and this meant he was again made of flesh and blood. And if he were mortal, that also meant it was possible for him to feel pain again. He was suffering.

The last I had known, Jonathan had been sent back to the underworld, to the land of the dead. It was his second trip, making him one of the select few—perhaps the only one, as far as I knew—to die twice. Four years ago, Jonathan had told the necromancer who'd brought him back that life continued on the other side, and in this life, he'd been made the consort of the queen of the underworld. When Jonathan had been dispatched a second time, I assumed he was gone forever, that his soul had gone back to the land of the dead, the queen's domain—whoever *she* was.

Now I was having these nightmares, and they came to me almost every night. I couldn't understand why I would dream of Jonathan—and why those dreams would repeatedly be filled with him being viciously tortured. He hadn't been on my mind at all. I'd forgiven him long ago. As a matter of fact, I'd been the one to dispatch him from this world the first time, and that was only because he had begged me to. Under the conditions of our strange curse, it was the only way for him to end his immortal life, which he deeply wanted. I still felt guilty for what I'd done; after all, who can take the life of the person they love—even if it's at his request—and not be torn apart by it? Still, I would've thought that if I were going to dream about anyone, it would be Luke, so recently departed from my side.

But it was Jonathan.

In my horrific nightmare that night, I tried (as always) to set him free. The chain that the manacles were attached to fed through a pulley in the ceiling that was affixed with a padlock to a ring bolted into a stone block. First, I tried to pry off the padlock but it held firm. Then, I began to search the floor on my hands and knees, groping in the darkness for a key, thinking I might find one for either the padlock or the manacles. The entire time, Jonathan stood quietly, his arms stretched overhead, oblivious to me, unconscious on his feet.

It wasn't until I heard him make a sound, halfway between a grunt and a gasp, that I whirled back to look at him and, for the first time in any of these dreams, saw a sign of another person. A hand snaked lovingly along the side of his face, cupping his jaw. It was a woman's hand, elegant and long, whiter than snow. He didn't fight her. He let her caress him. I would be lying if I said that the sight of a woman's hand didn't unnerve me. It wasn't because a woman was involved—this was Jonathan, after all; it was only natural that a woman would be involved. No, there was something strangely inhuman about that hand. I wanted to cry out and demand that she release him, but I couldn't. In that peculiar way of dreams, I couldn't scream. I couldn't make a sound. My throat was shut tight, paralyzed with fear and anger.

Then I woke up, exhausted and drenched in sweat. These dreams that continued to plague me night after night were taking a toll on me—and I was beginning to believe they were *meant* to, that they were a sign that Jonathan needed me. But Jonathan was no longer on this earth. He had gone to a place where I couldn't follow. Yet, if he needed me, how could I not go to him? And there was only one person I knew who could help me. Only one man could get me to where Jonathan was.

ONE

The sunlight glinting off the Mediterranean that afternoon was bright enough to blind, and the boat bounced hard off the waves like a broken-down carnival ride. I'd come halfway around the world to find someone who was very important to me, and I wouldn't let a little rough weather keep me from finishing my journey. I squinted against the headwind to the horizon, trying to will a rocky shoreline to appear out of nowhere.

"Is it much farther?" I asked the captain.

"Signorina, until I met you this morning, I never knew this island even existed, and I have lived on Sardegna my entire life." He was in his fifties if he was a day. "We must wait until we get to the coordinates, and then we will see what we shall see."

My stomach floated unsteadily, due to nerves and not the waves. I had to trust that the island would be where it was supposed to be. I'd seen strange things in my lifetime—my *long* lifetime—many of them stranger than the sudden appearance of an island that heretofore had not existed. That would be a relatively minor miracle, on the scale of such things, considering I'd already lived over two hundred years and was destined to live forever. But I was a mere babe compared to the man I was going to see, Adair, the man who had given me—or burdened me, depending on your point of view—with eternal life. His age was inestimable. He could've been a thousand years old, or older. He'd given differing stories every time we met, including the occasion of our last parting four years ago. Had he been a student of medicine in medieval times, devoted to science and caught in the thrall of alchemy, intent on discovering new worlds? Or was he a heartless manipulator of lives and souls, a man without a conscience who was interested only in extending his life for the pursuit of pleasure? I didn't think I'd gotten the truth yet.

We had a tangled history, Adair and I. He had been my lover and my teacher, master to my slave. We had literally been prisoner to each other. Somewhere along the way he fell in love with me, but I was too afraid to love him in return. Afraid of his unexplainable powers, and his furious temper. Afraid of what I knew he was capable of and afraid to learn he was already guilty of committing far worse. I ran away to follow a safer path with a man I could understand. I always knew, however, that my path would one day lead back to Adair.

Which is how I came to be in a small fishing boat, far off the Italian coast. I wrapped my sweater more tightly around my shoulders and rode along with the ship's rocking, and closed my eyes for a moment's rest from the glare. I had shown up at the harbor in Olbia looking to hire a boat to take me to an island everyone said didn't exist. "Name your price," I said when I'd gotten tired of being ridiculed. Of the boat owners who were suddenly interested, he seemed the kindest.

"Have you been to this area before? Corsica, perhaps?" he asked, trying either to make small talk or to figure out what I expected to find at this empty spot in the Mediterranean Sea.

"Never," I answered. The wind tossed my blond curls into my face.

"And your friend?" He meant Adair. Whether he was my *friend* or not, I didn't know. We'd parted on good terms, but he could be mercurial. There was no telling what mood he'd be in the next time we met.

"I think he's lived here for a few years," I answered.

Even though it appeared that I'd piqued the captain's interest, there was nothing more to say, and so the captain busied himself with the GPS and the ship's controls, and I went back to staring over the water. We had cleared La Maddalena Island and now faced open sea.

Before long, a black speck appeared on the horizon. "Santa Maria," the captain muttered under his breath as he checked the GPS again. "I tell you, signorina, I sail through this area every day and I have never seen that"—he pointed at the landmass, growing in size as we approached—"before in my life."

As we got closer, the island took shape, forming a square rock that jutted up out of the sea like a pedestal. Waves crashed against it on all sides. From the distance, there didn't appear to be a house on the island, nor any people.

"Where is the dock?" the captain asked me, as though I'd know. "There is no way to put you ashore if there is no dock."

"Sail all the way around," I suggested. "Perhaps there's something on the other side."

He brought his little boat around and we circled slowly. On the second side was another cliff, and on the third, a steep slope dropped precipitously to a stony and unwelcoming beach. On the fourth side, however, there was a tiny floating dock tethered to a rock outcropping, and a rickety set of sunburnt stairs leading to a stone house.

"Can you get close to the dock?" I shouted into the captain's ear to be heard above the wind. He gave me an incredulous look, as though only a crazy person would consider climbing onto the floating platform.

"Would you like me to wait for you?" he asked as I prepared to climb over the side of the boat. When I shook my head, he protested, "Signorina, I cannot leave you here! We don't know if it is safe. The island could be deserted . . ."

"I have faith in my . . . friend. I'll be fine. Thank you, Captain," I said, and leapt onto the weatherworn wooden dock, which bucked against the waves. He looked absolutely apoplectic, his eyes bulging as I climbed the staircase, gripping the railing as I struggled against the wind. When I got to the top, I waved to him, signaling that he should go, and watched as his boat turned back the way we had come.

The island was exactly as it had appeared from the sea. It seemed carved from one lump of black stone that had emerged directly from the ocean floor. It had no vegetation except for a stand of scraggy pines and a bright chartreuse carpet of moss spread at their roots. A few goats ran by and seemed to regard me with an amused, knowing air before they scampered out of sight. They had long, silky coats of many colors and one had a frightening pair of twisted horns, wicked-looking enough to be worn by the devil.

I turned to the house, so ancient and solid that it seemed to have grown straight from the bedrock of the island. The house was a curious thing, its stone walls so sandblasted by weather that it was impossible to tell much about it, including when it might've been built, though it resembled a fortress—small and compact yet just as imposing. The front door was a big slab of wood that had been thoroughly dried and bleached by the sun. It had elaborate ironwork hinges and was decorated with iron studs in the Moorish style, and gave the impression that it could withstand anything, even a battering ram. I lifted the knocker and brought it down once, twice, three times.

When I heard nothing from the other side of the door, however, I started to wonder if maybe I'd made a mistake. What if the captain had misread his charts and left me on the wrong island—what if Adair had moved back to civilization on the mainland by now? I'd tracked him down through a man named Pendleton who'd acted as Adair's servant until Adair chose to go into seclusion. While Pendleton wasn't sure what had caused Adair to withdraw from the world, he gave me coordinates to the island, which he admitted was so small that it appeared on no maps. He warned me there was no easy way to get in touch with Adair, as he didn't use email and didn't seem to have a phone. I had no intention of alerting him to my arrival anyway—force of habit made me wary of Adair still, but I also didn't want to risk being put off or dissuaded from coming.

I knew Adair was somewhere in the area, though, because I felt his presence, the unceasing signal that connected him to each of the people he'd gifted with eternal life. The presence felt like an electronic droning in my consciousness that wouldn't stop. It would fall off when he was far away—as it had the last four years—or grow stronger when he was close. This was the strongest it had been in a while—and was competing with the butterflies in my stomach in anticipation of seeing him again.

I was distressed to hear that Adair was living by himself, particularly because it was such a remote location. Now that I saw the island, I was more worried still. The house looked as though it had no electricity or running water, not unlike where he might've lived in the eighteenth century. I wondered if this return to a way of life that was familiar to him could be a sign that he was overwhelmed by the present and couldn't cope with the never-ending onslaught of the new. And for our kind, retreating into the past was never good.

I sought out Adair now after four years apart only because I'd been seized by an idea that I wanted to put into action, and I needed his help to make it work. I had no notion, however, if he still cared for me enough to help me, or if his love had dried up when it went unreciprocated.

I knocked again, louder. If worse came to worst, I could find a way into his house and wait for Adair to return. It seemed an arduous trip to make for nothing. Given my immortal condition, it wasn't as though I needed anything to live on, food or water, or that I couldn't deal with the cold (though there was split wood stacked against the side of the house and three chimneys, each with multiple lots, visible on the roof). If he didn't return after a reasonable length of time, I had my cell phone and the harbormaster's number, though the captain had warned me that reception was nearly impossible to get this far off the coast. If I was lucky, however, I might be able to flag down a passing boat . . .

The door flung back at that instant, and to my surprise, a thin woman with brassy blond hair stood before me. She was in her late twenties, I would guess, and though pretty, she was worn around the edges in a way that made me think she'd worked hard at enjoying life. She had on a wrinkled sundress and sandals, and hoop earrings that were big enough to wear as bracelets. Unsurprisingly, she regarded me with suspicion.

"Oh! I'm sorry—I hope I'm not on the wrong island," I said, regaining my wits in time to remember to be charming, all the while thinking: *In seclusion, my ass, Pendleton.* "I'm looking for a man by the name of Adair. I don't suppose there's anyone here by that name?"

She cut me off so sharply that I almost didn't get the last word out. "Is he expecting you?" She spoke with a working-class British accent. Over her shoulder, a second woman stepped into view at the other end of the hall, a full-figured woman with long dark-brown hair. Her skirt came down to her ankles and she wore embroidered Turkish slippers on her feet. Aside from their shared displeasure at seeing me, the pair of young women was physically as dissimilar as two women could be.

"No, he doesn't know I was coming, but we're old friends and—"

The two of them crowded the doorway now, shoulder

to shoulder, a barricade of crossed arms and frowns set on lipsticked mouths. Up close like this, I could see that they were very pretty. The blonde was like a model, thin and boyish, while the brunette was lush and womanly, and a picture of them in bed with Adair came to my mind unbidden, the three in a tangle of bare arms and legs, heavy breasts and silken flanks. Their lips on his chest and groin, and his head thrown back in pleasure. A wave of hurt passed over me, tinged with that particular sense of belittlement rarely felt out of adolescence. I fought the urge to turn around and flee.

Had I been wrong to come here? No, knowing Adair hadn't changed and had returned to his sybaritic ways made my task easier. There would be no strings, no possibility of reconciliation. I could forget about everything except asking for Adair's help.

"Look, girls," I started, shifting the weight of the knapsack in my hands. "Would you mind if I came inside to get out of this wind before I'm blown off a cliff? And if one of you would be so kind as to let Adair know that he has a visitor? My name is—"

"Lanore." His voice rang in my ear, rushing to fill a space left empty. And then he appeared at the end of the hall, a shadowy figure backlit by the sun. My heart raced, being in his presence once again. Adair, the man who'd hurt and deceived me, loved and exalted me, brought a man back from the dead for me, given me all of time in the hope I would share it with him. Did he still love me enough to help me?

As I stood in Adair's magnetic presence, everything that had happened between us rushed back to me in a tumult, all that passion and anger and hurt. The chaos of the strange world I had known when I'd lived with him tugged at me. I stood at his door ready to ask him to take a journey with me—a journey that wasn't without risk. The bond between us might be ruined forever. Still, I had no choice. No one else could help me.

A new chapter in our history was about to begin.

TWO

The girls stepped aside without a word, making room for Adair as he approached the front door. I could see him better as he moved out of the sunlight. I knew, of course, that physically, he would be unchanged from the last time I'd seen him. He was the same height and weight. His face was the same, with those arresting, wolfish eyes of green and gold. He wore his beard a little thicker, and had grown his curly dark hair to his shoulders, though at the moment it was held back in a loose plait. The only change—and it was striking—was in his manner.

Adair was one of those people who came off from the first as aggressive and intimidating, the kind of man who naturally set other alpha males bristling. Menace always seemed to crackle just under the surface, and once you got to know him, it only got worse. His moods were changeable and you were never quite sure where you stood with him. Remarkably, that tension was now nearly gone. His natural aggression was nearly undetectable. He was subdued, though I suppose it might've been from the shock of seeing me.

"I can't believe you came back—" Adair began, his voice full of emotion, but then stopped himself. He reached for my hand and drew me over the threshold, continuing in a more restrained fashion. "Come in, don't stand outside. A person could be killed by the wind out there."

"I hope I'm not intruding," I said as I squeezed past the two women, who stared down on me coldly.

"Not at all. We don't often get visitors—as you can imagine, given the isolation—so your arrival is a surprise, that's all." Adair closed the door, and the four of us looked at one another awkwardly. "Well, I should introduce everyone. Robin, Terry, this is Lanore McIlvrae, an old friend of mine. And, Lanore, this is—"

"Robin and Terry, yes." Terry was the brunette, Robin the blonde. They took turns shaking my hand limply, as though the last thing they wanted to do was to let me into their house.

"How long has it been since you last saw each other?" Terry asked, arching an eyebrow at Adair, her arms folded over her ample chest.

"Four years," I answered.

"It seems—longer," Adair offered.

The women made no attempt to mask their hostility, and I started to feel that I'd made a bad mistake by coming without warning. They both oozed sexuality—you could tell by their dress and body language—and I could only speculate as to what I might've interrupted. Before I could sputter another apology for the intrusion, however, Adair asked, "Will you be staying?" and gestured to the knapsack I was holding before adding, "Oh, of course you will. I shouldn't even bother to ask: unless you have a boat at the dock or someone coming back for you soon, you'll need to stay overnight, at least. Though you're welcome to stay as long as you wish."

"I realize this is terribly inconvenient of me, showing up unannounced," I said, looking gratefully at the girls before turning back to Adair. "This isn't purely a social call. There's a reason why I'm here, Adair. I need to talk to you."

His expression darkened immediately. "It must be important for you to have made this journey. Shall we do that now? We can go to my study—"

Robin sighed irritably, shaking her head as she reached for my knapsack. "For pity's sake, did someone die or something? Surely that can wait till later. We should get you settled, find you a room first." She then started up the stairs without waiting for anyone to agree. He gave me a nod, indicating I should follow. I was sorry to leave him so soon but followed the blonde, the soles of her sandals scraping on the treads.

I glanced into the rooms we passed as we walked down the hall, mildly curious about the interior of this odd domicile. Adair was a rich man, after all, and could live in luxury and comfort anywhere in the world, so why had he chosen to hide away on this rock in the middle of the Mediterranean Sea with these two women? The fortress was built in a rustic Moorish style and seemed as unimproved on the inside as it was on the outside. There were no clues in the bedrooms, as each was plainly decorated and obviously unoccupied. Wooden beams spanned the low ceilings, and the walls were white-washed stone. The furniture was all rough-hewn and probably had been made on Sardegna or Corsica a century ago. Simple woven blankets covered the beds.

Of all the rooms we passed on the second floor, only one appeared to be in use. In it, a huge feather mattress lay directly on the floor, the tangle of white sheets hinting of wanton abandon. Old Moroccan lanterns fitted with candles circled the bed, which faced a high, wide window dressed in gauzy curtains, through which you could see a panoramic view of the sea. Discarded clothing lay all over the floor, including a pale pink brassiere—Terry's, by the size of it. Two more Turkish slippers sat at odd angles to each other, as though they'd been kicked off in a burst of bad temper. Adair's unmade bed stirred something near my heart, but the casually tawdry display of the women's clothing extinguished that stirring as easily as one might squeeze out the flame on a match head.

"Looking for something?" Robin asked, suddenly beside me, catching me gawking outside their bedroom. "You can't have this room. It's already taken," she said in her sharp way.

"I didn't mean to pry, but the door was open," I said apologetically.

She had a funny way about her, guileless, like a child. She stared at me flatly, as though she was trying to tell what was going on in my head. "You came here hoping to get back together with him—that's why you want to see if we're sleeping with him, isn't it?"

Heat rose up my neck and across my cheeks. "Not at all. He's a friend. I've come to see for myself that he's happy."

"You've come an awfully long way just for that." She narrowed her eyes at me. "That's not the only reason you came."

"No," I murmured. I saw no reason not to tell her the truth. "I need a favor from him."

"Must be some favor," she said, then stuck a lock of hair in her mouth and began sucking on it, as though she was simple-minded. It was an unnerving gesture.

"It is." The same anxiety I'd felt when I'd made up my mind to find Adair rose up in my chest, beating frantically like a bird was trapped inside me.

"And after you get what you want from him, will you leave us alone?" She practically spat the words at me. I didn't know what to say, but before I could gather my wits to answer, she spun on her heel and started down the hall again, my knapsack banging against her shins.

Before Adair and I could speak in private, there was dinner with the girls to endure. The meal was set at a dining table that wouldn't have looked out of place in a castle. The chairs were as ornately carved as thrones, the windows covered with long, heavy drapes of burgundy and gold. The walls were still fitted with iron brackets meant to hold flaming torches, now made obsolete by a huge crystal chandelier. It was too grand a setting for our small party, and made for a strange, off-kilter meal.

For dinner, Terry had roasted squabs and fresh greens tossed with olive oil. I assumed all the food came from their larder as the island appeared to have neither a chicken coop nor a garden. Adair and the girls ate with their fingers like hedonists, and their mouths were soon slick with squab fat and oil. The girls kept Adair merry, joking and flirting, and something was going on under the table, too, no doubt, a bare foot nestled in his lap or an eager hand stroking his thigh. They did their best to make me feel like an intruder, but I would be damned if I would let them intimidate me.

"How did you two meet Adair?" I asked as I picked at my salad with a fork.

Robin and Terry exchanged looks before the blonde answered. "It happened here on the island, actually. We were staying on Corsica, on holiday. Terry and I always go on holiday together, ever since we were kids. We go anywhere there's sun and heat . . ."

"And pretty men," Terry added, winking at Adair.

Robin poked tentatively at a piece of arugula. "Anyway, by the middle of the second week, it was getting sort of boring—"

"Too many German tourists," Terry interrupted, rolling her eyes. "Hans and Franz with their wives and their little Hanslings in tow. And the men all squeezed into Speedos. Too much white, middle-aged flesh on display for my taste. And, besides, it's not a proper holiday unless you find a complete stranger to shag. . . ." Terry watched to see if she'd managed to shock me, but I betrayed nothing.

"We hired a boat to take us out on an excursion, you know, to explore the little baby islands off the coast," Robin continued, fishing a segment of tangerine out of her salad between thumb and index finger, "and we came upon the black beach below. We'd never seen nothing like it, so we talked the captain into dropping us off for an afternoon of sunbathing."

"Oh, but it was too bloody cold for sunbathing," Terry said.

"We thought the place was deserted. So there we were, lying topless in the sun," Robin went on as though she hadn't been interrupted, "when we see *him* wandering toward us, head down, all lost in thought. I couldn't believe my eyes at first. I mean, we thought this place was deserted. Who'd have thought someone was living here on this rock all alone?"

"He invited us in for a drink, and one thing led to another . . ." Terry grinned wickedly at me, to make sure I understood what "the other thing" had been.

". . . and we've been here ever since," Robin finished.

"How long has it been now? Three months? Four?" Terry touched Adair's arm lightly to get his attention. There was something possessive about her gesture and he didn't seem to care for it, but he didn't say anything to her. He was a gentleman—up to a point.

"Four months? That's an awfully long holiday," I said, looking from one woman to the other. "What about the people back home, your family, your jobs? They're okay with the fact that you seem to have—um—checked out?"

"I suppose they're wondering if we've gone mad." Terry laughed raucously, throwing her head back, apparently not concerned in the least what anyone thought of her. "But they know we're adventurous girls. We couldn't turn down the opportunity. There'll be time enough to settle when we're older. In the meantime, will we ever get another chance to have an island all to ourselves, and to live in a fortress—with a man like Adair? Not bloody likely."

Adair pushed back from the table and rose. From the smoldering look on his face, I could tell that he'd had enough. "If you don't mind, girls, I think Lanore and I have something to discuss in private." He helped me up from my chair. "Let me show you the island."

The wind had eased since the sun went down, making it mild enough for a stroll. We were finally alone together, Adair and I. I was curious: in the house, he had seemed so changed, but maybe that was an act. Maybe he didn't want to lose his temper in front of his guests. Now that there was no one nearby, he could say what was really on his mind. Given how we'd parted, Adair might do or say anything—he might take me in his arms and kiss me, or he might chastise me for leaving him without a word in four years. He could even keep me here against my will, as he'd done once, though I sensed that he'd lost that kind of fire. I tingled from head to toe with wild impatience, waiting breathlessly to see if Adair would do something—or if *I* would be the one to do something impetuous. It felt like a devil was whispering in my ear to open the door to trouble and tell him that I'd missed him, that I had feelings for him that I'd never confessed. I kept my hands shoved into my pockets and my arms pressed tight to my sides until the feeling passed, until I could be sure that I wasn't about to do something I'd regret later.

There wasn't much to see on the island or far to go, and before long we were at the black-pebbled beach watching the last wisps of periwinkle sky sink into the sea. For all its roughness, the island was stunningly beautiful. Stars were just starting to emerge from the velvet canopy overhead. There wasn't the least bit of Italian coastline visible on the horizon. We might as well have been a million miles at sea and staring off the edge of the earth into infinity.

I looked back over my shoulder in the direction of the house. "I don't think the girls are happy that we went off by ourselves. I didn't mean to cause a big disruption. I hope this

won't make trouble for you later . . ." I began, but then realized
the absurdity of my words, to think that Adair would let himself be bullied by two angry women. The Adair I knew had
once fearlessly surrounded himself with murderers and thieves,
keeping these villains as his servants, and not one of them had
ever dared cross him. Had he changed so drastically that he
couldn't handle two jealous girlfriends?

He shrugged. "If they don't like it, they can leave at any
time."

"Have you made them—companions?" I asked as delicately
as I could. "Companion" was the term we used to refer to ourselves, those whom Adair had bound to him through the gift
of immortality. That was what we called ourselves in our more
discreet moments; we'd also used "captives" and "concubines,"
but mostly "others," because, by taking our mortality away
from us, Adair had made us something apart from humanity.
We were the others, no longer human and not like Adair,
either.

"I have no need for any more companions. I only let them
stay because, well . . ."

I raised an eyebrow. "I've *seen* them. I can imagine why you
let them stay."

He looked at me with mild annoyance. "Don't tell me that
you're jealous. You have no reason to be—*you* were the one to
leave *me*, as I remember. You didn't expect me to be celibate
after you left and went back to that man, did you?"

I turned into the breeze to cool my cheeks. "Of course I'm
not jealous. Look, we haven't seen each other in four years—
let's not start off with an argument, okay?"

He let his hands hang in the pockets of his greatcoat as he, too, turned into the wind. The loose strands of his long dark hair whipped behind him. "Of course. I don't want to argue with you, Lanore."

I longed to tuck my arm under his as we used to do when we walked along the streets of Boston many, many years ago, but I knew it was one of those crazy urges I had to guard against. It wouldn't do to get too close to Adair; I could lose my perspective, and it would be that much harder to do what I'd come to do. Instead, I asked, with forced cheer, "How did you end up here, anyway, after Garda? I would've thought you would've gone to see the world."

He nodded at the endless horizon. "Don't you think it's lovely here?"

"Lovely in its way, I suppose . . . but so isolated, stuck out here in the middle of the ocean. Tell me you haven't been here alone the entire time since I last saw you."

He shrugged, a little bit embarrassed by my pity. "Yes, for the most part. After you left, I stayed at the castle at Garda with Pendleton, but I couldn't stand living there. Your ghost was everywhere: in the mezzanine where we sat in the evenings and you told me about your life, in the bed we had shared. You must admit, when you left I had a lot to think about. I wasn't going to continue living the way I had before. . . . So I sent Pendleton on his way and came here to be by myself, and every day I circle the stone path and stare at the ocean to clear my head."

That meant he'd been on his own on the island for nearly four years, if the girls had joined him only recently. "Weren't you lonely?"

"No, not really. I needed the solitude. I needed to understand myself better and I wouldn't have been able to do that surrounded by others." He turned back to the fortress and we started to wander inland again. "What about you?" he asked. "What did you do after you left Garda?"

The wind was at our backs now and blew my hair over my shoulders and into my face and I had to brush strands out of my eyes. "Do you remember, when you'd finally caught up with me, the man who came to my rescue?"

"The doctor. Of course I remember him. I almost killed him."

"His name was Luke. You made me try to send him away so we would be together, you and I. But I'd already told him about you, and he didn't believe that I'd stay with you freely and refused to go. So you made him forget me, took away all his memories of me." Adair had made that part of my punishment for betraying him, for walling him up and leaving him entombed for two hundred years. He'd meant to strip me of everything, property, freedom—but especially love, the love of the man who had given up everything for me.

In the end, however, Adair couldn't go through with it. When he saw that I'd never come to love him as his prisoner, he set me free and told me to go after Luke. To find him and tell him who I was and what we had meant to each other. "I knew he'd go back to be near his daughters," I said, "and that's where I found him. I begged him to remember me. And because it was meant to be—just as you said—he listened, and he forgave me."

Adair flinched. "So, you have been with him the whole time we've been apart. And was it as you hoped? Were you happy together?"

I bowed my head. I didn't want to hurt him, but he should know the truth. "We were happy, yes."

He started to turn away from me. "So why have you come here—"

"Luke died a few months ago," I said, cutting him off. "It happened very quickly. When he took me back, we ended up living near his former wife so he could spend time with his daughters. He was practicing medicine again, and we'd just gotten the house remodeled the way we wanted." The words spilled out though I hadn't planned to tell Adair these details. But once I started, I couldn't stop. I suppose it was because I'd had no one else to tell. "The illness came on very suddenly. He went into the hospital and never came out. First there were tests, round after round, until they found the problem. A brain tumor." I swallowed and stared at my feet. "His doctors argued whether it was operable or not, but by then it was too late. Everything started to fail: memory, speech, vision. He had seizures. It was hard to watch." And hard to relive now in the retelling.

Adair stared at me intently. "I am sorry."

"I stayed in the house for a while. I'd gotten close to his daughters and his ex-wife. They've been nice to me, but I think they were beginning to wonder why I was still hanging around. After all, Luke was my only connection to the area. Aside from the three of them, I had no one else, no friends. I'm sure it seemed odd to them, based on what they knew of my past life. They thought it was so glamorous, the home in Paris, all the travel, and after Luke died, I think they expected me to go back to it." Adair knew, however, that my Paris house was gone: he'd burned it to the ground when he'd been trying to find me, to flush me out, to burn everything I owned as part of my punishment for what I'd done to him.

"So, your man is gone and you've come to see me," Adair said. There was a tiny uptick in his tone, a hint of expectation.

"It's not like that. I'm not ready to be with anyone yet," I rushed to tell him, wanting to be honest with him. Believing that I was being honest. I was still raw from Luke's passing. It had been only a few months.

Oh, but it was the wrong thing to say to Adair. His face crumpled a bit, and I felt his mood deflate, almost unperceivably. He took a moment to compose himself. "Then why are you here? Don't play games with me, Lanore—why did you come looking for me?"

His questions set my heart pounding hard in my chest. The time had come to tell him, to throw myself on his mercy. It felt too soon; I'd expected that we would've spent more time catching up, that I'd have a better chance to see where I stood with him, to find out if he'd forgiven me for breaking his heart. I couldn't risk that he'd refuse me. I needed him. He was the only one who would be able to help me get to the cause of the nightmares.

The goats chose that moment to come over, staring at us as though they'd never seen humans before. The one with the huge set of horns snorted under his breath as though making up his mind about something, but he didn't run away when I petted his shaggy head.

"You're right." I dropped my gaze, cowardly. "I've come for a reason. There is something I need to ask you to do for me, Adair."

Before I could utter another word, however, we were hit

by a sudden gust of cold air. A huge dark cloud was sweeping toward us from the sea. It unfurled across the entire horizon, black thunderheads roiling like a cauldron at full boil, lightning bursts blinking deep within the gray swells. A heavy sheet of rain dropped from the sky and swept across the waves, heading in our direction. I'd never seen a storm break so swiftly, especially one that size.

"That looks dangerous," I said, pointing to the sky. "We'll have to go in."

"It's nothing to be worried about. We get weather like this all the time." Adair tried to sound nonplussed, but I noticed that, for some unknown reason, he seemed to be looking at the dark clouds with suspicion. The first huge gust rolled in off the water, sending the goats running for the shelter of the pine trees. Adair placed a hand on my back to gently guide me to the house. As we approached the French doors off the dining room, I saw the two women silhouetted in the yellow light watching for our return, the brunette twitching with impatience. As we stepped through the door, the downpour started behind us in earnest.

I brushed my windblown hair back into place while Adair bolted the door. The women glared at him. "We wondered where you were. You'd been gone so long," Robin said to Adair in a whiny child's voice.

"Quite a storm out there, wouldn't you say? And strange that it came on us so quickly," Adair said under a furrowed brow. He seemed to be probing for something.

"That's how it is here, on the water," Terry replied breezily. Of the pair, she was the bold one, the one who would stand up to Adair. "Good thing you came in. Winds could blow someone as small as her right over a cliff," she said, nodding coolly at me.

Robin took Adair's hand and began to tug him toward the stairs. "C'mon, Adair, say good night to your guest. She must be tired after all that traveling," she said, though plainly it wouldn't matter to her if I keeled over from exhaustion at that very second. Adair opened his mouth to protest, but I shook my head.

"That sounds like a good idea," I said. "Robin's right. It's been quite a day, what with the travel and all. We can finish catching up tomorrow." I needed time, anyway, to make sense of the strange situation in which I'd found him.

Adair capitulated, tucking the blonde under his left arm and the brunette under his right. Thusly propped up, he turned away from me. "I guess this is good night, then. We'll see you in the morning." I watched them walk away, three abreast, the girls' hips swaying as they climbed the stairs.

THREE

I waited a few minutes before heading to bed. I didn't want to run into any of them again tonight. It seemed fitting that I be alone, for that had been my choice, to leave Adair for Luke. Still, I'd been jarred by the sight of Robin and Terry; I don't know why I hadn't thought Adair would be with someone else by now, but it honestly hadn't occurred to me, and I was left feeling unsettled. I climbed the massive staircase and padded by the closed door to their shared bedroom, their muffled voices rising and falling as I passed. I imagined they were talking about me. I started a fire in the tiny fireplace, changed quickly, and slipped into the chilly bed.

I was smothered by a sense of incredible melancholy. I should've known that talking about Luke would stir memories, bringing to the surface everything that I'd tucked away in the back of my mind. It was the first time I'd spoken about Luke's death with someone who hadn't been directly affected by it; namely: his children, Jolene and Winona; his ex-wife, Tricia, and her husband; and the doctors and nurses who'd worked with Luke at the clinic. Of all those people, I was the one who was least entitled to anyone's condolences. Sure, Luke and I lived together as though we were husband and wife, but we'd been together for only a few years. I was practically a new-comer. Tricia had more of a claim on him than I, let alone his children. The sympathy belonged to them.

The first sign that something was wrong came when Luke collapsed at the clinic. He didn't tell me until he got home that night. "I passed out today," he said casually at the dinner table, not even looking up from his plate. "I woke up on the floor of my office. I don't recall how I got there." He tried to claim it was only light-headedness, because he hadn't eaten lunch or because he was dehydrated, but after a few minutes of cross-examination he admitted that he'd been having head-aches for days. I begged him to see a specialist, but being a man, and a doctor, he wouldn't listen. I think it was because he had an idea of what was wrong and he didn't want to have it confirmed.

I've been with a lot of people as they were dying and can attest: it's not like it is in the movies. It's not antiseptic or tidy. It is absolutely the lowest point in any person's life. They're either old and their body is starting to irrevocably fail, or they're young but very sick or have had an accident. In either case, they're afraid of what's coming, afraid and con-fused. I've learned through experience that there's nothing you can do for someone at the end except to try to keep them company so they don't have to make that passage alone. No one wants to die alone; I've held the hand of many a dying man. That's the price of immortality. It hasn't meant that death is a stranger to me; if anything, we are reacquainted frequently at the deathbeds of others.

As a matter of fact, I'd been through the death of a close loved one so many times that, during those last weeks with Luke, I went into a kind of autopilot. I knew what was expected of me in those situations. The dying wanted unfailing support. Luke wanted me to be stoic in the face of his emotional ups and downs. He wanted me to be practical and logical, to be a rock at a time when his life was falling apart. He wanted me to be in the waiting room while he was undergoing tests. He didn't want me to freak out when he suddenly couldn't speak or use his right arm. He never had to ask for any of this; I just knew it was what he needed from me. He was too smart to worry that I would be unhinged by his passing; he knew I'd lost plenty of others before him.

It seemed that immortality—rather than make me more sensitive to the pain of losing a loved one—had robbed me of the ability to feel real emotion in the face of death. When my lovers and friends died, my feelings were always muted and distant. I'm not sure why this was. It might have been to protect me from being swamped by grief, so I wouldn't relive the sadness I'd felt for each of the people I'd lost over the course of my life. Or maybe it was because I knew from experience that, soon enough, another person would come along and—if not take Luke's place, not exactly—at least distract me from missing him. Because I had no choice but to live on and on.

Immortality had made me less human. Instead of giving me greater perspective on what it meant to be human, which you'd think would happen when you had such a long life, immortality had put me at a greater distance. No wonder Adair grew to be insensitive to the suffering of others: immortality forces you to become something other than human. I felt it happening to me, even though I didn't like it. I came to see it was inevitable.

That night as I lay in bed, I thought back to one afternoon in the hospice. The doctors didn't expect Luke to last more than a couple of days, and he was unconscious most of the time due to the morphine drip easing his pain. He wore a knitted cap for warmth as almost all his hair had fallen out from chemotherapy. What was left had turned shock white. He'd lost a lot of weight, too. His face was shrunken like an old man's and his arms seemed too thin for the IV needles and the sensors that fed his vital signs to the monitors.

I'd taken to curling up in a lounge chair by the window, reading or knitting while he slept. I was grateful for the sedatives and painkillers making his last days more comfortable. After all, I'd sat with loved ones dying of tumors and tuberculosis with nothing stronger than Saint-John's-wort and fortified wine to see them through it. The nurses, when they came in to check on him or change the drip bag, would invariably comment on my seeming calmness—backhanded compliments all; I think they thought I should be more upset, like Tricia and the girls. They couldn't understand how I could be so detached. I'm sure they thought me cold-blooded. I wondered if Luke thought so, too.

This one afternoon, however, Luke was more lucid than usual. When I saw him shift restlessly in bed, I put down my book and went over to him. "How are you feeling?" I asked, taking his hand gingerly to avoid jarring the IV needle.

His eyes were feverishly bright. "I have a question for you. Are we alone?"

I looked through the open door toward the nurses' station down the hall. They were engaged in their work. "Yes. What do you want to ask?"

He licked his lips. He seemed to be looking past me, as though he could no longer focus his eyes. "Lanny, I was wondering, now that I'm dying . . . if you had the power, would you make me like you?"

I hated that question. It wasn't the kind of thing I would have expected from Luke, either. He'd always seemed too sensible, too down-to-earth. I tried not to miss a beat, however. "But I don't have the power. You know that. . . ."

He was impatient with my evasiveness. "That's not what I asked. I want to know if you *would*."

I reached up to tuck a few loose white hairs under his cap. "Of course I would, if that's what you wanted."

He snorted and closed his eyes. "You're just saying that."

"Where is this coming from?" I asked, trying not to sound as tired as I felt. I knew why he was being peevish: he was afraid and exhausted. It was the end. It hovered in the darkness every time he closed his eyes. The waiting could bring out the worst in people.

His breath grew louder, ragged. "You know who *could* make me like you. Adair. He'd do it if you asked him."

This time, I paused. Was Luke asking me to track down Adair and beg him to give me the elixir of life? It made me see Luke in a completely different light. Not only had I never suspected that he cared about living forever, I thought he would have sooner chosen death than ask me to go on his behalf to this man who frightened me so much. But death plays us cruelly at the end. "Is that what you want?" I asked, waiting.

But he'd slipped into unconsciousness. His hand went lax in mine. By the time he woke a few hours later, he'd forgotten ever asking me and I was spared from having to come up with an answer.

I remembered Luke's question that night in the fortress, though, as I tossed and turned in bed. For here I was at Adair's house not for Luke's sake, not to beg for Adair's favor so that Luke could spend eternity with me, but to ask him to help Jonathan, a man who was dead and gone and surely beyond our help.

And I did not want to ask myself why.

The house was very quiet when I rose the next morning, though I wasn't surprised, not after listening to women's voices and squeals of delighted laughter late into the night. I trotted down the stairs to the kitchen and made coffee, looking forward to time alone to sort out my thoughts without being reminded that Adair was finding ways to pass the time without me. My disappointment was understandable, then, when I found Terry lounging at the old farmhouse table in a pair of men's pajama bottoms and a tank top too small to do much besides decorate her breasts. As the coffee brewed, she watched me out of the corner of her eye and popped tangerine segments into her mouth. Once the coffee was ready, I slid into a chair opposite her with a mug in my hands.

"There's coffee," I said, to be sociable.

She said nothing.

"It's a lovely day," I tried again, taking a sip from my mug.

She snorted and tore off another segment. "It's bloody windy and cold, same as it is every day."

"At least it's sunny."

"It is that," she said, looking down at the tangerine peels, flicking them with a fingernail. Then she fixed her merciless stare on me. "So, don't take this the wrong way . . . it's not that Robin and I aren't delighted to have you stay with us so completely out of the blue and all. But what made you decide to come looking for Adair, anyway?"

I could've pointed out that it wasn't her house and it didn't matter what she and her friend thought of me, but I reminded myself to look at it from her point of view. They'd all been having a wonderful time until I showed up. "I got the urge to see an old friend," I said.

"Old friend, eh? How far back do you go, you and Adair?" Okay, that probably was the wrong excuse to use with her, given that I looked to be in my early twenties on the outside, and Adair not much older than that. As a matter of fact, we both appeared to be younger than Robin and Terry. "Are you childhood friends, then?"

"He was one of my first lovers." It was the truth; I hoped that by letting her know we were intimate once but no longer would satisfy her. There was a time, in the beginning, when life with Adair had been thrilling. When I came to him, I was a young girl from a small, isolated town of people with Puritan forebears. I had been raised to work hard, not to question either my elders or the Bible, and to have few expectations of life. I knew nothing about desire or physical pleasure. Life under Adair's roof turned all that upside down. Adair taught me about pleasure and showed me that it was possible to enjoy my body as well as other things in life—beautiful clothes, a fine wine, a good book, gay company—things the good folk in St. Andrew would've condemned as frivolous. To want such things was a sign of moral weakness. Life hadn't always been easy in Adair's house, but had it been any harder than the life I'd had in St. Andrew? I looked up to find Terry regarding me hostilely and added, "I haven't come back for him, if that's worrying you. I swear."

Her aggression subsided upon hearing this. "I know I'm being awfully rude. It's just—we're having a good time here. And I've gotten very fond of Adair. Still, we know fuck all about him—he won't talk about himself at all. We'd like to know more." Her tone took on a conspiratorial warmth.

"There's not much I can tell you," I said, conscious that I was walking a tightrope. Adair didn't like to be talked about behind his back. He'd impressed upon all his creations, we immortals, that we were never to share our secret with anyone outside our circle or risk terrible consequences. The result was that I tended to be tight-lipped around people. I saw in Terry the same frustration I'd seen in my friends over the years. They'd been hurt by my wariness and unable to understand why I put a barrier between us. I hadn't been able to get close to anyone in a long time—until Luke.

I think Terry was starting to realize that what she had with Adair was all she'd ever get. It would never go on to greater intimacy; he would never let her get truly close to him. Now here I was—the first person from his past to show up on the island and probably the last. I was her one opportunity to learn more about the man she loved and, as much as she disliked me, she weighed the benefit and risk of sharing her fears with me. She nervously jammed her hands between her knees like an anxious child, before she spoke. "It's been fun staying here with him, you know? He's a good bloke, and we're having a fine time, all carefree and easy. And it's a nice place to live, isn't it? Better than some filthy youth hostel. We thought we'd only crash here for a short while, Robin and me. That was the plan, anyway. We stayed for the laughs and"—her eyes flitted over my face—"good sex. It wasn't love at first sight or anything. Things have changed, though. We feel differently now. He grows on you, doesn't he? He's so mysterious, and smart—and dead sexy, too. I've never met a man who could do the things he does in bed. . . ." She caught herself and gave me a brief, embarrassed smile. "Let's just say they don't make them like that in Bristol, where we come from."

"They don't make them like him *anywhere*," I offered.

"Which is why we figured you came to get him back."

I shook my head. "Adair and I found out the hard way that we're not right for each other. We're just friends."

"If you say so . . ."

"Look, he's wonderful—in some ways. He's all the things you said of him, but there's more to Adair than meets the eye. I'm not trying to talk him down, but . . . you can trust me on that."

I was trying to convince her that she had nothing to fear from me, but everything I said seemed to have the opposite effect. Maybe she thought I was being patronizing, maybe she thought I was trying to trick her, for she jumped off the stool, bristling. "You talk like you're done with him, but you're not. I can tell. I can see it in your eyes plain enough, and if you really believe what you just told me, you don't know your own mind. You're fooling yourself if you think it's over between you."

"You're wrong, Terry," I said, trying to calm her, feeling as though I'd been pushed into a fight I didn't want. "I'm not trying to come between you and Adair. You'll see: once I'm gone it will go back to the way it was, and you two will have Adair to yourselves."

She tossed back her hair, defiant. "Oh no, it won't. Everything's changed. Can't you feel it? The minute you walked into the house it's like something came between us, me and Robin and Adair. And it's because he's still in love with you—but you don't need me to tell you that. You know it already." Her face was flushed; her anger rose up like a storm inside her, fighting to get out. She looked at me sharply one more time, hatred in her flashing eyes, before bolting from the room.

It took a few minutes for me to calm down after Terry left. The house fell silent again. I sat at the table listening for noises from the floor above, straining for some sign that Adair had risen. I waited patiently until, sip by sip, I'd emptied my cup. Still, there was no indication that he was about to come downstairs. Restless, I decided I might as well go exploring.

To say the house was peculiar would be an understatement. It seemed to have once been a fort before it was converted into a residence. The house was deceptive; like a handkerchief tucked up a magician's sleeve, you didn't know what might be hidden inside. From the outside it looked small, but inside was another matter. As I meandered down long, lonely hallways and went up and down winding staircases, the house seemed to unfold continuously before me as though it sprang to life from an M. C. Escher design. As best I could tell, the house's four wings made a perfect square, with a courtyard at its center.

On the first lap, I managed to lose my way somehow, and though surprised, I was amused by my inattention. However, it stopped being funny when, on the second lap, I still hadn't found my starting point. By the third lap, I was near panic, thinking I might never find my way through this strange, telescoping maze. That is, I *think* I made several laps of the building, but I couldn't be sure because I never seemed to take the same hall twice. Nor could I reliably say how many floors there were, or if these were floors in the conventional sense, as some staircases were only a half flight in length before stopping abruptly and leading to yet another hallway.

I noticed something else strange about the house, too: there were no maids, no housekeeper. There was no sign that there was anyone in the house except Adair and the two women, and yet *someone* had to be taking care of the place. A house this size undoubtedly needed a number of servants; Terry and Robin hardly seemed able to handle the job, and in any case the two women didn't seem inclined toward housekeeping, aside from the kitchen, that is. From what I'd seen the night before, they seemed quite at home there, concocting splendid meals.

I don't know how long I'd been lost in the house and was really starting to break into a panic when I finally stumbled on a set of stairs that brought me back to my starting point. I emerged in the entry hall just as Adair was descending the main staircase. Tousle-haired, he was pulling a shirt over his chest, and the sight of his bare skin reminded me of when he used to parade around the mansion in Boston in a state of undress, a silk banyan doing a poor job of hiding his nakedness, looking for all the world like an indolent pasha traipsing from one concubine to the next.

I must've looked a bit wild-eyed after being lost, because on seeing me he said, "You haven't been exploring on your own, have you, Lanore? You really shouldn't do that. The house has been renovated so many times and built onto over the years that there's no longer any rhyme or reason to the layout. It's easy to lose your way, and I don't think I'd be exaggerating if I were to say there's a good chance we'd never find you."

If I hadn't just spent the better part of an hour or so lost in that maze of staircases and long, empty halls, I would've thought he was making it up in an effort to keep me from finding something he didn't want me to see. Now, of course, I knew he was sincere. He led me to a cozy room past the kitchen that appeared to be his study. The far wall had a big window that looked out on a stand of pine trees, the only shady spot on the island. Two walls were dominated by shelves, each shelf full of old, leather-bound books. I glanced over the spines, wondering if these were Adair's or had belonged to the previous owner of the island. I realized with a blush that, subconsciously, I'd been looking for titles that had something to do with alchemy or magic, signs of his past life, but there were none that I could tell. Nor was there any evidence that he was dabbling in magic again: no bottles of mysterious liquids, no glass jars of seeds or roots, or unidentifiable animal parts as I'd seen in the hidden room in the mansion in Boston all those years ago. The room was reassuringly normal.

"The two books you left with me," I said, referring to the ancient tomes filled with his alchemical secrets that he had given to me on the day of my departure, a token of his intent to forego magic. "I brought them with me. They're up in my room."

Adair wrinkled his brow. "I gave them to you. You didn't need to return them."

"I don't feel right keeping them. Besides, it doesn't matter where I put them or what I do with them, they look out of place. They're meant to be with you, I think." I pulled down a book, flipped the pages until I got to text. I didn't know the language, but from the way the lines broke, I could tell it was poetry.

He crouched in front of the hearth to build a fire. "Did you sleep well last night?" he asked over his shoulder.

"I slept fine."

"I am glad to hear that. Most people don't when they first come here. They complain of bad dreams. The girls did." He nodded in the direction of the kitchen. "The locals have all kinds of reasons why this is. Some people say the bad dreams are caused by vapors given off by the rocks here, that the island has these hallucinogenic properties because it is made of an unusual combination of minerals. Others say it has to do with the precise longitude and latitude being in some strange magnetic field. Still others say it's because of its ominous past."

"Did you have bad dreams when you arrived?" I asked, even though I couldn't imagine he'd say that he did. I didn't think it would be possible for Adair to have nightmares any more than I thought he could be frightened. To me, he was so intimidating that it seemed impossible for him to have those sorts of weaknesses.

He drew sheets of old, brittle newspaper from a wooden

box next to the fireplace and crumpled them for kindling. "It's not something I like to talk about, and not something I would discuss with anyone else, but I will tell you, Lanore, since you ask. When I first came here, what I experienced was worse than bad dreams. I couldn't close my eyes and not feel something of the terror I felt in my tomb in the house in Boston. It's hard to explain, but it was as though whatever it was that had me in its grip there had followed me here. It felt as though the space around me would open up and try to swallow me whole." There was an edge to his voice and I worried that I was getting into dangerous territory, since I was the one who had put him in that tomb. "It would come and go, and lasted for a few months, but eventually it went away. Maybe it was magnetic fields or vapors, and I got used to whatever was causing it."

I went over to the window. The horned goat had appeared out of nowhere and was staring thoughtfully at the house, as though he was considering whether he had business inside. There was something surreal and hypnotic about the goats, especially the horned one, who seemed particularly devilish, and whenever they were in view I found that I couldn't tear my eyes away from them. "How did you find out about this place, anyway?" I asked Adair while still looking out the window at the goat, waiting to see what he would do. "I don't think you could've picked a more obscure location if you tried."

"It is a bit infamous," he answered as he stacked wood on the grate. "Supposedly, the Romans sent a theurgist here in exile. He had been quite notorious, apparently, upsetting everyone with his heresy. They'd banished him to this rock without food or water, and expected him to die quickly, but legend has it that he lived on for centuries."

So Adair wasn't the first long-lived magician on the island. Perhaps it held a special allure for them. "Pretty nifty trick," I said, finally breaking away from staring at the goat to watch Adair build his fire. "I wonder how he managed that."

"With the protection of a powerful sorceress, or so the story goes." Adair smirked at me over his shoulder. "The last person to live here had been a disciple of Aleister Crowley's, the great English sorcerer. He had been with Crowley at his temple in Cefalù. The man came to live here after the Sicilian authorities shut down the temple and threw Crowley out of the country. The furniture, the books you see here—all in Italian and mostly having to do with magic and the occult—are his. When I bought the house, it had been untouched for fifty years."

"The house has a very magical history," I murmured as my stomach tightened in reflex.

"So it would seem." Adair struck a wooden match and held it to the kindling.

No wonder he wasn't in a hurry to get his books back from me. "So that's why you came here: to do more research?"

He took one of the chairs by the fireplace. "That wasn't my intention. I wanted to get away from everything, and this little island seemed exactly what I was looking for. It wasn't until I'd decided to move here that I found out about its past. But I suppose there's something about this place that drew me, just as it drew Crowley's disciple."

"So you've moved on from alchemy? Now you believe in magic?"

He gave me a tiny frown. "They're both parts of occult philosophy. 'Magic' is just a word. I believe there are things that we don't have the means to explain—yet." He patted the chair on the other side of the hearth. "But enough about that. You didn't come all this way to talk about magic. Why don't we continue the conversation we started last night?"

I slipped into the chair, my heart pounding. I could put it off no longer: the time had come for me to tell Adair about the nightmares. I assumed that he would be none too pleased, because the dreams involved his rival, Jonathan. Adair wouldn't care if Jonathan was being tormented in the depths of hell—he might even get a measure of satisfaction from it—and I hadn't yet thought of a way to make him care enough about Jonathan's fate to help me.

"I need your help," I said timidly. That made his face light up; my request had made him happy. He wanted to be of service to me. Perhaps he thought I'd come to ask for money or some other little thing that he could easily grant. It wasn't going to be that simple. I took a deep breath, and began to tell him about the dreams.

FOUR

dair did nothing as I spoke. He kept a neutral expression fixed on his face as he listened, sitting with one leg crossed over the other, his hands clasped and index fingers steepled. Occasionally, he tapped his index fingers together or bounced his right foot up and down. His unresponsiveness made me nervous, and the possible reasons raced in the back of my mind: he must be disappointed to learn that I'd come because of Jonathan, not for him. Or maybe he thought I was foolish to presume the dreams had any meaning at all. I worried, too, that after giving him the reason for turning up unannounced on his doorstep, my audience with him would be over. Or worse, that the truth might reawaken the sleeping dragon that was his fierce temper, and that was the last thing I wanted to do.

But he didn't appear to be angry. When I'd finished telling

him about the nightmares, my voice tapering off to embarrassed, self-conscious silence, he said, "Why, Lanore, I'm surprised that you would let something like this bother you! You
said so yourself: these are dreams, nothing more than that."

"I'm not so sure," I replied.

"Of course they are. And you know as well as I do that
you're having these nightmares because something is bothering
you. Perhaps there is something on your conscience? Something you feel guilty about?"

My cheeks warmed at the thought. The list of things of
which I was guilty was very long indeed. "Of course I do. I'm
only human."

He knew I was being evasive. "What I meant is: Do you
feel guilty about something that deals with Jonathan? Something that also has to do with this dead man, the doctor?"

There was. It was a shameful secret that I'd carried in my
heart ever since Luke helped me escape from St. Andrew four
years ago. He smuggled me past the police and held me together emotionally after I'd given Jonathan the mercy killing
he wanted.

I never got over the feeling that I'd used Luke in the most
horrible way, charming him into becoming a fugitive in order
to help me. Sure, he had wanted to do it; it wasn't as though
I could force him to do something against his will. But I saw
that he was vulnerable: his wife had left him for her high-
school sweetheart and moved far away with their daughters,
and his parents—for whom he'd relocated to that tiny, isolated
town, in order to care for them—had just died. He was alone
and morbidly depressed; anyone who looked at him would've
been able to see it.

After he transported me out of town and across the border to Canada and safety, I should've sent him back. I often wondered if it wouldn't have been kinder if I'd slipped out on him while he'd slept at the motel. On waking and seeing I'd gone, he would've returned to St. Andrew, embarrassed and resentful for having been duped, but he'd go on to have a normal life. It would've been like releasing an animal back into nature instead of trying to keep him as a pet.

But Luke wasn't the only lonely one: until Jonathan had come back into my life at the very end, my life had been empty. What had life become for me except a series of relationships, going from one companion to the next to keep loneliness at bay? When the companion was young, life would be a series of fiery distractions, nightclubs and dinner parties, teary spats and passionate reconciliations. And then when the companion grew older, if we were still together, life mellowed into quiet evenings and crossword puzzles, and then at the end the hospital, always the hospital. But I'd grown tired of it. My emotional well had run dry and, for the last stretch, I had lived alone.

So I thought—I *honestly* thought—that here was a chance to try again with Luke, this nice man who'd put himself on the line for me. He had proven himself dependable; why not stay with him? I owed him my loyalty—after all, he'd saved me from prison. I told myself that it didn't matter if I didn't love him. He didn't love me, either—how could he when he barely knew me?

And it wasn't as though I'd deceived him. He knew that I loved Jonathan; I'd *told* him so, spilling my story out to him on the drive to Quebec as we ran from the law. I confessed what an unhappy, possessed creature I'd been for two hundred years, in love with a man who could not remain faithful to me. Anyone with eyes in their head would've been able to see that I would be unhappy, and maybe even a little bit insane, for some time to come. You could argue that, in some ways, Luke was as much to blame as I.

When I confessed this to Adair, however, he cocked his head at me in confusion—or maybe he was only pretending to be confused. "Back in Aspen, when you were pleading with me to spare this man's life, you told me that you loved him," he said pointedly.

"I did. I do," I fumbled. "I came to love him dearly."

"But not passionately," he countered. "So you feel guilty because you stayed with Luke, even though you didn't love him with your entire heart and soul."

I gave a helpless shrug.

"Because you still loved Jonathan." His voice went flat.

If Adair could see into my heart, he'd know that it was divided. I'd loved Jonathan once, but that love had faded. I loved Luke, too, but he had never stood a chance to be the great love of my life. There was something growing in my heart now, something that had the potential to push everything else aside—but I wasn't sure I should ever tell Adair about it, and certainly not at that moment. "Yes, because I still loved Jonathan. I've felt guilty about it ever since. I'd always felt as though I'd entered into a relationship with Luke under false pretenses, even if everything turned out okay in the end."

"Did it?" I'd disappointed him and so he was being mean, poking a spot he knew was tender. "By the time he died, you loved this Luke with all your heart?"

With *most* of my heart—but that was not for Adair to know. "Yes."

This was not what he wanted to hear, of course. "Then there's no reason for you to have a guilty conscience, is there?" he said impatiently. "How did you sleep last night? Did you have one of those nightmares?"

I shook my head. "No, but that's because I took a sleeping pill."

"Well, there is your answer. Sleeping pills."

"I don't want to take sleeping pills forever," I said sharply, almost in despair.

His beautiful eyes filled with sadness. He may have thought me a fool, a pitiful wretch for being hopelessly in love with the wrong man; he may have been moved because I sounded so utterly forlorn in asking for his mercy; or I may have been breaking his heart all over again, but he put his anger aside. "It won't be forever," he said, trying to reassure me. "I expect these dreams will fade away soon enough. But in the meantime, stay with me. If you have any more dreams, I'll be right here."

Adair's plan was to distract me until I stopped having the dreams. The island was at my disposal, he said. I could do whatever I pleased. It was the perfect place to get away from the world, that was for sure. Its desolateness made it ideal for losing one's self in a book or being alone with one's thoughts. If I wanted to be distracted by crowds and foreign sights, he said he could radio for a boat to take me to Sardegna or Corsica, where there were casinos and shops, movie theaters and fancy spas. If I craved anything, food or drink, trinket or treasure, from anywhere in the world, he would be happy to send for it. All I had to do was ask.

All that I wanted, however, was to follow him around. It was ironic that, after hiding from him for so long out of fear, here I tagged along after him, never letting him out of my sights. He was my protector and could keep my bad dreams at bay. That didn't mean I wasn't still a *little* afraid of him; I was only too aware that he was capable of turning on a dime. But here, on this island, he seemed in control and—dare I say it?—at peace. He was a rock, under which I could take refuge.

We spent most of our days together. For Adair, there was no television or idle surfing on the computer. It turned out that he read constantly. He'd stored all the books he never read, poetry and literature, on the highest shelves in his study but pulled them down to read to me, translating from the original French, Italian, or Russian. When he tired of reading aloud, he read to himself, studying whatever had caught his fancy, while I lounged nearby like a companionable cat. Rather than feel as though I were imprisoned in a small space for hours on end, I came to enjoy it. The wind howled outside the window, but Adair kept the fire built up, and so I felt snug and cozy. There were two stout armchairs beside the fireplace in which to relax and a window seat, tucked between two bookcases and outfitted with a deep box cushion, covered with an old kilim. Pillows and rustic blankets were piled in corners. It reminded me a little of Adair's old boudoir in the Boston mansion. All it needed was a hookah.

We managed to have quite a bit of privacy, as Robin and

Terry were used to Adair keeping to himself during the day. God only knows what they were up to, wherever they were in the fortress. At first they checked up on us regularly, knocking on the door to see if we wanted to join them for tea or lunch, secretly looking for signs of growing intimacy between Adair and me. They couldn't force themselves on us, however, and Adair never invited them to join us, and so after each innocent inquiry the girls had no choice but to leave us alone.

Between books, we'd talk. Not about whether there was the chance of a future for us—no, nothing as weighty and frightening as that, as much as it had to be in both of our thoughts. Conversation started tentatively, as we figured out where the land mines lay. There was so much history between us, after all, so much that was too sensitive to discuss so soon. Once we'd started, though, conversation came easily. We reminisced about life in the old days, how hard everything was before electricity and plumbing, motorcars and airplanes. Adair had a wealth of stories; he'd lived for such a long time and had experienced things I knew only from books. He could be funny; he could be thoughtful. He could even be philosophical.

And, for the first time, he acknowledged remorse for things he'd done. This was quite a shock, though I tried not to show it on my face, for in the past Adair had never expressed regret of any kind. He'd always had reasons for his actions—whether moral or just in the eyes of other people, it didn't matter to him—and once he'd embarked on a course, he rarely let doubt stop him but, rather, swatted it out of his path without so much as a backward glance. This was a fundamental change in his nature, and as I listened, I felt a creeping sense of relief and optimism that perhaps there was hope for him yet. That, given enough time, the leopard could evolve and change its spots: anyone could change, even Adair.

Being together like this reminded me of our time in Boston, when I had been part of his strange household, one of five people to whom he'd given eternal life in exchange for blind obedience and service. I asked Adair whether he had been in touch with the others and he admitted that he avoided Alejandro, Tilde, Dona, and Jude. "I can't abide their company anymore," he confessed, saddened. "There was a time when I needed them to be a buffer between me and the rest of the world. They served a purpose, but that time has passed. I'd rather live simply and privately."

I thought about inquiring after my dear old friend Savva. He, too, had been one of Adair's companions once, and we'd spent a lot of time together when I was on the run from Adair. Savva had fallen very far from the brilliant, irascible, and maddening young Russian I'd known a hundred years earlier. He had turned to narcotics for respite from his demons and become a bad heroin addict. He'd driven away all his friends and could no longer cope with the ever more complex demands of modern life. Savva was living proof that eternal life was not a gift to everyone—for the very unstable, it could be a neverending hell. When Adair and I had last parted, I'd asked him to show mercy and release Savva. Now, I couldn't bring myself to find out if Adair had done as I'd asked.

No, I wouldn't ask about Savva. Since I'd come to the island, I'd seen many promising signs that Adair had truly changed; it gave me hope. If only every day could be like this: the two of us lying together in the sun, enjoying each other's company.

A dangerous and seductive thought had begun to take root in my mind: I started to think how nice it might be to stay right where I was. After all, I had nowhere else to go and no one waiting for me. I could put off the lonely job of building a new life—which, frankly, got more tedious and seemed more pointless each time I had to create a new identity. If I could put out of my head all the bad things that had happened between Adair and me, if I could pretend that there was only the here and now, then I might be able to manage it. I could live with Adair day to day, never needing to look ahead, never daring to look back.

I knew that if I asked, he would make it happen. He would send the girls away so I could take refuge in his bed, where the nightmares would never dare to follow me. And what waited for me in his bed but days and nights of stupendous sex? Sex so pure and powerful that it would keep me focused on the moment, on the physical pleasure of the body, and free me from my overburdened mind. More than any man I'd ever known, Adair had the ability to turn sex into both a physical and spiritual act. We would stay in the bedroom for days at a time, feasting on each other, right down to our souls. I ached to give myself up to Adair like this. It would make life so much simpler. . . . As long as I *remained* in that state, as long as I could stay drugged up on pure experience, it could work. It would be like being drunk and never sobering up. It was very tempting to consider and if I'd been just a little bit weaker, or more selfish, I might've let it happen.

But then I remembered all the terrible things we'd done, Adair and I, and I knew we wouldn't be so lucky. Fate would not let us be happy, not truly, not when so much remained unaccounted for. My sins were slight—minor deceptions, a white lie told here or there—compared to Adair's, which ran past duplicity and theft, all the way to murder. Fate could not possibly be finished with the two of us. Besides, I didn't come here looking to escape. There was something I *had* to do, and I would never find peace until I followed through with it.

FIVE

I was playing solitaire with a worn, old deck of cards I'd found in a desk drawer, while Adair read, reclining on a bower of pillows on the floor. He broke from his reading to roll onto his back and cock his head in my direction, as though he was about to speak. I don't think he was aware of how very appealing he appeared at that moment, his hair loose and leonine, the first few buttons on his shirt undone to give me a peek at his chest, and his jeans twisted so they were tight across his hips. He'd thrown an arm over his face to shield his eyes against the sun, but I could still see the lower half of his face, including his strong mouth, and I recalled how kissable it was. The sight of him was tempting.

Where's the harm in a cuddle? I thought, even though I knew we probably would not stop there. And if we were to indulge this once . . . if I leaned over him for a kiss and took the opportunity to press full against his chest . . . if I reached down to undo the fly of his jeans, and unleash the passion that I knew was inside him . . . would I be lost to him for good? Could we stop again after having done the deed once?

But why not try it and see? a voice in my head asked. *After all you've been through the past year, nursing your dying lover, it is time for you to be reborn. And you know this man; you've been in his bed a thousand times already. Stop thinking and do something about it. Go over and kiss him. Tell him you want him to take you right here, now. Tell him that you want him inside you, like the old days. Where is the harm?*

I was about to abandon my cards and slither over to him when he said unexpectedly, "There's been something I've been meaning to talk to you about."

"Oh?" I said, already half risen to my feet.

"It has to do with the girls."

Ah yes, the two women who had fallen for Adair and were sharing his bed. I had somehow forgotten about them in the heat of the moment. *There* was the harm in succumbing to temptation: it would be an entirely impetuous and selfish act with consequences that would harm *them*. A chill settled over me. It would be irresponsible to just do as we pleased. We both had responsibilities, after all: he, the girls; and me, rescuing Jonathan.

He sat up and leaned forward, his forearms resting on his knees, oblivious to the thoughts I was battling. "It's hard to explain, but ever since Robin and Terry arrived, I've had the feeling that something—strange—is going on. I've had no one to discuss it with, but now you're here, I thought . . ." He shook his head, impatient with himself.

To be honest, I was annoyed that he'd brought up the girls. I felt as though I'd been doused with cold water, though it was undoubtedly for the best. I quickly regained my composure. "What is it?" I asked, pushing the cards aside. "Out with it. You can tell me."

"All right. Just remember—you asked for it." He hesitated. "The story of how we met, me and the girls, all that was true. They turned up on my doorstep, just as they said, but at the time, I sensed that there was something familiar about them. From the moment I met them, I knew that I'd seen them before. And then it dawned on me"—he flicked an unsteady glance my way a second time to make sure I was still following him—"they reminded me of a pair of sisters I knew centuries ago."

"So? It was déjà vu; they reminded you of someone else. That's not uncommon."

"There's more to it than that. You see, these sisters were witches." He rushed the words out of his mouth as though he was embarrassed to say such a thing. "Their names were Penthy and Bronwyn. Robin is very much like Penthy. They have the same blond hair, both high-strung and flighty. Terry is just like Bronwyn, bossy and headstrong. They lived in the English fens land, out in the woods"—here he hesitated, avoiding my gaze—"in a giant tree. They admitted to being witches right away. They said they'd come from a long line of witches, and had been banished to the forest by the townsfolk, who had been afraid of their mother. They were something, those sisters. Beautiful, but a touch mad, I think. You could see it in their eyes.

"That night, I stumbled through the fens wood in the

dark, lost, sure I was going to fall into a bog and never be heard from again, when I heard them call me. Like sirens, they were. They wanted me to come down from my horse and spend the night with them. They tried to enchant me, feeding me wormwood tea and poppy-seed cake, and salads of nasturtiums and morning glories. You know me, Lanore; you know I have a strong constitution, but after a meal like that, I was stoned out of my mind and tame as a house cat. They waited until we were in bed to tell me that they were witches. I'd never been around women magic-handlers before. The great alchemists I'd met had all been men." He stroked his beard thoughtfully. "I grant you, there might have been a few female alchemists back then, though I would imagine that they'd have hidden their interest, as it wouldn't have been to their advantage to be discovered, but more than one or two? I doubt it. And if there were, this very practice of keeping apart from other practitioners, the *great* practitioners, would have been their undoing. Because that is how you become great. Alchemy is not something you can master on your own. You must learn from the discoveries of others.

"I found the witch sisters' magic disconcerting at first, but got used to it soon enough. Adepts called it 'kitchen magic,' the kind that's passed from one generation to the next without formal training; it's roundly thought of as primitive. The sisters didn't want to hear that, of course. They were proud, and didn't want to be judged or looked down on, but I had something they desperately wanted: a book of spells. That's like the holy grail to them, and once they found out I had one on me, they came up with a plan to rob me. They tied me up, but I managed to escape."

I settled close to him on the pillows, to share his sunny spot. "You couldn't have been too pleased about that."

"I didn't appreciate it, no. I let my anger get the better of me, I'm afraid. I destroyed their home," he admitted sheepishly. That sounded like the Adair of old, the Adair I knew, with a temper as explosive as a nuclear warhead. "And they swore to take revenge on me one day."

"And you think these two girls are Penthy and Bronwyn, come back to make good on their threat?" I asked, dubious. "Reincarnation?"

I felt his weight shift restlessly beside me. "Maybe . . . why not? There's something about this island that makes things happen. This place has a magical history, but I think there's more to it than that. I think there's a strong magical force here. That's why Crowley's disciple came here, that's what drew me here. That force could have enabled the witch sisters to come back."

"I suppose anything is possible," I said, trying not to sound as uncertain as I felt. "Let's say, for argument's sake, that it's true, that these witches have come back through Robin and Terry. Have they *done* anything to you, done anything malicious?"

"Not that comes to mind," he admitted.

"What do you think they'd want from you?"

"I don't know." I could tell I'd vexed him by the dark look that clouded his face. "Look, I realize it sounds far-fetched, but I know how I feel and I think they're Penthy and Bronwyn. But as to why they've come back . . . well, that part I don't know *yet*, but whatever it is, it won't be for the good," he said, and sounded a bit slighted by my skepticism. "I grant you that I might have it all wrong. Maybe it's just the island making me feel this way. There's something uncanny about it, almost as if it has a will of its own. Perhaps the barrier between this world and the next is at its thinnest here . . . or it's positioned at a special confluence of stars. Or it's a combination of magnetic forces, or a balance of elements found nowhere else, as legend has it. You'll have to take my word for it. I can feel it."

I didn't want to tell him, but I could feel it, too, just as I could see there was something peculiar about the British girls. When they were in high emotion, it seemed they could make the air crackle and pulse and practically *warp* around them in a way that made the hair at the back of my neck stand up. No, I didn't think Adair's hypothesis was incorrect, but I also couldn't allow myself to agree with him for fear that it might be true.

"You look exhausted," he said, perhaps trying to change the subject so we wouldn't be at odds any longer. "Why don't you try to take a nap? I'll be right here while you rest."

I'd been awake for more than two days straight. I *was* exhausted, though I was used to going without sleep for long stretches at a time; I'd often had bouts of insomnia, or perhaps it was just that in this strange immortal form, we didn't need sleep the way mortals did. Still, I could tell I was on the brink of impairment, of falling into that surreal state where you couldn't trust your senses and it was difficult to collect your thoughts. I did as Adair suggested, and snuggled under the arm he wrapped protectively around my shoulders.

It came within seconds of falling asleep, as though the dream had been hiding in the closet or floating along the ceiling, waiting for me to close my eyes in order to pounce. I had no sooner closed my eyes than I was dragged down, down, down into pitch blackness, quickly drawn along the now familiar stone passageway against my will.

I would've dug my heels in if I could, but it was impossible to resist, as though the dream had me by the arm and was pulling me forcibly to my destination. My head was clouded with the usual feelings of fear and dread, but beyond this I sensed something else was with me in the passage. There was a malevolent presence hovering over and around me, a spirit or spirits hurrying down the passage with me, excitedly feasting on my fear.

In a flash, I was at the hated door and it swung open at the slightest touch. I stepped inside and followed the same wandering torchlight from my earlier dreams. The room had been strangely reconfigured, furnished like a boudoir even though the walls were still made of the same filthy stone blocks and the floor was still packed dirt, loosely strewn with straw. Directly in front of me stood a handsome mahogany bed, one befitting a king's bedchamber. Luxurious red-and-gold curtains hung from the four posters, the curtains drawn back to reveal gleaming white sheets betraying not a speck of dirt from the filthy surroundings. The sheets were rumpled: obviously, someone had recently been sleeping there. A voluptuous chaise longue upholstered in red velvet sat at the foot of the bed, and off to the side was a folding screen, three large panels covered with silk painted with a river scene. Items of clothing had been thrown haphazardly atop the screen, as though someone had undressed hastily. All the pieces were men's clothes from the period of my youth: breeches, an embroidered turquoise waistcoat and navy frock coat, a long white stock tie still pleated with wrinkles from when it had been wound around someone's neck. No, not "someone's" neck; I knew whose clothes these were. These clothes belonged to Jonathan.

I knew for certain, in that strange way of dreams, that Jonathan had been in this room not long ago. He had been in this bed, and he had been forced to undress. But where was he now? Then I caught movement out of the corner of my eye, a ripple of black disappearing behind the edge of the door. Jonathan; again, I knew with certainty that he was being taken somewhere. I knew this just the same as I knew I had to catch up to him, or lose him forever.

I hurried after them, Jonathan and his captor. I was led into a part of the passage I'd never been before, never having gone beyond the door in my previous dreams. The passage seemed to get narrower and narrower, until I could barely squeeze between the walls, and it twisted and turned so that I couldn't see very far in front of me. Every once in a while I would turn a corner and see part of a figure—the point of an elbow, the heel of a foot—disappear as it turned a corner and was, once again, beyond my reach. The dream teased me, letting me get close enough to see a snippet of Jonathan, then it pulled him far away until all I could hear was the echo of footsteps up ahead. All the time, my chest squeezed tighter and tighter as I feared that if I awoke before catching up to him, I'd never have the chance to see or speak to him again, in this life or the next.

I spun around a corner in a headlong rush but somehow managed to have the presence of mind to realize that a shadow fell into the passage in front of me. Someone was coming for *me*, and I could tell by the gigantic form that it wasn't Jonathan. Sensing great danger, I quickly stepped back and slipped around the corner, pressing up against the cold stone blocks and holding my breath, praying not to be detected.

I could tell by the sound of footsteps that whatever had been coming for me had paused in the passage directly ahead. I listened for breathing but heard nothing. What could it be? So far in my dreams, I'd seen only Jonathan and a woman's hand, which I assumed belonged to the queen of the underworld. But by the size of my pursuer's shadow, it seemed unlikely to be her. Still, who else could it be? As unnerving as the whole thing was, this was exactly what I'd hoped for, wasn't it, to confront the queen and ask her to release Jonathan? Perhaps I didn't need to ask Adair to send me to the underworld. Perhaps I could confront the queen in my dreams and find peace for Jonathan and for myself.

I drew in a deep breath and stuck my head around the corner—but only for a split second, before drawing it back in complete horror. It wasn't the queen of the underworld waiting for me in the passage. And it wasn't Jonathan.

It was a demon. It had to be a demon—what else would look like this? He stood seven feet if he stood an inch, so tall that he had to crouch in the tight passageway. He was so broad-shouldered and deep-chested that he might've been a bull standing on its hind legs. His face, too, was not unlike a bull's, broad and snoutish and ugly beyond belief, and, to complete the bullish appearance, long horns protruded from the top of his head. The demon had a man's arms, though massive as tree trunks; hands that were clawlike, with fingers ending in razor-sharp talons; and an animal's legs, literally: thick, muscular hindquarters, huge sickle hocks of tendon and bone, fierce-looking cloven hooves. A long tail snaked behind him, twitching. He was all red flesh, as you'd imagine the devil to be, red flesh singed to blackness at the extremities, black legs up to his hocks like boots, black forearms as if gloved, black tail tufted at the tip. Red and black, except for his eyes, which were glittering topaz and had a vertical slit, like those of a reptile. His barrel chest heaved with every breath, as though he had been running or was sniffing the air to pick up a scent. My scent.

I turned and ran down the hall the way I'd come, as silently as I could, though my head clamored with the sound of my ragged breath, the thumping of my heart, blood sluicing in my ears. *Don't look back,* I told myself over and over, sure that something terrible would happen to me if I did, that I'd turn to stone or salt, or would be sentenced to remain in the labyrinth forever. *It's only a dream,* I also tried to tell myself. Yet I ran hard, sprinting down the passage, my soles barely touching the packed dirt floor.

When at last I thought I was a safe distance away, I stopped, panting heavily now, doubling over with my hands on my knees and nearly retching from the effort. In my dream state, I tried to recall what I'd seen exactly. The sight of the demon was already growing wispy. The residue of fear stayed with me, though. Dream or not, he was truly something to be afraid of; I felt it to my bones. However, as I stood there, doubled over and breathless, I berated myself. What kind of behavior was this? Did I honestly want to help Jonathan or not? I had to screw up my courage and go back down the corridor and face the creature. For Jonathan's sake.

I stood up and took another deep breath. The pounding of

my heart began to slow. *Courage.* I'd just about gathered my wits and was about to head back the way I'd come when, suddenly, the demon appeared around the corner. He was closer now, and I could see him in more detail. He had an obscene air about him, due no doubt to the genitalia openly displayed between his legs, swaying heavily with each step. There was no mistaking his yellow eyes falling on me heavily, deliberately, and I thought I saw the corner of his brutish mouth turn upward. *He is coming for me.* My scream froze in my throat. I couldn't move and it was only with great luck that before he could lay one of those large, maniacal claws on me, I lurched awake in Adair's arms.

SIX

"It was a dream. Just a dream."

Adair meant to be reassuring. I knew that he wanted me to blink my eyes and see that I was in his study and not the horrible dungeon of my dreams; to catch my breath and say with an embarrassed chuckle, "Oh, you're right of course. I see that now." But I didn't.

I didn't need him to tell me it had been a dream. I *knew* I was awake now and on the other side. However, wisps of the dream were still trapped in my head, making it hard to separate nightmare from reality. I could still see the demon's rippling red haunches and shoulders, as well as the golden eyes that had sized me up with such calculation. I could still smell the monster's ashy, earthen odor.

"It was more than a dream. I know it." I shuddered against the memory.

He didn't release me. Instead, he started to rub my back as you might to console a child. "It was a *bad* dream, I'll give you that. You had me worried . . . you were making horrible noises in your sleep. I thought you were choking. I tried to wake you up, but it was as though you were in a trance. I called your name and I even shook you, but you didn't respond."

"That's what I mean—if it had been a regular dream, you should've been able to wake me. Something's going on, I can feel it." I let him hold me for a long moment and buried my face against his chest, breathing in his once familiar scent.

After I'd had a minute to gather my wits, Adair gently pulled me to my feet. "We've been cooped up in here too long. We should get out of the room for a while. Clear our thoughts. I think the girls have made lunch. There's something delicious in the air, mushroom soup, perhaps? Why don't we see what they're up to?" He was trying to take my mind off my fright, and was probably right about our needing a change of scene: I couldn't hide in the study forever.

We followed the aroma down to the cavernous kitchen, where the two girls were huddled over a huge stockpot on the stove. They lifted their heads when we entered.

"Ah, look who's here. Come to join us?" Terry asked, stepping to the worktable. She wiped her hands on her apron before taking up a massive chef's knife to mince parsley.

"Still among the living, are you? We thought maybe you'd died in there." Robin's rejoinder fell flat, like the taunt of an insecure young child.

"We're catching up on old times," Adair said. A wooden bowl held slices of rustic homemade bread. He fished one out.

"If you can bear to come up for air, you are welcome to join us for lunch," Terry said briskly as she scooped up a handful of parsley and dropped it into the pot. "It's just about ready."

"It smells heavenly," I offered, and then I thought of Adair's description of the hallucinogenic meal the witch sisters had made for him and wondered where the mushrooms had come from, if they could've been gathered on the mystical island.

Robin danced up to me, and said, "I was about to go down to the wine cellar to get something to go with lunch. We've nothing suitable up here. Do you want to come with me? It's quite impressive. I've never seen so many bottles in one place at one time before, except at a grocer's."

I'd been into the labyrinth belowstairs only once, the morning when I'd gotten hopelessly lost, and had resolved not to venture down again, but there didn't seem to be any danger in going with Robin. "All right," I said. "I'd like to make myself useful."

She took me through a nondescript door at the rear of the kitchen, which opened onto a long set of stone steps descending into darkness. Robin didn't seem intimidated by the cellar in the least; she knew where all the light pulls were, and what's more, she kept up a stream of chatter as she led the way deeper and deeper under the fortress. The plaster walls eventually gave way to brick, and then stone. It felt as though we'd burrowed straight down toward the center of the earth, a strangely far distance from the living quarters for a wine cellar, but perhaps necessary due to the vicissitudes of the rock and creeping seawater. The halls here were very dark, with few overhead lights. I was starting to wish that she'd brought a flashlight.

"This way," she said cheerily as we entered a very narrow hall. I was seized by a sudden feeling of claustrophobia, as though the walls were starting to press in on me. Then we passed a door that seemed familiar, though I knew I hadn't been this way before. I stopped to take a closer look, letting Robin go on ahead. The door was old and scarred, gouged by something very sharp by the look of it. I put a hand to the wood and it swung open, as though whatever was inside had been waiting for me.

I groped along the wall for a light switch, but there was none. The light from the hall, dim as it was, was sufficient; as I looked around, I again felt a sense of déjà vu. It was then I realized that the floor underfoot was packed dirt, smooth from disuse. And the walls were stone, made of very large, precisely cut blocks. In a flash, I knew it was the room from my dreams.

I wanted to scream but it was as though I was back in my nocturnal prison and I couldn't, my voice trapped in my throat. I turned to the door and it suddenly swung shut in front of me. I thought I'd seen the fleetest glimpse of Robin at the door, a smile on her sly face, her hand on the iron latch. I started pounding on the door, calling, "Let me out, let me out!" as soon as my voice came back to me. I struggled with the latch but it wouldn't work, the mechanism frozen in place. "Robin, this isn't funny. Let me out now!" I shouted, but I heard nothing on the other side of the door, not even the patter of retreating footsteps.

I kept pounding, all the while telling myself to stay calm, not to lose my head. It wasn't the room from the dream, it couldn't be. That was just a dream and this was reality. And yet . . . I could swear that I was beginning to smell the same dark aroma from my dream, the smell of ashes and earth. And I thought I heard something coming toward me from the dark recess of the room, a heavy, blunt footfall, one deliberate step at a time, and the snort of animal breathing. I shrieked in earnest, kicked and banged, jerked on the latch so mightily in an attempt to fling the door open that I might've dislocated my shoulder. To no avail. The acrid smell of scorched earth wrapped around me, and the heavy breath washed down my neck in cascades as though the monster was standing right over me . . . and just as I thought I felt the brush of its taloned hands reaching for me, I was pulled under by blackness.

"Dear God, Lanore, you gave me a terrible fright," Adair said as soon as I opened my eyes.

Where was I? Not in the dungeon, I saw that right away. I was lying in my bed in the guest room, Robin and Terry visible over Adair's shoulder, hovering at the doorway. Adair sat on the edge of the bed, watching me intently.

I bolted upright, but the sudden movement made my head spin, and Adair grabbed my shoulders to keep me from tumbling out of bed. "The cellar—"

"You're safe," he said, trying to get me to lie back. "Robin came to get me. She said you were trapped in one of the storerooms. The door shut behind you and she couldn't get it open."

The fleeting glimpse of her sly smile was frozen in my memory. "She's lying," I countered. I was ready to throw back the blanket and climb out of bed to confront her, but Adair held me in place. "She locked me in there! She did it on purpose. She wanted to frighten me," I insisted, pointing in her direction.

"What cheek!" Terry shouted at me from the doorway, but I noticed that Robin scurried backward into the hall, out of my view.

"Now, Lanore, really," Adair said, trying to soothe me. "Why would she do that?"

"How should I know?" I snapped. "All I know is that she did."

"You're tired, and you've had a lot on your mind lately, Lanore," he said loudly enough to be overheard by the girls, then added under his breath, "Are you sure it's not your imagination?" But he had been heard after all, for there was a giggle at the door, mean and childish and meant to intimidate me.

I grasped Adair's shirt and pulled myself closer to him. "Adair, we need to speak *in private*. Please," I said in a low voice.

He twisted in his seat and barked at the two women to leave us alone and, once they'd slunk away grumpily, got up to close the door after them. "Are you quite sure that you saw Robin close the door?" he asked skeptically as he resumed his seat.

I wanted to remind him that he was the one who suspected the malevolent witch sisters of possessing the Englishwomen in some way, but didn't want to be pulled into an argument on the matter, not at the moment. "Never mind about that—that's not what I want to talk to you about." I closed my eyes and an image of the ochre stones rushed up and sent a fresh shiver through me. "That room in your basement, the room where I was trapped . . . it's the place in my dream. The dungeon."

He stared at me uncomprehending for a minute, and then shook his head. "You must be mistaken. . . . It can't be."

"It *is*. I'm not imagining it," I said hotly.

"Not imagining, but maybe it's the power of suggestion. You told me that you got lost in the basement the other day—maybe you're only remembering what you saw then. Maybe that's why the room seems familiar to you."

That sounded reasonable, but—no. I hadn't been lost in the basement for long, and besides, I hadn't gone nearly that far down the passage on my first morning here. The hall in my dream looked precisely the same as the one snaking beneath Adair's home—they *were* the same. I didn't have the slightest doubt. I was going to tell Adair all about the demon I'd seen in my dream and whose presence I'd felt underground, but I decided not to mention it lest he refuse to send me to the underworld, thinking it too dangerous.

"Something's going on, Adair. These dreams are a message. I know it, I can feel it." The dreams were coming fast and furious now, and what's more, they were breaking through to the daylight world, having followed me to Adair's island—or lured me here. I was beginning to believe there was some kind of intelligence behind them. Someone was trying to communicate with me. It was time to lay my cards on the table. I was going to need to ask Adair for his help at some point, and it seemed that the time had come. I took a deep breath. "I don't think they're dreams, not exactly. I think they're something else. I think Jonathan is trying to contact me."

This was not going to be an easy topic to discuss with Adair, no matter how I brought it up. Jonathan was the last person in the world Adair would want to talk about, especially with me. He'd never liked Jonathan; what's more, I don't think he forgave Jonathan for breaking my heart (and, to an extent, never forgave *me* for falling in love with Jonathan in the first place). To say that the three of us had a complicated history was an understatement, and I'm sure Adair had hoped that was behind us now that Jonathan was dead. Only here he was again, still coming between us even in death.

Adair gave me an incredulous look, as though he couldn't believe his ears. "You think he's trying to reach you?"

"You sound as though you don't believe it's possible, but why not? You brought him back from the dead once, proving that he continues to exist—why shouldn't he try to contact me?" Adair started in surprise and tried to cover it up, but I had been waiting for this. "Yes, I know all about it, Adair. I knew that you brought Jonathan back from the dead, thinking he could tell you how to find me. And I know what he told you, too, once you'd resurrected him."

"That he'd been brought to the attention of the queen of the underworld," Adair said tensely, as though even the words—"queen of the underworld"—spooked him.

"I heard how this queen had learned about him, too," I went on, pressing the momentary advantage I had while Adair was still in shock over how much I knew. "It was because of the tattoo, the tattoo you gave him, like the one you have on your back. This queen must've been looking for it—looking for *you*."

At this last part, Adair grew grave and tense, his cheek twitching involuntarily. But he seemed to want to deflect attention and said to me, briskly, "It seems you know a lot for someone who wasn't there. How did you learn of this, Lanore? It had to come from one of the others who had been with me at the time. So, which one was it? Was it Pendleton, Alejandro? Or was it Jude?"

There was a time when Adair couldn't stand for his minions to talk about him behind his back, and if any of us were caught doing so, it would've been grounds for a most unpleasant punishment. So the minions rarely shared confidences with one another, and on that rare occasion when we did, we kept that secret sacred, on pain of torture. It was Jude who had told me, but I had to wonder if it mattered now. Adair seemed much changed from his old self. He'd set the others free to live their own lives, and here he was, living on the island, in seclusion. Still, it felt like a betrayal to give that name up. "I can't tell you and I'm sure you understand why," I said after a second's hesitation. "But you shouldn't doubt that I know it all, everything that happened between you and Jonathan."

As Adair's face clouded with shame and uncertainty, I leaned even closer to him and held his hands tightly so he couldn't pull away. "I don't care about anything that happened in the past, Adair," I said hotly, pleading with him. "I don't care if you kept Jonathan from me, if you want to keep everything he told you a secret from me forever. But I know about this queen and that she's made Jonathan her prisoner, and all this time it's been preying on my mind."

I could tell Adair wasn't happy to hear that I'd been thinking of Jonathan, that I'd never *stopped* thinking about Jonathan, but he tried to hide his concern behind a breezy wave of his hand. "I don't know why you call him a prisoner. . . . The word he used was 'consort.' I suppose you don't like to think of him as her consort, however. And as for this queen, why concern yourself with her at all? There are endless myths of devils, demons, and gods who oversee the transition of souls to the next plane of existence. In some religions, the figure that rules the underworld is a woman, yes. I must say that I wasn't surprised to hear that this queen had been taken with Jonathan—why shouldn't she be susceptible to his charms, like every other female who has crossed his path?" I detected a note of exasperation in his tone. There was another pause, a gaze askance. "I sent him back, yes, but you should know that he *wanted* to go back. And . . . Jonathan told me the queen would come looking for him, and you must understand, I did *not* want that to happen."

A flush of color bloomed on Adair's face and he ducked his head so I couldn't study his face while he spoke. "What I have to say isn't very flattering, Lanore, but I'll tell you to prove that I'm being honest with you. In the course of my life, I've done things that others might call questionable. I did so always thinking I was in the right, of course, that these things were necessary for the betterment of science, to improve what we knew about the world beyond our natural world, the *supernatural* world. If I felt a qualm for what I've done, well, I told myself it didn't matter because I was going to live forever. I would never see the judgment day. Only that wasn't strictly true, was it?

"I've been outrunning death for centuries now. For a time, I didn't believe that there would be anyone to answer to. I've had my doubts that there was anything waiting on the other side of the veil, but Jonathan's taken care of this, hasn't he? He tells us that there's something, *someone,* waiting for us on the other side. I should've gone there—to the underworld, the domain of this queen—centuries ago. Surely if the queen came looking for Jonathan and found me, she would take me with her. But I wasn't prepared to be held accountable for my sins."

I lifted an eyebrow. Even a man as unrepentant as Adair could be afraid of judgment and punishment. Except he had proof now, didn't he, once he'd spoken to Jonathan. Something waited for us on the other side, and he was afraid of it. "That's why you sent Jonathan back—not because you didn't want me to see him again."

"He said this queen would come looking for him, and I *knew*—I felt in my heart—that I could not let this happen. We cannot meet." He seemed embarrassed by his admission. I wanted to assure him that everyone is afraid of dying and of the unknown, but I knew he didn't want to be comforted by me. It would make him appear weak, and he hated weakness in anyone. He absolutely wouldn't be able to tolerate it in himself.

Adair looked at me, ashamed. "Is this what you wanted to hear from me? A confession? To learn that I have fears, too?"

I still held his hands, and now gave them a squeeze. "I don't want you to hide your feelings from me, Adair. It's in these moments that I feel closest to you, I think," I admitted. He colored again, this time in surprise. "Anyway, that's why I've come to you. I'd heard that Jonathan was being held prisoner by this queen of the underworld and I want to see if I can help him."

He shook his head. "Leave it be, Lanore. You don't owe Jonathan anything. Let him take care of himself."

"It's not a matter of owing him anything, Adair. I haven't been able to stop thinking about him, trapped in purgatory. I was willing to put all that had happened aside and accept that I'd done the best I could, that Jonathan was gone from my life. But then these nightmares started, and they were all so vivid and so—obviously directed me. At first I thought it was a guilty conscience, just as you said . . ."

"What else could they be?" he asked, still skeptical.

"I think it's a message. He's being held prisoner in the underworld—and someone wants me to know it. Maybe it's Jonathan, maybe it's someone else, but I think somebody wants me to act."

"And what makes you think it is Jonathan?" Adair asked.

"Well, we have a bond between us—more so than the presence," I added, referring to the almost telepathic signal that existed between the person who had bestowed immortality and the recipients of this gift. We companions had always called it "the presence," an ever-present electronic vibration in our heads that tethered us to Adair. There had been one between me and Jonathan, but it had been broken the day I'd released him from his human form. The bond I was referring to now was the bond that had existed between Jonathan and me from childhood, a special love that had survived infidelities and blistering honesty, a bond that seemed indestructible.

"It would be unwise to assume that Jonathan is behind these dreams," Adair warned.

"It doesn't matter where the dreams are coming from. They're terrible, and getting worse. I can't ignore them any longer. I want to go to the underworld, Adair. I'm going to get this queen to release him."

He stared at me as though I had lost my mind. "And what do you think this would accomplish? Your loyalty to Jonathan is admirable, but . . ."

"Don't try to talk me out of it, Adair. I know it's foolish, but I feel in my heart that it's what I need to do."

"And how do you plan to do this? How do you propose to find this woman?"

The moment of truth had arrived. "That's why I've come to you. I want you to send me to the underworld."

He drew away from me as though I'd turned into a serpent before his very eyes. "You say this lightly, as though it is an easy thing! And how do you propose I do this? There's only one way that I know of, and that would be to release you—to *kill* you."

"No, that's not what I'm asking for," I said, rushing to reassure him. "I wouldn't ask you to release me, not after having gone through that hellish ordeal myself. I know better now." I killed Jonathan and carried that guilt with me every day since; I knew I would never be entirely happy again.

"I think there's another way to accomplish this." Adair listened skeptically as I explained how I thought he could assist me. "When I heard that my house in Paris had mysteriously burned to the ground, with no trace of arson, no sign of any accident, I knew it had to be you. Somehow you'd been able to do this even though you were nowhere near the city. I didn't see how this could be possible, so I thought and thought about it until I saw that the only explanation was that you must've been able to *will* your consciousness outside your body. That somehow you were able to reach across an ocean and start this fire in the real world, the physical world. I think that's the answer. Do you think you can do that for me, or teach me to do it? To send my consciousness to the underworld?"

He looked at me, still stricken. "I wish you wouldn't ask me to do this, Lanore. There are so many uncertainties, I don't know where to begin. . . ." He broke away from me and rose from the bed, and went to the window, rubbing his chin distractedly. "I might be able to send you there—it is not a given, not by any stretch—but more worrisome still is, how would you come back? What if I couldn't bring you back? You could be lost to the other side forever."

I don't think I'd ever seen Adair so distraught, not even when he released me from the palazzo at Garda. He paced in front of the window. "The only answer would be for me to go with you to the underworld—but I cannot do that. I have explained to you already."

"I understand, Adair. I'm not asking you to come with me," I said gently.

"How can you ask me to do this, Lanore?" he asked, his voice taut with anger and distress. "I might be the instrument of your destruction."

"I wouldn't let that happen. I wouldn't want to make you suffer."

"And what if Jonathan did not wish to come back? Have you thought about what you'll do then? Will you stay with him forever in the afterlife?"

"I'm not looking to stay with Jonathan, Adair." I lowered my gaze so he wouldn't see the love in my eyes. "I want to come back here."

He continued, carried away by his worry. "We've no idea what would be waiting on the other side. It could be the very end of you, but it's obvious that you won't let me talk you out of it. Why should I be surprised that you're willing to risk everything for Jonathan?" His voice was heavy; I'd hurt him deeply. "If you've nothing left in this life to live for . . . nothing at all . . ." I could have said something to him then, perhaps I *should* have, but if I told him that I had feelings for him—dare

I say that I *loved* him—he would never let me go. He'd never risk losing me. So I held my tongue.

He turned away from me. "I can see you've made up your mind and so . . . I can only tell you that I'll think about it. That's the best I can promise you at the moment."

"Adair—" I started toward him.

He held up a hand to make me keep my distance. "No. I need to be alone to think. Don't come after me, Lanore. I'll let you know when I've made a decision." He turned around and swiftly exited the room, closing the door behind him.

SEVEN

G ape-mouthed, I watched Adair leave and resolved
to let him go. He was obviously upset but wouldn't
want me to see him this way, and I didn't wish to
push him any further. I wished it hadn't gone so badly and
had to stop myself from rushing after him to try again, as I'd
undoubtedly only make things worse. There was no easy way
to ask a man who loved you to help you reunite with a rival,
but there was nothing to be done for it. No one else has Adair's
powers. A more rational person wouldn't have approached
Adair at all, no doubt, and would've given up Jonathan for lost,
but when it came to Jonathan my thinking was skewed.

He had been my first love, after all. Growing up in the
wilderness of the Maine territory in 1800, it was inevitable
that a boy of Jonathan's qualities would become the prince
of St. Andrew, our little town. For one thing, he was the

eldest son of the man whose timber business kept the town afloat, and many families with eligible daughters would've been interested in him for that reason alone. But in addition to being heir to a fortune, Jonathan had been blessed with formidable beauty. Indeed, even though none of us girls had ever been outside of our isolated town, we knew instinctively that Jonathan was uncommonly handsome. It wasn't until I was banished to Boston and had seen thousands of men that I understood how exceptional he really was.

While I didn't love Jonathan only for his looks, I won't lie and say that they didn't matter at all. You cannot imagine the force of Jonathan's appearance. Adair had been so jealous of him that he nicknamed him "the Sun God." He was like a master work of art or sculpture: one never tired of looking at him. I was always finding new depths to his beauty, too; I'd see him in a new way when a trick of light played over his hair, or as he stretched across a divan while reading a book. I wish I'd been an artist and able to capture all those moments on paper. It was a shame now that he was gone, there were so few records of him.

Ironically, Jonathan had hated when people stared at him. He learned to bear it with grace as he got older, but as a child, it used to upset him terribly. He would make a fuss, demand that people stop looking at him, and run away if they didn't. When he got a little older, it brought out a mean streak in him, and he would sometimes treat his smitten admirers poorly— until, with adolescence, he understood what it was they *really* wanted from him. And what these girls wanted was his atten- tion, to have this beautiful man treat them as though he was theirs, and theirs alone. They wanted to feel his mouth on theirs and his hands on their breasts, and they wanted to hold the firm measure of his masculinity in their quaking hands. They wanted to wrap their legs around his waist and feel him empty himself into them. They wanted him to make them squirm with pleasure before sighing with contentment. Oh yes: Jonathan came to understand their desire better than they did themselves, those girls who trailed in his wake like moths love-drunk on the flame.

Some people despised Jonathan for seducing women who ached to be seduced, angry because he did so on his terms, and to this I say: What of it? The women were happy—oh, there might have been a few tears when a girl realized that she would not be able to change his mind, and for God's sake, no one knew that better than I. But he never tricked any girl to get her into his bed. He was always up front with his intentions. His partners knew not to expect fidelity from him: How could they when there was an endless stream of women who begged and schemed for his attention? I learned the hard way that the clamoring and come-ons would never stop and that fighting human nature was futile. You might as well try to hold back the tide.

But of all those doe-eyed maidens and bored wives in St. Andrew, in the end I was the only one to be seriously hurt because I was the only one foolish enough to try to make him stay with me. Then Adair came into my life. His potion seemed tailor-made for my conundrum: it promised not only to bind Jonathan to me, but that we would be together *forever*. Leave it to Jonathan, slippery as an eel, to wriggle out of ties as ironclad as these. He left me after only ten years, left me to figure out how to survive in a world that was not kind to a woman on her own.

That had been my comeuppance for trying to trap him: a few unhappy years together and an eternity in which to miss him, and the presence in my head to remind me that he was alive but choosing that we live apart. It was a hellish punishment, though some might argue I deserved it for what I'd done to him. And for those who despised Jonathan for being a cad who seemed to flit through his life unscathed, they can take comfort from knowing the elixir kept him from outgrowing his beauty, as he would've in the natural course of things. If I hadn't given him the elixir, Jonathan would've gotten jowly and wrinkled, and would've found peace in his later years. As it was, he was trapped with all the attention he didn't want, with no way to make it stop.

Did either of us deserve our punishment? I'd turned this question over in my mind for nearly two hundred years, and the longer I lived, the more I'd begun to believe that I was not being punished, that this curse was not a judgment. If there was a God, it seemed ludicrous that he would single me out for such an extravagant punishment when there were people who'd done far worse. It used to be that when I met someone who was greedy or predatory, I'd wonder if someone like Adair might be keeping him in secret torment. I wondered if there were more people with my exact dilemma than I thought. Maybe the bad *were* cursed to suffer until they paid for their sins. For a while, I wished I could peel back the veneer of other peoples' lives to see if they, too, had a devil riding on their back. Until one day, I decided to stop thinking about it. To stop looking for evidence. It was driving me mad.

After Adair brought Jonathan back from the underworld, I could ignore it no longer. I tried to tease apart the few details I had to make sense of this unknown world. The fact that there was a queen seemed to indicate that there was an order to our existence, a grand plan. I began to wonder again if there was a reason for everything I'd been through—and if so, where I stood now. Did we carry our sins with us, like the chains of money boxes shackled to Jacob Marley's ghost, and if so, had I done enough good to atone for any of my sins, or had I only added more to the invisible chain I dragged behind me? I could imagine, too, how Adair felt at news of this queen, how it must've frightened him. And why he didn't want to send me into this shadowy netherworld, not wanting to draw the queen's attention; for his sins had to stretch behind him in chains so long they circled the earth; even Atlas would barely be able to stand the weight.

Now I had to wait for Adair's answer. After my earlier experience getting lost in the house's labyrinth of stairways and floors, I was loath to go exploring on my own again. It was midafternoon when I trotted downstairs. First, I checked in the kitchen for Robin and Terry and later went back to Adair's study and rapped on the closed door, but there were no signs of anyone. All was quiet and empty. Knives were left on the cutting board next to minced parsley, a book open and turned facedown, as though Terry and Robin had left in the middle of preparations.

Finally, I decided I might as well finish touring the island—if Adair's attitude toward me darkened, I could be leaving it at any time. I borrowed a heavy shawl left hanging on a hook by the door and went outside, only to be immediately assaulted by a wind so fierce that it seemed to want to drive me back into the house. I wasn't about to give up that easily, however, and head down, started off for a walk.

The terrain was uninviting, no matter which direction you went. I headed for the stand of pines, as it was the only windbreak on the island, picking my way over moss-covered rocks and holding my breath each time I almost slipped. On the other side of the trees was the long black beach. The slope made the approach bad for boats, as did the whirlpools and swells and rough currents that made such an approach impossible. Landing at the dock was the only way onto the island and made the island easily defensible. No wonder some earlier settlers had put a fortress on it.

I followed the beach until the shore became rocky, then cut inland to a worn, uneven trail that led over rocks stacked like giant children's blocks. When the rocks became cliffs I retreated farther inland, parallel to the coast, until I was back where I started. At this point I was mildly tired and wind-blown and the weather was picking up, and with the house staring down on me like a strict governess, I gave up and went inside.

Chilled to the bone, I kept the shawl wrapped around my shoulders as I wandered down the hall, calling "Hello? Hello?" even though I knew by the silence that there was no one about. As I passed the dining room, I saw that the table had been set with one plate holding a sandwich of cold meat on bread and a small haystack of dressed greens. One very full goblet of red wine and a damask napkin completed the vignette. Being hungry, I sat down and ate, pausing now and then to listen for evidence of someone else in the house. There was none.

I left the crusts on the plate, pushed back from the table, and took the goblet upstairs with me to my room. The bed had been made and a fire started, but it could not have been burning for very long, as there was still a chill in the air. I was beginning to feel like Goldilocks in the bears' house. The others had to be around; there was nowhere else to go on the island and nowhere to hide, except in this fun house of a dwelling. I had the feeling they were all around me—I just couldn't *see* them. As darkness fell and the house settled into creaks and groans, I downed a sleeping pill—no, two—with the last of my wine and crawled into bed, and before long was asleep.

I decided the next morning to bring Adair's books to him, even if he didn't seem in a rush to get them back, perhaps because he no longer needed them, surrounded as he was by Crowley's assistant's collection. I slipped them out of my knapsack and went downstairs to leave them in his study.

I went to Adair's study, knocking once before pushing back the old wooden door to find him sitting in a chair, staring into the fire. It was an incredible relief to see him, as I was half-afraid the room would be empty and I'd have another lonely day in front of me.

He looked up at me wanly. I hid my surprise and held the two books out to him. "Good morning. I'm returning these to you."

"Ah. You can put them over there." He nodded toward his desk.

Books held tight to my chest, I brushed past him. "I hope you don't mind that I didn't wait for you to send for me. I'm not trying to rush your decision, Adair, it's just that I was so lonely yesterday. This island is a spooky place when there's no one else around. Where did you go, anyway? I didn't see a soul the rest of the day."

"I was never far from you. I needed time and space to think."

It was a relief to know I hadn't imagined his absence or that the house, which I trusted less and less, hadn't spirited him away to its deepest recesses. "If you don't mind, may I join you for a while? I'll sit in the corner; you won't even know I'm here. It's just that, with the nightmares and being locked in that room in the cellar . . . I'd rather not be left on my own."

He continued to lean against his clasped hands as he studied the flames. "You can imagine how it's been for me, then, these past few years."

"I don't know how you could live here alone."

He glanced up at the shelves, at the rows and rows of books looking down on him. "It served me well at first, because I was trying to get away from the world. There was this trove of books to keep me busy in the beginning. So much to read. I was starting to get restless when the girls arrived. They've been a pleasant diversion, but they won't be staying much longer."

"Won't they?"

"No, I don't think so," he replied cryptically. Then he gestured for me to take the chair next to him by the fire. "Come here, Lanore, and sit with me. I want to talk to you. I've made my decision."

I did as he indicated and watched him anxiously, unsure if I was more afraid of being turned down or being told that I would get what I'd asked for.

He looked me over, as sad as I'd ever seen him. "I will do as you ask."

Relief broke over me and I simultaneously erupted in a cold sweat. "Oh, Adair, thank you—"

He held up a hand, interrupting me. "With conditions," he added quickly. "Conditions you must agree to, if I am to help you." He turned his head coldly so I couldn't look into his eyes. "First of all, you must promise to come back to me. No matter what you find there, even if Jonathan begs you to stay, you must promise that you will return. I will not deliver you to Jonathan only to lose you to him forever."

"I already told you that I will return," I said. "But, I swear."

He didn't seem especially pleased by my agreement, and continued solemnly. "Nor can you remain with the man you just lost, this Luke, if you should see him. I couldn't bear it if you disappeared in the underworld, not knowing what happened to you."

"Of course," I said, agreeing readily.

Adair turned his full attention to me, those green-gold eyes churning with a mixture of emotions—anger, remorse, helplessness. "I want to tell you, Lanore, that I knew right away what my answer would be. After everything we have been through, you should know already that I would deny you nothing. Whatever you ask of me, I would do it for you." His voice broke as he confessed that he was helpless, perhaps for the first time in his life. "But what I had to think about—what hurt me to the quick— was that you could ask this of me, *knowing* what it might cost me. It appears I was lucky with Jonathan—there have been no repercussions. But if she finds out about me, how I have cheated death . . . I can't imagine I will be that lucky a second time."

He was right, of course. Why hadn't I thought of that? No wonder he was hurt and upset with me. I had forgotten that he would be taking a risk, too. How could I be so inconsiderate? How could I take him for granted like this? And here I thought I'd changed from the selfish woman I was two hundred years ago.

I felt as though I'd gotten the wind knocked out of me. "Adair, forgive me. Forget what I said—I can't ask you to do this. That was thoughtless of me."

He looked at my stricken face and gave me a sad smile. "It is kind of you to offer to put your mission aside, Lanore, but I cannot accept. If we do not do this, the idea of Jonathan in the underworld will prey on you constantly. You'll never be able to get it out of your mind. If you're brave enough to go to the next world to save the man you love so dearly, I should be brave enough to send you."

And at that moment, I understood that Adair truly had changed. He had no reason to test fate and risk drawing the wrath of a powerful cosmic entity. He could've turned me down without an explanation. But he was willing to do whatever he needed to make me happy. The Adair of old would've thought it foolish and dangerous, and would not have considered my request, not for an instant. By acceding to my wishes, Adair had proven that he'd undergone a tremendous transformation and he had done it for me. What more could anyone ask of another person? I thought as I blinked back tears. I knew I could trust him completely, trust him to send my soul out into the unknown on a tether as fragile as a cobweb and he'd find a way to bring me back. I could trust him with my heart, too, if I ever was brave enough to give it to him. I rushed into his arms, briefly, pressing my face to his, and brushed his lips with a fleeting kiss. "Thank you, Adair. Thank you."

He closed his eyes, perhaps to hold on to that kiss an instant longer. "I'll make the necessary preparations for your journey. Just remember your promise. Come back to me."

EIGHT

⟨———————————————⟩

Now I had nothing to do but wait for Adair to figure out how to do what I'd asked of him. I had no doubt that he would find the right spell, whether it was hiding in one of the two books I'd returned to him—the one that was no more than a collection of loose sheets held between ancient wooden covers, or the meticulously hand-written, perfectly bound book of secrets with its peacock-blue cover—or somewhere in the house's many volumes on the occult. Adair would need to go through hundreds of books, thousands upon thousands of pages in an assortment of languages, modern and archaic, while my only job was to let him get to work.

The hours of waiting to hear from Adair were not empty; no, anxiety rushed in to keep me company. I was about to be sent to the next plane of existence, and it was impossible not to worry. It was, in some ways, like being an astronaut or intrepid adventurer, getting ready to venture into uncharted territory. Or, to look at it more grimly, it was not unlike dying, and dying was not a complete unknown to me, since I had died once already when Adair gave me the elixir of life that made me immortal. It struck me suddenly that all this time I'd been living an unexplainable paradox—being dead and yet not dead—and I was about to do it *again*, further complicating the complicated question of my existence.

Dying had been painful; even two centuries later, I remembered it well. The terror of being trapped in a body that was shutting down, fighting for breath as my heart failed and could no longer pump blood to my brain and lungs. Struggling to free myself of the weight that settled, heavier and heavier, on my chest. Clawing at the blackness that closed over me like cold water and tried to push me into a frightening void. Would it be like that this time?

Perhaps death wouldn't even be the worst of it, for I was traveling beyond death this time. What lay on the other side could be even worse. I thought of all the representations of the afterlife described in stories and poems. The nine rings of hell in Dante's *Inferno* came to mind, and I supposed that if I were lucky, I would be consigned to the second ring, the repository for those who have given in to the sin of lust. It seemed pretty tame compared to the ninth ring, the place where those guilty of treachery were kept. For I'd been treacherous, hadn't I? Most notably by imprisoning Adair behind a stone wall for two hundred years (for which he'd forgiven me, remarkably).

It didn't matter that I tried to turn my mind to more benign depictions of the afterlife: my thoughts stubbornly returned to hell, as though it was predetermined that this was the place where I would go. Maybe my dreams were a warning to me. The underworld would be a dark, cold place. The queen was surely there—the demon, too, and here I was, rushing toward what other people (those with common sense) would flee in terror. As frightened as I was, I knew I would go through with it. I was like a soldier collecting my thoughts in the moments before leaping into battle: there is no turning back, there is no getting out of it. I would never be able to live with myself if I gave up now, and, for me, never would last forever. I could just manage to keep from panicking by reminding myself that I had survived the unknown and the impossible the first time.

As I sat in the sunlight streaming through the window, eyes closed and absorbing heat like a cat on a sunny ledge, I half expected Adair to show up at my door with a certain request, one that I was surprised—and a little disappointed—that he hadn't made already. I could understand why he hesitated to invite me into his bed, constrained as he was by the presence of two Englishwomen and by my recent widowhood. But we were about to be separated by a huge cosmic gulf, the future uncertain. Although I had great faith in Adair's powers, I had to accept the possibility that we might never see each other again. Surely he would want us to be intimate at least once before he sent me into the unknown. When I considered that I might never have the chance to experience Adair's love again, I was starting to feel this way strongly, too. I would regret it forever if I was unable to return to this life. Besides, for all I knew, it might even strengthen his link to my soul and enhance his ability to transport it back and forth from the underworld.

Desire awakened inside me like a thousand tremulous butterflies as I warmed to the idea of going to bed with Adair again. As Terry had pointed out, he was a very good partner (as well he ought to be: he'd had a thousand years of practice and, in all that time, probably let few opportunities to practice pass him by). He didn't lack for confidence, or the right equipment, and the cock between his legs was a magnificent thing with such heft that it had to be held with two hands. He had been a good teacher, too. Jonathan was my first lover and had been good in his way (though, as a seventeen-year-old, I'd hardly known the difference), but he could not compare with Adair for technique or sheer lustful enthusiasm. From Adair, I learned to enjoy sex and not to fear it. In many ways, it was Adair who ushered me into adulthood.

Since coming to the island, I'd felt there had been moments when he was waiting for me to relent, to take him by the hand and lead him to his bedroom. Or maybe to my room, where there wouldn't be the scent of the other women infused in the bed linens or stray hairs of brown and gold on the pillows. We would go to my modest room and lock the door against surprise, and he would pull me on top of him on the narrow bed as he looked deeply into my eyes. In bed, he could have any of a hundred different moods, but he was always eager for more: more tactile sensation, more cresting pleasure. Thinking about him made the urge all the harder to resist. How easy it would be to give in. I suppose it meant my heart was healing after Luke's death, that I would even consider it.

Adair had probably known all along that I'd wanted him. He would've only needed to kiss me and I wouldn't have been able to resist him. Should I find him now and have one last pleasure with him before heading to the underworld? I was struggling to extinguish this spark of desire when there was a knock at the door, jolting my eyes open. Adair stood in the doorway as though he'd been summoned by my thoughts. Only he didn't look aroused. He didn't even look happy. He was glum and fretful, full of misgivings. In one hand, he carried a mug.

"Is it time already?" I asked weakly. "You found the spell so soon?"

"I already had an idea where to look. It was only a matter of putting the ingredients together," he said as he entered the room. He put the mug on the table next to the bed, then ran his hands over the mattress, smoothing the sheets. "You will lie here, on this bed, while your soul is in the underworld. Come, sit." I did as I was instructed and perched on the edge of the bed.

Adair reached into his pocket and pulled out something that he pressed in my hand. "I've been thinking about your return, about how I will know to bring you out of suspension. We need some kind of signal. I want you to hold this. Carry it with you at all times, wherever you go. And when you are ready to come back, just let it go. I will see it fall from your hand, here, and I will know to bring you back." He closed my fingers around the object, looking earnestly into my face. "Will you do that for me?"

"Of course," I said. When I opened my hand, however, I couldn't believe what I saw: it was the vial that he'd worn around his neck when I first met him, the vial that had contained the elixir of life. The one I'd stolen from him and used to make Jonathan immortal—to make him *my* immortal consort, with disastrous results.

"This is impossible," I gasped as I held it up in the light so

I could get a good look at it. It was the same filigreed cylinder of silver and brass, its stopper and chain intact. "It can't possibly be . . . Luke told me, on his deathbed, that he'd found it among my things. He said he'd crushed it under his heel and threw it out the window."

"I found it on the beach here when I was out walking one day," Adair said, not astonished in the least. As though he knew all his possessions would come back to him, given enough time. Like the books of secrets I'd returned to him. Like me.

I turned the vial around in a complete circle. It wasn't crushed. It wasn't damaged in the least. "I don't understand . . ."

Adair closed my fingers around it again. "Understanding is not necessary for this spell to work. Faith is." He handed me the cup. "Drink this."

Like his previous elixirs, it smelled of grass and mud, things of the earth not meant to be ingested in such a raw form. I wrinkled my nose at it. "Another potion? Why must it always be a potion?"

"I suppose you'd rather have it be a dram of whiskey," he observed.

"Or even a piece of cake," I said, and sniffed.

He tapped the mug. "Drink up."

If I had reservations, now was the time to bring them up. If I didn't wish to go, I could've handed the cup back to Adair. I could've asked him to assuage my fear of pain or of being lost forever and wandering like a ghost between the planes of existence. I could've encouraged him to climb onto the bed with me and blank out all my misgivings.

But I did none of those things. The abyss was waiting for

me, yawning before me like a great black chasm, and I knew if I hesitated now, I might not go through with it. I took a deep breath and swallowed the potion as quickly as I could, so as not to taste it. Despite my efforts, I caught the tail end of it, and to my surprise it didn't taste of weeds and dirt but of the finest vanilla cake frosted with buttercream. I wiped the last drop from my chin with the back of my hand as I handed the cup to him.

As he took the cup from me, I couldn't resist . . . I gazed deeply into his eyes as I leaned against him, and kissed him. For one moment, we were locked together and made one, and it was as though I could feel every emotion he was experiencing at that instant: surprise, elation, gratitude, longing, regret—so much regret—and happiness. I felt happiness, too, and it surged between us for one long minute, even after our mouths had parted. That kiss was all it took for me to know that I loved him, despite all that had happened between us, despite any doubts I might still have had. I loved him and there was nothing I could do to change that; I'd been stupid to try to deny it.

Adair felt it, too, in that kiss. He knew that something fundamental had changed between us and he hesitated, waiting for a sign from me. I could've stopped it right then, I think. I could've told Adair that I'd changed my mind and that would be that. We'd start to explore what could be between us—but it would be tainted from the very beginning. Adair had said as much himself: not knowing what happened to Jonathan would prey on my mind. Adair understood when I said nothing, did nothing, and without another word, he helped me lie back on the bed, and spread a blanket over me as though I was only about to take an afternoon nap.

I held on to the edge of the mattress to steady myself. "Something's happening already," I told him. "It feels like the bed is falling, as though the house is collapsing underneath me." I tried to smile reassuringly as I spoke, but there are few feelings as frightening as suddenly losing all sense of balance.

"Will you be okay?" he asked, closing my hand tightly around the vial.

"I'm a little scared," I admitted.

"I'll be right here. I won't leave your side. Don't forget: the vial. Release it and I will bring you back in a heartbeat." He ran a fingertip over my forehead, brushing a lock of hair aside in a tender moment of concern, my last image of him as I felt myself falling for real, halfway inside another world, with the world I knew galloping away from me. Adair disappeared from my view and I saw nothing but blackness, walls of blackness falling away from me. I held on to consciousness a moment longer, enough to realize that it didn't feel like the transformation at all. There was no pain, only the feeling of being pulled along at an incredible speed through utter darkness—where was the light everyone talked about seeing as they were dying? And then, just as suddenly, there was nothing. No reassuring presence at my side, no vial in my hand, no lingering taste of vanilla on my lips. No blackness or the rush of wind on my face as I fell. Nothing at all.

NINE

When I regained consciousness, I saw that I was in the fortress. I was surprised; I'd expected to be transported to another world, one that was familiar and biblical in nature, like that of Dante's *Inferno* or Milton's *Paradise Lost*. I don't know why I'd made this assumption, though it seemed to prove that old saying that wayward souls will turn back to God on their deathbeds. Given my nightmares and the role that the fortress had played in them of late, I probably shouldn't have been surprised to find myself there, and at least I was on the upper floor and hadn't woken in the hated cellar.

As a matter of fact, I shouldn't say that I "woke up," as though I'd been asleep, but instead was suddenly aware of my surroundings, as often happens in dreams. Everything looked just as it had in Adair's house. I was in a wide hall with a long red runner under my feet, and the familiar wooden doors to the bedrooms faced me on either side. The same iron sconces hung on the wall, the same rough-hewn Italianate chairs sat at intervals the length of the corridor. It was so clearly Adair's home that, for a minute, I wondered if the elixir hadn't worked and I had only sleepwalked from my room. But when I looked at my surroundings more closely, I noticed that the hall ran longer than the ones in Adair's house; as a matter of fact, this one seemed to telescope out like a fun house in both directions. If I took a step toward either end, it seemed to snake out farther still.

The hall was as quiet as a library. I walked up to one door and put my ear close, listening for sounds on the other side, before trying the handle. I strained, but I heard nothing. Had I any reason to choose this door over the one next to it or the one down the hall? I considered this predicament for a minute, but reasoned that I had been set down in the fortress at this precise spot for a reason, and that was to go into the room in front of me. I gripped the cold metal doorknob, gave it a turn, and stepped inside.

It was obvious that I'd stepped into another dimension. The room I entered wouldn't have existed in Adair's fortress. It seemed like the lobby of a grand hotel with groupings of chairs, rattan with pale green silk cushions, flanked by potted palms. The ceiling was high, the room itself very wide. Tall shuttered windows held back harsh white sunlight, throwing sliced shadows onto the floor. Huge ceiling fans circled overhead, pushing around hot, humid air. Streams of people walked by in all directions wearing clothing from an earlier era. The women wore dresses with long, full skirts and wide sleeves, and tall hats perched on elaborately done hair; the men wore tight-waisted morning coats and long trousers, despite the heat. The crowd consisted mostly of Westerners, but there were a number of Arabs, too, in spotless white tunics as a kind of livery. It was a hotel, obviously one that catered to Western travelers, and by the looks of the people and the surroundings, not to mention the heat, it appeared to be somewhere in North Africa or the Levant. As I stumbled along, trying to make sense of the location, I realized that I recognized this place. I'd been here before.

As I walked slowly down the lobby, gaping at the hotel guests passing by, it started to make sense. This was the hotel in Fez where Jonathan had abandoned me nearly two hundred years ago. I felt a jolt of pain at the recollection, but I told myself that it was only the last, lingering traces of an old embarrassment and didn't mean that I was still hurt by his cruelty. However, I couldn't imagine what it meant that I'd been brought here to this time and place. That fateful day, the day I woke to find Jonathan had abandoned me, was not one I wanted to relive. I'd already felt the pain of that betrayal a thousand times. Perhaps that's what happened in the underworld; perhaps I would be forced to relive all the worst moments of my life. The thought terrified me; I tried not to panic. *Hang on and let's see what happens next,* I thought gamely to calm my nerves.

As I walked through the lobby, I realized that the people all around me couldn't see me. They couldn't hear me or feel my presence, either. I was like a ghost to them, here to observe them, not vice versa. But why I'd been sent to this place at this particular moment in time, I couldn't guess.

I was about to turn around and look for a way out when my

gaze fell on a man in a tall, fan-backed rattan chair. I knew this man. He wore an impeccably tailored suit of light wool, a swallow-tailed morning jacket in a dove gray, with a pale-pink-and-gray foulard silk cravat wound high around his throat. His blond curly hair was tamed with pomade, and a charcoal top hat sat jauntily atop his head. His gloved hands rested on the silver handle of a fine gentleman's walking stick, and he looked at me over the rim of a pair of dark spectacles, with an amused look on his face.

"I was wondering when you were going to turn up, Lanny. I've been waiting for you for a whole five minutes. You're late." It was my old friend Savva.

I took the chair opposite him, as I'd done in an earlier life when he found me in this same lobby and brought me back from the brink of despair after Jonathan had left me. That was the first time I'd met him, and it was this meeting that made me realize there were more of Adair's companions walking the earth than I'd hitherto guessed. After our initial meeting, Savva and I traveled together for a number of years, through northern Africa and along the Silk Road for the most part, trying to avoid detection and eke out a living. It had been a precarious existence, mainly because neither of us had any useful skills beyond being decorative and charming. I was only a woman, a fact that counted for little in those days, and Savva was a wildly unreliable drunkard, opium fiend, and homosexual. We were, in short, a suspect pair as far as society was concerned but not a threat to anyone. As long as no one took special notice of us, we managed to skate by.

The man who sat in the chair in front of me was nothing like Savva as I'd last seen him four years ago, ravaged by heavy drug use and alcoholism. By then, it was clear that what had been thought of as his nature—indolent, capricious, and naughty, by nineteenth-century standards—was actually a serious personality disorder, bipolar or some other manifestation, which he'd tried to endure through the increasingly heavy use of drugs. The man in the chair opposite me was the Savva of old, charming, devilish, and sweetly beautiful. He was like a boy bent on playful anarchy, who—with a mischievous glint in his eye—beckons you to join him.

"I thought I'd never see you again!" Savva exclaimed, at the same time I said, "What are you doing here?" and we both laughed.

"Are you dead?" Savva asked delicately.

"No, I'm not. Are you?" I asked, even though I knew the answer.

Savva nodded. "Yes, for . . . well, a short while. One loses track of time here, one day bleeding into the next, if there are actually 'days' at all." He pulled a gold watch from a vest pocket and waved it nonchalantly on the end of its little chain. "Completely useless here. It reads the same all the time, regardless of whether it's light or dark. Doesn't matter if I look at it all day. Useless."

"If you're dead, then it must've been . . ." I'd been putting the pieces together and broke off, unable to finish the sentence.

"It was Adair, yes. He found me and released me," Savva said calmly. "He told me that *you'd* sent him. Now, don't look so shocked; I know you meant it as a kindness. It was a very *enlightening* encounter and I will tell you all about it, but not right now. I would much rather hear your news. How in the world did you come to be here if you haven't died? Wait—don't answer that yet. I want to show you something first. Come with me. We're going for a *stroll*."

Miraculously, when we stepped through a door, all of Fez unfurled before us, Fez of 1830, better than my memory could ever capture. The city was exactly as it had been, as though it had never evolved, as though it had been someone's intent to capture it this way for eternity so it could be bookmarked and called up instantly, perhaps for a purpose very much like this— and I wondered if all of history was indexed like this, and for what reason.

We took to the thoroughfare in front of the hotel. Carriages clattered by, carrying Western tourists out to see the sights of the day, but Moroccans comprised most of the traffic, traveling by foot or the occasional donkey-drawn cart. There was dust everywhere, a fine white powder raised by traffic, floating at knee height in perpetual clouds. Savva hooked my arm under his and we started along the street, the merciless Moroccan sun beating down on our heads. As we walked, Savva shot his walking stick out smartly, the polished wood glinting in the sunlight.

"How can this be? How could we be back nearly two centuries in time?" I asked, gesturing to the scene around us. "It's not possible. It can't be Morocco. We must be in heaven or hell. Which is it, Savva?"

He gave me a thoughtful frown. "Why, I've always assumed I was in heaven, for how could hell possibly be like this?"

"And have you been here the entire time you've been, um, deceased?"

"In Morocco? Goodness, no." He chuckled drily. "If I had

to spend the hereafter in just one place, I would hardly pick that dreary hotel. No, I suspect I was brought here because of *you*, to see you."

"Is that how it works? Are you summoned to a particular time or spot every time someone once close to you dies?"

The brilliant sun glinted off Savva's dark spectacles as he shook his head. "No, I don't think that's the case. When Adair killed me, I first arrived at a lovely mansion, one of those white palatial affairs, set on a huge green lawn with a hedgerow maze and clouds of sheep grazing off in the distance. I thought I'd been brought to the English countryside, that heaven was an English country manor—one teeming with gorgeous men. The best part was that they were all gay—or if they were straight they found me *irresistible*, because all I had to do was smile at them and we'd be off shagging in one of the upstairs bedrooms." He smiled glassy-eyed at the memory of those early happy days after death.

"Really? Only men—no women?" I asked, thinking maybe he'd just overlooked them.

"Maybe it's heaven for homosexuals. Maybe there is a different heaven for straight people, or lesbians," he replied, astringent as ever. "Or maybe it was tailor-made for me, I don't know. I can only tell you what I've experienced. As you can imagine, it took quite a while for all this nonstop shagging to get tedious enough for me to take a break and explore the rest of the mansion. That's when I began running into people I knew, people who'd passed before me, and that's when this thing would happen"—he gestured to the scene surrounding us—"when we'd suddenly be transported back to the time and place where we'd known each other. I have no idea why

that happens, unless it's to make it easier to remember who
the other person is, or to ease the reconnection, or just for the
cosmic hell of it. Oh, you know me, Lanny—I never wonder
about these things, I just accept them for what they are."

Yes, this was Savva's nature, for better or worse. Easygoing
and not one to question his situation, Savva wasn't going to be
much help in explaining the reasons behind the events taking place in the afterlife. I had so many questions for him but
couldn't let myself get sidetracked. I had to find Jonathan and
return to Adair. I could almost feel Adair's impatience like a
string tugging at me.

"There's a reason I'm here, Savva," I said, getting straight
to the point. "I'm on a mission. I'm here to find someone and
I could use your help." I explained my current predicament as
best I could, giving him a detailed account of the nightmares.

He snorted in mild disgust at the mention of Jonathan's
name. Not that I could blame him after all the evenings he'd
spent nursing me through fits of weeping. Jonathan was the
root of all the evil in my life, as far as Savva was concerned. I
pushed on to avoid yet another discussion about my blind de-
votion to a man who did not return my affections; this time, it
wasn't about love—it was about duty.

"What about the queen of the underworld?" I ventured.
"Have you heard of her?"

Savva drew back like a man who'd almost stepped on a
snake. "Oh yes, I've actually seen her. Not everybody does, you
know. It's not as though she's Saint Peter, administering your
test before you're allowed to pass through the pearly gates," he
said with a snide laugh. He continued to hustle me along, his
walking stick shooting forward in time with his stride. "I'd

been here for a while before hearing about her. As I said, it's impossible to judge how much time has passed here, but I was at a party one night, in the mansion. There were bar dancers wearing little, tiny short shorts and a mirror ball flashing light all over the room—just like the halcyon disco days in the 1970s. The place was packed and we were all dancing with abandon. Then, all of a sudden, there was a commotion on the other side of the ballroom, the sound of excited murmuring, like a swarm of angry bees."

Savva became quite animated at this point, caught up in his tale, and he sped up his gait, hurrying me along even faster down the street. "One of my friends grabbed my hand and said we've got to go, that the queen was coming. And he pulled me toward the exit at the back of the room, only everyone was headed in the same direction, and before we could get to the doors we heard someone call out, 'Make way! Make way for your queen!'

"And then the crowd parted and I saw *them* step onto the dance floor, the *demons*." Savva tried to suppress a shudder. "That was the first time I saw them, but it wouldn't be the last. Hideous things, they are, half-man, half-beast. They were the embodiment of evil. There were two of them, snorting like horses and scanning the crowds as though they were looking for someone. Then this woman stepped on the dance floor between them.

"I could tell she wasn't human right from the start; she was so tall and thin and spectral. She was wrapped in a black cloak that covered her from her throat to her shoes, and in the darkness it just looked like her head was floating through space. She had flaming red hair that danced about her head as though it were alive, like Medusa's snakes. The queen has the face of a predator, high cheekbones and hungry eyes. Sharp, cunning. She, too, was looking over the crowd. You could tell by the delighted expression on her face that she was on the hunt, looking for prey.

"She finally found what she wanted, a handsome boy with blond curls and blue eyes—a boy who didn't look all that different from me, really. I sometimes wondered if she *hadn't* been looking for me that night, though I can't imagine why she would. She snapped her fingers at her demon guards and they took hold of the boy, each hooking one of his arms in theirs, and dragged him away."

"What did she do to him?" I asked, aghast.

"I don't know. Nobody knows what she does with the unfortunates, though it's rumored that she makes them *disappear*. My friend told me that whomever she chooses is never seen again."

The queen's inclination for pretty men could explain why she was holding Jonathan. "What about the demons? Do they roam around freely?" I asked.

"No. You never see them except in her company. I assumed they were her bodyguards or something like that. Her royal guard. She is the queen, after all." He tilted his head thoughtfully and laid a hand on my arm. "Are you sure you want to do this? Go up against the queen and her demon guards? Oh, but what am I saying. It's Jonathan we're talking about. Wild horses wouldn't stop you."

We were back at the entrance to the hotel, the sun starting to slant sideways, the day half-gone (or pretending as much). I squeezed both of Savva's hands in mine. They were fine-boned and silky, and I noticed he had on his old rings, a gold signet and a large, square-cut emerald, ones he'd sell to secure our freedom from an Algerian pirate, later in our personal timeline. "It was good to see you, Savva. And thank you for the information. But I'd better be going. . . ."

He held me fast. "Don't go yet, Lanny. Who knows when we might see each other again, if ever?" His eyes got a little damp. "You can give me an hour more, surely you can. Let's order tea. They do a fabulous high tea here, you really must indulge me," he said, ignoring my weak protests and raising a hand to flag down one of the hotel staff.

Plates of butter cookies layered with raspberry jam and lemon curd and dusted with sugar. Scones and clotted cream. Crustless watercress-and-cucumber sandwiches cut into tiny batons. A pot of luxuriant Ceylon tea for me, better than any I could recall ever having in real life, and for Savva, a tall sparkling gin and tonic (for "tea" would never mean tea for Savva). This banquet was brought to us on a large brass tray made into a table with the addition of a little wooden tripod, and was placed between our two chairs. The fact that the hotel did not serve anything like this proper English tea in 1830 was not lost on me, but I took a page from Savva's book and decided to suspend disbelief and go with the flow while I was here in the underworld.

Amid the lush spread, I asked Savva how he'd met his end, curious to know how Adair had handled his release, whether he'd treated Savva kindly. By then, Savva had been in worse shape than the last time I'd seen him, and had moved from his apartment in the medina to a tenement building in a rough neighborhood outside of Casablanca. It was the very last thing he could afford, Savva admitted, the next step being squatting with other junkies in an abandoned, condemned building. Adair must've been shocked to see what had become of the charming boy he'd once known, the bon vivant who had grown up on the fringes of aristocracy in the beautiful city of St. Petersburg.

According to Savva, Adair had turned up out of the blue at the apartment one evening. He didn't have to break in, as the door had been open; more often than not, in a drugged stupor Savva failed to remember to latch the door. Adair found him asleep on a bed in the filthy, disheveled apartment, fully dressed except for shoes and socks, his face blank and dreamless. A few objects had stood on the nightstand: a candle stub, still burning, and his rig—a syringe, a spoon, and a shoelace, much used and fraying.

"Is it you, Adair, really you, come to see me after all these years?" Savva had muttered to his visitor, eyes rolling under half lids. He'd thought he imagined Adair at his bedside, the man who had lost interest in him long ago.

But Adair had kept staring at him, horrified and speechless. "It was so obvious that he was pitying me. It was unsettling," Savva confessed. "I never would've thought it possible, you know. To him, pity was a useless emotion. I must've been nearly unrecognizable to Adair, jaundiced and drawn by long weeks—months!—without so much as a bite to eat." I pictured his blue eyes gone dull, his skin as lifeless as a dried corn husk, his hair thin. "Adair couldn't believe I'd gotten that bad. He thought we would *never* change, no matter what we did. I think he was shaken that I had managed to spoil his handiwork."

Adair had explained how he'd come at my request, Savva told me. "It's not as though I *wanted* you dead," I protested, coloring at having been found out, but he waved my concern aside. "I understand why you did it, Lanny, and I'm grateful. I didn't want to live forever. We're not meant to, we're not built for it, some of us less so than others. I'm a weak vessel; I accept that. Life had become unbearable for me and you knew it. I was glad that Adair had come. Strangely, though, he didn't want to end my life, even after seeing what had become of me. He talked of helping me, rehabilitating me—Adair, can you believe it? He even told me that he was *sorry* for having caused me to suffer, which made me laugh out loud. I couldn't believe my ears. Adair, apologizing. Can you imagine it?"

Savva's words comforted me. I was glad for proof that Adair had changed beyond what I'd seen for myself on the island. The fact that he could have compassion for someone besides me proved that he didn't act only in his own self-interest. He was willing to change in order to make me happy. The reserve I held in place, to keep from completely falling in love with Adair, melted a tiny bit.

"I finally did it, you know," Savva continued in a serious tone, snapping me out of my reverie. "I confronted him. 'I never understood why you chose me,' I told him, 'or why you let me live when you so obviously stopped having any need of me. I shouldn't have been a coward, that day I left your household. I should've asked you to kill me instead of letting me go. I've been trying to kill myself, anyway, ever since. So, yes, I want you to do as Lanny asked,' I told him. 'I want you to kill me.' And he did." Savva took a long drink from his gin and tonic, happy in a childish, spiteful way.

"How—how did he do it?" I asked, barely able to ask and yet possessed by morbid curiosity. Would there be some kind of ceremony to it? It couldn't be as straightforward as ending a mortal life, could it?

Savva became still. "He made me close my eyes. Then he put his hands around my throat—those strong hands, so deft—and broke my neck. It was over in a second." He snapped his fingers and I jumped at the sound. "Adair was gentle as a lamb about it, so concerned that he might cause me a second of pain. He was almost the way he'd been at the beginning when he first saved me and made me immortal—courtly, you know? When he loved me. Funny—Adair was always a bit like a father to me. I suppose that sounds horribly twisted, but there you have it. To me, he was the capable older man who was going to take care of me. I think he saw himself that way, too, and that's why it bothered him that I'd been stumbling around, lost, feeling unwanted. It was like he just realized that he'd failed me."

"Is *that* what this has all been about?" I asked softly. Savva's self-destructiveness and unhappiness: Had it all been because Adair had ceased to want him? Had he been wandering the world unhappily because he had been cast out of Adair's life and forced to go on without him?

Savva laughed archly as he tossed his napkin to the table. "Oh, my dear, you needn't be so melodramatic. It isn't entirely Adair's fault, as much as we like to blame him for all our troubles. I brought baggage of my own: I was looking for a big, strong man to make me feel safe and secure." His words resonated with me more than I wanted to admit.

We spent the next half hour nibbling on tea cookies and

analyzing the man who fascinated us both. "It is always a case of mutual attraction," Savva said with conviction; it was obviously a matter to which he'd given considerable thought. "Attraction is a very curious thing, you know. We're rarely attracted for the reasons we think; it's the subconscious at work. In all our cases, we were drawn to Adair, and he to us. There was something in him that we were looking for, each of us in our way. I wanted a father—I admit it—and he, perhaps, wanted someone who would adore him like a son. Tilde admired his power because it was what she wanted for herself." I hoped he'd stop short of psychoanalyzing me. I didn't want him to peer into my heart and pluck out the weaknesses that had drawn me to Adair. I'd rather not think that I was drawn to Adair out of weakness. I wanted to believe that I knew Adair now, and was falling in love with him with eyes wide open—nor did I want to admit to Savva that I'd fallen in love with the man I'd once feared and loathed.

"Adair needed us to do his dirty work, yes, but he needed us to adore him, too. He liked to be adored, the same way a king likes to be surrounded by flattering courtiers and boot-lickers," he said, meanly enough to make me squirm. What place had I held, then, in this unflattering gallery? Savva rose then and bent down to kiss me on the cheeks as he prepared to take his leave. "Be very careful, Lanny. I wish I could talk you out of this crazy mission of yours. You don't want to run afoul of the queen." He tugged on his gloves, looking the very picture of a gentleman. "Anyway, I hope we see each other again, but I don't know that you'll be able to recognize me at all, if we do. I feel as though the most peculiar changes have been coming over me lately."

"What sort of changes?" I asked, suddenly seized with anxiety now that Savva was leaving me to navigate the underworld alone.

He made a face, coloring high on his cheeks. "I don't know if I should tell you this—it's rather embarrassing—but I think I'm beginning to grow a *tail*. There seems to be the littlest nub at the base of my spine. I can't imagine for the life of me what that must mean."

We kissed good-bye again and I let him melt into the crowd before I collapsed back into my seat. *Growing a tail.* There was no doubt what it meant: he was turning into a demon. If this was the case, it meant that the demons Savva had seen accompanying the queen and I had seen in my dreams might have been Adair's companions, too. His companions had been hurtful beings in life, and it seemed they would go on to fill an even worse role in the afterlife. A horrible thought, that we had an assignment waiting for us in the underworld.

It wasn't until I rose to leave that I realized I had no idea where to go next. I doubted I was meant to remain in 1830, and yet I had no notion how to leave. I tried to retrace my steps, moving slowly down the lobby. Finally, I came to what, I was pretty sure, was the door I'd originally come through. When I gripped the doorknob, it tingled in my hand like a premonition, and I knew it was the right door. I pushed it open and stepped over the threshold.

TEN

Adair pulled an armchair next to the bed where Lanny lay. At the sight of her face, tranquil but motionless, he groaned with displeasure. He couldn't help but be upset at the sight of her: though pink-cheeked and dewy-fleshed, she was so still, she could be mistaken for dead. And as unsettling as it was to see her like this, he found it more unsettling to leave her. He sat at her bedside with the tense, expectant air of a spouse in a hospital room. He stared at her for hours on end, watching her face in the hope of seeing a twitch or flutter of an eyelid, the first sign that she was on her way back. When his anxiety got to be too much to bear, he would remind himself that he could always revive her. It was within his power—theoretically. True, she'd be mad at him for bringing her back too soon, but if he claimed he'd acted in her best interest, she wouldn't be able to stay mad at him.

Still, he'd given her his word and could only hope that Lanore intended to keep her word, too, so he continued to be patient and wait.

Nonetheless, he still had misgivings about the mechanics of transportation to the underworld, the science of moving someone through planes of existence. It was as though he'd sent her off in a car that he'd cobbled together from spare parts without quite knowing how it would actually work. She might end up in a ditch on the side of the road with no way to ask for his help . . . except that she had the vial. The fact that it had washed up on the shore here gave Adair some hope, as though it had some special homing property with magical powers all its own.

Days passed, Adair parked in her bedroom like a worried dog waiting on its master's return. He was shocked to realize only a few days had passed when it felt like an eternity.

He looked down on Lanore, laid out like his own Sleeping Beauty, fully clothed, her blond curls spread over the pillow like twisted ribbons, her pink lips moistly parted. He watched her bared sternum rise and fall. The edge of her bra was just visible under the neckline of her dress, tempting him to touch it, to finger the lace and the soft flesh under it. She was achingly molestable. If only they'd had sex before she'd left, he thought, this waiting might be easier to endure. He kicked himself for not bringing it up at the time, afraid of what she'd think of him. It made it all the harder to sit next to her now without imagining what it would be like to have his way with her. He was seized with the idea of taking his clothes off and lying next to her. If he could hold her body against his, he'd be able to half sate this intense need for her.

As he sat thinking slightly obscene thoughts, Adair realized Terry was beside him, appearing out of nowhere and twitchy as a snake about to strike. "No change? Is she still asleep?" she said with what he was sure was false solicitousness. He'd told Robin and Terry that Lanny had taken ill and was sleeping off her sickness. "You might as well come to bed. It won't change things, you watching her like this . . ."

"Someone should be here when she wakes up."

"We can leave the door open. We'll hear if anything happens." Robin had edged up on the other side and now was massaging Adair's shoulder a little too desperately.

"No, you two go to bed. Maybe I'll join you later." It was a complete lie, as he had no intention of going to their bedroom tonight or, in all likelihood, any other night. He didn't want them hovering at his elbow, waiting for him to betray so much as one lovesick look at Lanny.

Terry ran a hand over his shoulder, then his chest. "Come to bed," she protested. "It's been days and you've barely left this room. This is getting—weird."

Robin tried, too, tugging his arm. "I want you. I'm horny," she said plaintively, like a child asking for a glass of water.

The thought of having sex with the two of them was, frankly, mildly revolting. He had no appetite for anyone except Lanore. How could he go off and enjoy himself with these two while his love was submerged in the underworld and might need his help? Adair felt displeasure bubble up inside him, ready to explode.

"Not tonight. Don't wait up for me," he told them.

"Adair—"

"Enough! Leave me!" he bellowed, impatience crackling

in the air between them. They scurried out quickly and he closed the door and then, after a moment's consideration, braced a chair under the doorknob. He climbed into bed next to Lanny and lay on his side with his head resting on one arm, his topmost arm lying on her stomach. His head was even with hers and he noted the details of her face, the way her eyelashes fanned against her cheeks, the rim of her lips. He wished for her eyes to open as nothing he'd ever wished before.

Wake up, he thought. *Be here with me.* He wanted to gather her body in his arms and pull her to him, cradle her to his chest like a big, limp doll. The sight of her, corpse-like, had disturbed him so much that he needed the comfort of her touch, for reassurance that he hadn't lost her completely. He remained pressed against her on the narrow bed, his face buried in her hair, and listened as the wind shook the glass in the window and howled as it soared to the roof, as angry as a woman scorned. Slowly he drifted off to a space in between sleep and wakefulness, hoping it would bring him all the closer to her.

VENICE, 1262

Adair crouched on the landing of the back stairway in the doge's palace. He was a boy, fifteen, gawky and thin, a scarecrow in a nobleman's finery. He hid in the shadows, listening for the footsteps of a guard that might be between him and the door to the alley. He heard nothing. The palace was quiet.

He had been living for a month in the household of the

doge of Venice, Reniero Zeno. The doge was doing this as a courtesy to Adair's father, a Magyar lord, the equivalent of a duke in Italy. It was a curious practice of noble families, this shuttling of family members around like pawns. Daughters barely out of swaddling clothes were betrothed and left with a family of strangers, growing up alongside their intended spouse like brother and sister. Sons were sent to serve in a powerful competitor's court as a token of good faith, a hedge to keep one realm from attacking the other.

In Adair's case, there was no betrothal or enmity: it was pure courtesy and nothing more. His father needed a place to send his youngest son away from the wagging tongues at Magyar court after his tutor, the crazy Prussian Henrik, was arrested for heresy. Bad enough the lord had a son who did not wish to rule, but to make the matter worse he was interested in *science*. He had been born curious about everything. Always asking too many questions, eager to take a thing apart to see how it was put together, and that included dead animals, live reptiles, pig and sheep fetuses cut out of the womb. The clergy at court were angered by his experiments, fearing they disrespected God.

Adair had found a new alchemy tutor since coming to Venice. Officially, he was studying medicine with Professore Scolari, the doge's physician, known for his learned lectures on medicine and physiology. But Adair had been thrilled to find out that one of the bishops often seen in court, Bishop Rossi, was a devotee of alchemy, and managed to get Rossi to invite him to his private laboratory. It wasn't entirely surprising that Rossi, a clergyman, had an interest in alchemy, as it was the fad of the day and nearly everyone practiced it—well, anyone with a lick of education and any intellectual curiosity at all. The pope himself was rumored to dabble.

Sure that the doge would not want his ward practicing alchemy—it had to be part of the bargain with Adair's father, he was sure—Adair began sneaking off to the bishop's palazzo. He wasn't too nervous about being stopped along the way as he had nothing on him that would merit being brought up before the inquisitors. He had in his satchel only a few bottles, each containing drams of rare metals to share with the bishop as thanks for this hospitality and to signal that he was not a complete novice. He wanted to show the Venetian noble, whom he imagined to be well versed on the subject, that while he might come from the dark Magyar mountains, he was not backward and ignorant.

Nonetheless, Adair was careful on his journey, for he was alone and the city was notorious for its cutpurses and thieves. He listened carefully for any whispers or scrabbling of movement in the shadows and kept one hand on his sidearm at all times. After what seemed like entirely too long a journey along shimmering, black-faced canals, he came to the bishop's palazzo, not far from the Rialto Bridge. A footman led him into the house and asked him to wait in the entry hall while he informed the bishop of Adair's arrival.

Adair had just slipped out of his cloak when he caught a glimpse of movement overhead, and glanced up to see a beautiful young woman crossing the mezzanine. She wore a gown of ivory silk and her dark hair was pinned up with pearls. She looked as luminous as a ghost in the darkness. When she saw that he'd caught her staring down at him, she hurried away like a doe running for the cover of the forest.

Just then the bishop entered, and following the trajectory of Adair's upward gaze, registered the source of his attention, as a knowing smile crossed his lips. "Young lord! I am so glad you are able to join me in the laboratory tonight." He tossed back the voluminous satin sleeves of his robe to take Adair's hand. With a forthrightness that Adair appreciated, the bishop added: "I see that you have noticed my goddaughter Elena."

Adair nodded. "She would be hard to miss. Your god-daughter is very beautiful, sir."

"She is indeed. Elena just arrived this week from Florence. Her father is an old friend of mine and wanted to get her out of the city for a while." Rossi nodded to his young visitor, dropping his voice to a stage whisper. "A less than desirable young man has formed an attraction to her, her father says, and he hoped that some time apart will weaken her suitor's ardor."

"I see. . . . Is the attraction mutual?" Adair asked as he followed his host down a corridor and deeper into the palazzo.

"I blame it on Elena's youth. At her age, when a boy turns her head, she is sure there will never be another. She has found her soul mate, the man she is meant to be with forever, and all that rubbish," the bishop scoffed, and then abruptly changed the subject: "Come, my young lord. A fire has been building in the furnace for some time now and it should be of a sufficient temperature to begin our experiment."

As the bishop prattled on, describing the recipe he wished to attempt, Adair quickly realized that Rossi had miscalculated from the start. They would need to begin by reducing mercury to its essence, a tricky and time-consuming process: it could be ruined in an instant and thus required constant watching, which meant they would spend the entire evening on this *one* step. Adair fidgeted as his host went through his preparations for the experiment. Between the bishop's dithering and the obvious newness of the equipment, Adair came to the conclusion that Rossi was a rank novice. When Adair's father had informed him that he was being sent away, the one hope Adair was able to salvage was that he'd find someone more experienced to tutor him in Venice, so that he might advance more rapidly. Since arriving in the city, however, he'd had no luck, and it seemed Rossi would be no help in this regard. Adair tried to mask his disappointment.

"The doge has told me a little bit about you," the bishop said as he tapped out a tiny measure of quicksilver. He seemed to be intent on making small talk. "He says your family is one of the oldest and noblest in Hungary, and that your father is a duke and trusted adviser to your king—King Béla, if I'm not mistaken."

"Yes, that's correct."

"Did your father send you here to make an alliance of some kind with Zeno's court? Are you on a diplomatic mission?"

Adair cleared a spot on the table to rest his elbows, pushing aside flasks and bottles. "I wouldn't say that, your grace."

"Oh—so, your family is expecting you to return before too long?"

He wasn't sure where Rossi was going with this line of questioning, but Adair answered anyway. "I daresay they do not. And it's not as though I'll be missed. I have two brothers, both older than me, and my family looks to them to manage our estates and continue our line. I have no designs on my father's title. He knows I wish to become a physician."

"A physician!" the bishop said with forced cheer. "It's commendable that you wish to minimize human suffering—though some might argue that a physician only serves to *prolong* a patient's suffering—but I must say, it's an odd choice of profession for a nobleman's son."

"Perhaps. But I have a passion to know things, especially to figure out how things work. I have been told that the human body is the most complex subject there is, and being one who likes a challenge, I decided to study medicine."

The bishop frowned. "Isn't one normally drawn to medicine in order to help his fellow man?"

Adair shrugged. "I decided to become a physician because I am seized by the mysteries of life. I cannot help but feel that we, the living, are allowed to see only *half* of what goes on around us. The world runs by a vast set of rules by which the tides turn, the seasons change, the sun rises and sets, plants grow and then wither, we live and die. There is a rhythm to all these things, a rhythm and pattern to life so complicated that we can't begin to decipher it. Everything we see is bound by these rules, which are perfectly integrated one to the other, and they are all kept secret from man. I want the universe to share its secrets with me. I want to know who we are and how we came into being."

Adair's passionate soliloquy seemed to make the bishop see his guest for the first time—and he did not like what he saw. "Take care, young lord, for it seems to me that the half of the cosmos you wish to know is the realm of the Lord our God. We are not meant to know the ways of the Lord; we are only to accept his will. The church might deem your line of questioning to be quite blasphemous."

Adair rankled at the warning. "I meant that in the *context* of the Lord, of course, for he certainly must be the source of these rules. And yet he moves in mysterious ways—ways I would like to understand better. For instance, what is the soul and where does it reside in us? Is it a physical piece of us, like the heart or the brain? I would think it cannot be, since the Bible tells us that the soul cannot die. So it must go on, *persisting*, after the body has ceased to function."

"And if the Bible tells us so, it must be true. If you have questions about such matters, you should feel that you can ask them of me," the bishop said with an air of smug superiority.

The bishop's lack of intellectual curiosity made Adair respect him less, and he let himself get a little impatient with Rossi. "Then, you can tell me where the soul goes after death? We don't see them here with us on earth, so they must go *somewhere*, yes?"

Rossi made no attempt to disguise his irritation. "*The Bible* has your answers, my young lord: souls go to heaven, hell, or purgatory. Those are the choices. There are no others."

"And all I wish is proof of it."

The bishop gawked at him in amazement, too surprised by his guest's temerity to be outraged. "Proof? You want proof? There is no proof."

Adair knew he was skirting a run-in with the inquisitors, but he couldn't stop. "As men of science, it is our duty to look for proof, don't you think? Otherwise, what is the use of all this?" He waved a hand at the bishop's assortment of fancy tools and props.

"I am interested in knowledge the same as you, but my interest lies in learning more about the things that God set on this earth so that I might understand God's ways," the bishop retorted, his voice trembling with indignation. "The minerals, the waters, the things that can be touched, not matters of the spirit. That is a realm that can't be seen. That is the realm of faith. The way you talk, sir, it is as though you have no faith at all. When you question faith, you question God, my young lord, and to question God is to play into the devil's hands. Do you mean to court the devil, with such heretical talk?" Rossi asked, aghast. "Tell me it isn't so."

Adair was about to give the bishop a contemptuous reply when he thought the better of it. Rossi was a superstitious fool who would not change his ways, but there was no sense in antagonizing him. If Adair argued too strongly against religion—a direction in which he seemed more inclined every day—Rossi might bring it up to the doge. It would be more prudent to string the bishop along. Why, Rossi—having the doge's ear—might even come in handy one day.

Adair pressed a hand to his sternum as he made a low bow. "Oh no, your grace, I believe that you misunderstand me, no doubt due to my poor grasp of your language. Rest assured, our aims are the same, to better understand the ways of our Lord. Indeed, I am impressed by your knowledge of the Bible. It is so much stronger than that of my family's priests." Adair, still bowing, looked up to see how his words were being received by the bishop, and by the expression on the Italian's face, Adair could tell that Rossi didn't doubt him in the least. "Doubtless there is much I can learn from you, in religious matters as well as in the practice of alchemy. Perhaps I can prevail upon you to be my spiritual adviser while I am in Venice?"

His request had the desired effect on Rossi: flattered, the bishop preened like a swan. "Oh, my boy, I would be only too happy to be your adviser. Your spiritual guide, as well as your friend." The bishop clasped one of Adair's hands in both of his and gave it an affectionate shake before the two men continued in their work.

Once the mercury reduction was under way in earnest, conversation petered out. As Adair sat with the older man in the dungeon room, breathing in the noxious air and sweating like the devil from the heat, he considered his position once again. Salvaging his relationship with Rossi had been an astute move: the bishop would've said something to the doge, undoubtedly, and Adair thought of his father and how mad he would be if his son were arrested for the very thing they'd tried to avoid by sending him to Venice.

He left the bishop's palazzo in the hour before dawn, his host fallen asleep in a chair by the sweltering fireplace. With Adair's attention elsewhere, the reduction was ruined, seized up solid into a tiny rock smaller than a baby's fist. Good for nothing now. Adair left it on the worktable and slipped out of the sleeping household to make his way back to the doge's palazzo.

In the weeks that followed, Adair noticed that whenever he went to see the bishop, usually late in the evening after one of Professore Scolari's lectures, Elena would be waiting for him, laced into one of her beautiful silk gowns, her hair pinned and her skin bathed in lavender-scented oils. Adair noticed that the bishop always managed to be detained each time he arrived, and wondered if his delay wasn't intentional in order to give his ward a few minutes alone with the Hungarian nobleman. Adair couldn't help but wonder why the bishop would encourage these unchaperoned exchanges with his goddaughter. After all, he was a foreigner; surely Elena's family would prefer to see her wed to an Italian lord and not whisked off to a kingdom far away, where it was possible they'd never hear from her again.

In any case, Adair had no intention of returning to Magyar territory if he could help it, and without property of his own, he certainly could not take a wife. Besides, he was tiring of Rossi's company—the bishop warming to his new role as Adair's spiritual adviser and taken to repeating his favorite sermons during their sessions in the laboratory—and didn't want to complicate matters with Elena when her godfather clearly had ulterior motives in having them spend time getting to know each other.

That evening, as he traveled through cobbled alleys in the dark, he realized he must make this plain to Elena, if not Rossi. He practiced what he would say to her: *Do not set your sights on me, because I have no interest in acquiring a wife, not now, not ever.* Huddled inside his great cloak, with his face hidden under the brim of his hat, he marched briskly through the square to the bishop's handsome palazzo, summoning the courage to set Elena straight.

Telling her to her face would be another matter, however.

He had no sooner surrendered his cloak and hat to a servant than Elena hustled down the staircase, her timing so perfect it was as though someone had rung a bell to let her know he was there. She was more radiant than usual tonight, in a pale yellow gown that set off her dark hair, and his throat caught at the sight of her. He bowed low to her, heat rising to his cheeks. As always her beauty brought out something awkward in him, made him clumsy and thick-tongued. His mother had always kept her sons from spending time with the ladies at court, and frowned on too much familiarity with serving girls as well. As a result, even though Adair and Elena were close in age, he felt that she had an advantage over him when it came to dealing with the opposite gender.

"Good evening, Elena," he said cautiously. "How have you been since we last saw each other?"

Her dark eyes latched onto his as she described how she'd passed the time: going to mass in the morning, afternoons spent working on an embroidery project with the old nurse for company, dinners at the bishop's table hearing about his day. Her days never changed. How boring it must be for her, he thought, shut up in her godfather's bachelor household with no girls her own age with whom to gossip and play. Did Rossi let her go to balls or dances? What had she done to cause her family to send her away to Venice, he wondered? There was something about the girl's and the bishop's behavior that made him think there was more to the story. Or perhaps they'd sent her in the hope that she'd make a better match under the bishop's guidance?

She placed a hand on his forearm to get his attention, and Adair imagined he felt the heat of her tiny hand through the layers of his clothing. "Tell me . . . don't you wish to visit with *me* one evening, instead of my godfather? I think I would be much better company. You might read to me from your favorite poems. I would like that very much," she said.

"Why certainly, Elena, if your godfather would permit it," Adair replied. Though he knew he shouldn't encourage her, he felt pity for the girl. At his positive response, her pretty face lit up and she dropped her gloveless hand on his, so their skin touched for the first time. She might as well have set his hand on fire. After a momentary dizziness, he recalled his earlier decision—to never take a wife and be married instead to science—and opened his mouth to speak. It would be caddish to mislead her.

"Elena, there is something I must tell you, however—"

Her dark eyes widened at his words. "Oh no. You are already betrothed! Is that what you were going to say?" She clutched his arm, this time digging her fingers into his sleeve.

"No, Elena. It's not that, not at all." The emotion in her voice caught him off guard. With Elena, his head clouded. She was a thing of both extraordinary liveliness and tempting softness, from the glossy dark curls on her head to the organdy tucked along the neckline of her gown. The scent of warm lavender oil rose from her bare throat. She was a beautiful little present, wrapped in silk and lace.

"Then there is no problem if you were to kiss me." She smiled at her own daring. She lifted her chin and closed her eyes, clearly expecting him to take up her offer. He tingled with fear and desire. He had little experience kissing in passion aside from a few experiments with his cousins back in Hungary. The few whores he had known did not expect, or even particularly want, to be kissed. He tried to put these thoughts out of his mind as he looked at Elena. Why *not* kiss the girl? They were alone, no chaperones hovering at their side. The bishop's footsteps echoed down the hall, but he was still a distance away.

The seconds ticking by, Adair closed his eyes and kissed her. Her softness yielded to him. He felt as though Elena wanted him—perhaps even more than he wanted her—and the idea of being desired stirred him. He leaned into her, pulling her tighter, and she responded, her mouth opening for him. And just as he felt he could pour himself into her until they became one, a hand fell on his shoulder. It was the bishop.

Adair sprang back, his heart leaping, but there was no enraged outcry from his host, no shove propelling him away from the young woman. Adair expected Rossi to lose his temper and accuse Adair of taking advantage of his hospitality, but no—Bishop Rossi was smiling. He clapped Adair on the back. "My boy, don't be embarrassed on *my* account. It is only natural to have such feelings for a young lady as beautiful as my goddaughter." Why, he practically beamed with happiness, and Elena, for her part, stood behind her godfather, blushing so furiously that her cheeks were like two perfect red apples.

In the laboratory that evening, the bishop's mind seemed to wander, and so Adair took command of the experiment, measuring ingredients onto tiny silver salvers and tending the furnace while the bishop continued to wax eloquently about his ward. "Have I told you about her family, back in Florence? It's very old, a fine family. It goes all the way back to the duchy's beginnings. Her family has had their estate in the valley for as long as anyone can remember." Adair listened but didn't respond; the girl's pedigree meant nothing to him since he had no intention of lengthening her family tree.

"And Elena is such a clever girl. She knows a little French, and Latin, of course, for mass. But she has other talents, too. . . . She dances like an angel, and sings beautifully. I always have her sing at my dinner parties for my guests and—why, we must have you over for one soon. We shall make you the guest of honor. Would you like that?" the bishop asked excitedly, as though the thought—after weeks of Adair's company—had only just occurred to him.

"Certainly," Adair replied, but only to end Rossi's chattering. Even Elena's kiss and snowy-white décolleté were fading from memory, unable to compete with the allure of the laboratory.

"Excellent! I will speak to my housekeeper to make the arrangements," the bishop said, and beamed. Rossi clearly had no interest in their experiment that night; he was on a mission of a different kind. The old cleric studied Adair with an appraising eye. "She is a very lovely girl, wouldn't you say? She's considered one of the most beautiful girls in Florence, you know."

She certainly spent enough of her father's money on gowns and jewels, Adair thought. He put down the tiny pair of pincers he was using to count out crystals of salts of alum. "If that's the case, why has she been sent here to live with you? If she is one of the most eligible girls in Florence, shouldn't she be betrothed already?"

The bishop colored, having been caught. He leaned back into his chair, fussing with the billowing sleeves of his tunic to deflect scrutiny. "Well, if you wish to hear the whole story, she's the youngest of three sisters, and neither of the other two has yet been betrothed, you understand. Elena's father has his hands full right now finding suitable young men for the older two. And though it pains me to make any comparisons between the sisters, Elena is the fairest of the three. My friend needed to send her away until the other girls' matches could be made, her beauty being something of a distraction. . . ." The bishop gave a craggy smile, showing his yellowed teeth, and there was something about the way his eyes settled on Adair, watching carefully for his reaction, that Adair had to think there was more to the story than the old bishop was admitting.

They wrapped up the experiment that night—slightly more successful than the rest, but still a disappointment in Adair's opinion—and on his walk back to the doge's palazzo, Adair realized that he needed to find someone else with an interest in alchemy, so that he would continue to have access to another laboratory. It was plain that the bishop meant to arrange for Adair to marry his goddaughter, and Adair had already resolved that this was not going to happen. There was another reason that he wanted to quit Rossi, however, and that was because it was obvious that Adair was more skilled than the bishop, and Adair had no desire to waste his time with a dilettante. He wanted to work with someone better than himself. Henrik, his former tutor, had had his limitations, but he'd shown Adair how to use the instruments correctly and gotten him off to a good start. Adair's skills in the laboratory were solid: he was a competent journeyman alchemist, but now he needed to study with someone with greater knowledge or risk wasting precious time floundering about on his own.

Adair knew that he couldn't quit Rossi abruptly; he didn't want to make an enemy of the man. In any case, he knew it would be difficult to find someone to take Rossi's place. He'd have to find someone in Venice with a laboratory, and then he'd need to convince this person to share it. Without a laboratory, Adair couldn't continue his studies in alchemy. Try as he might to think of someone to replace Bishop Rossi, Adair came up empty-handed. While he kept his ear to the ground for potential mentors, he began to reconnoiter in merchants' alleys, the more obscure the better, looking for booksellers' stalls where he could spend his spare hours searching for books of secrets that would allow him to teach himself while he still had access to the bishop's laboratory.

There were few books of any kind for sale, let alone books of occult secrets. Most books of the time were religious in nature: Bibles, or excerpts of Scriptures and sermons. He began to feel as though he was picking through the same moldy tomes over and over, his quest destined for fruitlessness, until one day when he stumbled across a shop buried in the basement of a dingy building on a side street. The shop carried a sparse and odd assortment of merchandise. There were a few books, yes, but also bits of the arcane: a crystal ball, a skull inscribed with runes, a writing stylus made from polished bone. There were chests lined up behind a counter, and when Adair looked inside, he saw they were filled with all sorts of unidentifiable things, dark and dried until wizened to unrecognizability, but with smells that promised unknown properties, unknown delights. Adair's heart raced as he poked about, each discovery more interesting than the last.

The proprietor came down the stairs into the narrow shop just as Adair was riffling through one of the wooden chests behind the counter, clearly shocked by the young nobleman's presence. With this trade being dangerous business under the scrutiny of the church, he probably knew all his customers well and so he would be greatly surprised to see a stranger visiting him—and a nobleman at that.

"You've nothing to fear from me," Adair said to put the man at ease, though his words seemed to have little effect. He recognized there was a dance to be done when it came to wares such as these, if the shopkeeper wished to be spared a visit by the inquisitors. This was Venice after all, and citizens were encouraged to tattle on their neighbors. There were even letter boxes at the doge's palazzo for that express purpose.

The proprietor was an older man, bald with great wiry white whiskers, and over his tunic he wore a much-battered leather apron. He bowed his head in a show of deference. "Good day, my lord. To what do I owe the honor of your visit to my shop? Perhaps you came here on the recommendation of one of your lordship's friends?" the shopkeeper asked, watching Adair closely for a reaction. "If you would be so good as to tell me the name, that would clear the matter up."

Adair had no name to give and saw no sense in lying. "No, good fellow, I have no such recommendation to vouchsafe me. I was walking by your establishment and what I saw from the doorway intrigued me." He gestured to the dusty shelves. "I've seen similar items before, you see. I come from another kingdom far away . . ."

The shopkeeper nodded. "I thought as much, from your accent."

"Such objects are not as uncommon in my homeland as they are in Venice. I thought perhaps I might add to my collection, and came in to get a better look at your wares."

"Your collection, you say?" the shopkeeper said, now curious. "And is there anything in particular you might be looking for?"

Adair leapt at this opening like a cat onto a mouse. "Why yes: I am looking to purchase a book of secrets. Have you heard of such a thing?"

The shopkeeper's face clouded. "I've heard of them, yes . . ."

"Has one ever come into your possession?" Adair pressed.

The old man was obviously made uncomfortable by the subject and pursed his lips until his mouth almost disappeared in the thicket of his whiskers. "I have seen one or two, but never have had one to sell. These tend to be the property of collectors, such as yourself, and rarely are made available to purchase. It happens sometimes when a practitioner passes away, if the book is found among his things. But more commonly, the book is burned"—the shopkeeper glanced quickly again at Adair—"by the family, so as to hide the loved one's interest in the occult."

"Such a waste of knowledge," Adair said, shaking his head.

"Indeed," the shopkeeper agreed. But there was a fresh gleam in his eye now that they had an understanding. "But knowing of your interest, my lord, I shall keep an ear out should any such item find its way on the market. And in the unlikely event that one of these books should come into my possession, how might I get in contact with you?"

"You might send word to me." He took the quill from the ink pot on the man's desk and scribbled his name and address on a scrap of rough paper. He blew on the wet ink before handing it to the shopkeeper.

The man squinted at the writing before exclaiming in surprise, "But this address is for the doge's palazzo!"

"Yes," Adair said, his cheeks singed with embarrassment. "It is. I am a ward of the doge."

The shopkeeper peered at him curiously. "I doubt you are a fool, sir, so I can only surmise that you find great sport in playing with fire."

Adair thought about it and answered honestly. "Such is my interest in the topic, sir. I would risk everything in its pursuit."

Before the new cycle of the moon, Adair received word from the bookseller, a cryptic note delivered by a kitchen boy that said he should come to the shop at his earliest convenience, but to come alone—as though Adair needed a reminder that such interests were best kept concealed. He went to the shop late in the afternoon on his way to a medical lecture at Professore Scolari's.

The shopkeeper threw a bolt across the door after Adair entered, and led him to his residence on the upper level. It was a very modest dwelling, from what Adair could see, and very dim. There was only one window, which made for privacy. The shopkeeper gestured for Adair to sit at the table and went off through a doorway, and within a few minutes came back with a parcel in his hands.

"This book only recently came into my possession. It is one of the finest examples of its kind that I have ever seen," he said as he put it on the table and peeled back the deerskin wrapping. The book's cover was such a brilliant blue that it cut through the room's murkiness and commanded Adair's attention. He held his breath as he picked it up, opened it carefully, and began inspecting the pages. It was so beautifully and precisely constructed that it had to be the work of a monk. The pages were parchment and adorned with bits of gold leaf inserted here and there. There were illustrations, too—magic circles, runes, and all manner of pictures Adair couldn't make sense of it without further study. It smelled of candle wax and incense, and whispered of late hours in a scriptorium as its creator worked in secret, after his brothers had turned in for the night. Someone had risked his life and possibly his soul to make this book.

Adair's hands closed around the book. "I must have it. What is your price?"

At this, the shopkeeper's face puckered as though he'd bitten a lemon. "So, this is the tricky part, your lordship, which I beg to explain to you. There is another gentleman who is interested in the book as well. He is a longtime customer of mine. I dare not anger him by refusing him."

"Then why did you bring me here if you have no intention of selling it to me?" Adair demanded. He felt his blood boil in his brain.

"It's not that I have no intention to sell it to you. I wish that it were possible. I will speak to the other man, but I cannot see him stepping aside. He is a rabid collector, you understand. It's just that I . . . I knew you would like the opportunity to see it, as you've surely never seen a book of its kind before," he said, trying to assuage Adair's anger. "I was acting in what I judged to be your interest, my lord."

Youthful desire seemed to short-circuit Adair's ability to reason. "I've dealt with crafty merchants before: you are obviously hoping to drive up the price by having us both make you an offer on this book," Adair said impatiently, his grip tightening around the volume. "Very well, let me cut to the chase: I will pay double whatever your other customer offers. You have but to name your price and I will pay it." His offer was reckless and he knew it. He had only so much money at his disposal.

The merchant's face glowed pale in the dimness of the shop. "You're very generous, my young lord, but I can't accept your proposition. I beg you, let me speak to my other customer—"

"Consider this a deposit." Adair dug his money purse from a pocket and slapped it on the table before the shopkeeper, who let his gaze rest on the plump sack for a long, silent moment.

Adair began wrapping the book in its deerskin cover, anxious to escape with his prize while the bookseller was distracted. "And need I remind you in whose house I am a guest? The man who rules the principality, the doge of Venice. Don't be a fool. It would only take one word from me for you to end up in the dungeons . . ." he said, his bravado betrayed by a slight quaking to his voice.

At those unfortunate words, the bookseller's servile demeanor changed. He gave a long, irritated sigh and stiffened underneath his leather apron. "Ah, my lord . . . I wish our discourse had not deteriorated so quickly. I'd hoped you would not besiege me thus with idle threats that would only harm us both. Getting the law involved in our private transaction would get *both* of us in terrible trouble. And which of us is the more serious heretic? I may be a peddler of the occult, but you are the sinner who wishes to give over his soul to the devil, or so the inquisitors will see it. So while I doubt that you would make good on your threat, I prefer not to do business with men who would treat me thus."

Though he sensed it would do no good, Adair decided to press his bluff. "I will not be made a fool of, or cheated. You summoned me here and dangled your wares before me. I've offered you good golden ducats at a more than fair price. If you wish to avoid any unpleasantness, I suggest you act like a merchant and sell the book to the first customer who offers to buy it, and that is I. I consider our business concluded." He tucked the package under his arm and tried to brush by the shopkeeper, but the man put out his hand, catching Adair in his chest.

"I'm sorry, my lord, but I cannot let you have the book. Take back your coins and leave the—"

Adair's dagger was drawn before the shopkeeper could finish his sentence. Because Adair was flustered, his hand was unsteady and he was not as precise as he would've preferred: he only meant to send the man back a step or two, but ended up driving the tip of the blade into the man's chest. The leather apron saved the shopkeeper from serious harm, but he staggered to his knees, clutching the wound. In the moment of confusion, Adair darted out of the shop, his treasure hidden under his cloak.

With such a rare and damning book, Adair knew he had to take special precautions to keep it from being discovered. While he appreciated the book's beautiful construction, its peacock linen cover was something of a drawback as it made the book stand out no matter where you placed it. When he tried to hide it among his other books, the bright cover invariably drew the eye, and then of course the hand was sure to follow. It pained him to tuck it beneath floorboards or behind a loose rock in the wall, but there was no way to leave it out in the open. It was too conspicuous. He was careful to move it between hiding places in his bedchamber: it was the doge's palazzo after all, with more servants than the population of entire villages, and people were in and out at all hours, tidying up the room when he was not around. He stayed up late at night to read the book in secret by candlelight. Each page revealed whole new areas of alchemical thought and practice for him, for which he was amazed, and grateful. It was as though he was given all the sweet water he could drink after a prolonged and painful drought. Adair took the example of the monk who created this book and copied out his favorite recipes on rough paper in his native language so that he would have a spare copy in case something happened to the original.

He was returning late one night to the palazzo from a lecture at the home of his tutor of medicine, Professore Scolari, when he became aware that he was being followed. He was in a lonely alley at the time with only a quarter moon overhead for light. The alley had been so quiet that he had felt certain there was no one else with him, and sure enough, when he turned to confront his assailant, there was nothing there but blackness.

Then, without warning, a man Adair had never before laid eyes on stepped out of the inky emptiness. Adair could not believe his eyes: it was as though the man had been hiding inside a black cloud that completely obscured his presence. He was older and imposing, tall and broad as a church door. He had piercing gray eyes and a thick mustache, his long black hair streaked with silver. He wore a cloak of burgundy velvet trimmed in ermine, fine enough for a king to wear.

The conjurer pointed a finger at Adair. "Stand right where you are, you devil's stripling. You will not pass. I believe you have something that belongs to me."

Adair stepped back, his hand on his sword. "How can that be when I don't know you, sir?"

The man continued to glare at him. "Don't feign ignorance; you're not that good an actor. The book, sir. You took it from a friend of mine. You have frequented a shop near the Plaza Saint Benedict, have you not? You know the shopkeeper, Anselmo?"

"I didn't take it from your friend, I *bought* it. He was more than fairly compensated. I would be careful, sir, for I am a ward of the doge—"

"I know all about your place in the doge's household," the conjurer said with a sneer. "And we both know he would cast you out and return you to your heathen family's estate if he found out about your extracurricular interests. And I also know that the doge currently has at least a dozen such young men living under his roof, too many to keep track of. Zeno probably wouldn't even be able to identify your body—if you were to come to such an unfortunate end." The stranger was right: he had seen through Adair's bluff. "Don't worry, boy— I'm no assassin. I'm only here to take what's rightfully mine. Do you know what I am?"

There was little question that this old man was a mage, a

practitioner of some skill and ability, and angry with Adair for being so presumptuous as to buy (or, rather, steal) the book out from underneath him. He'd come to settle the score. Adair sheathed his sword quickly and made a low bow. "My sincere apologies, sir. I meant you no disrespect. The shopkeeper had summoned me to his store, had he not? I thought the man was merely trying to force an exorbitant sum from me with the pretense of having another buyer. I will return the book to you without argument if you return the sum I paid your friend Anselmo."

The large man relaxed, shifting his weight to his back leg, his hand dropping from his sword. "I'm glad you're being so reasonable," he said with some caution.

"Obviously, I do not *presently* have the book with me. Let me deliver the book myself to your house tomorrow evening," Adair said.

The old man narrowed his eyes. "Is this a trick? You want me to tell you where I live so you can send the doge's men to arrest me? How do I know I can trust you, after what you did to Anselmo?"

Adair bowed low again in a show of deference. "By the fact that you were able to follow me unseen within your ingenious black cloud, I can tell you are a man of considerable expertise in the magical arts, whereas I am a novice and have only begun in my scholarship. You would do me a great honor if you would allow me to set this matter right between us, sir."

"That black cloud is nothing, a minor trick. You'd do well to remember that imbalance in our powers; I would not hesitate to bring the worst punishment imaginable down upon you should you betray me." The old man thought, rubbing his grizzled chin. "All right, since you plead so prettily, I'll let you bring the book to me. But I warn you: I'll be watching your every move through the soothsayer's bowl and if you cross me, it will go very badly for you. Do you understand?" He watched Adair nod. "Come to the Plaza Saint Vincent tomorrow at midnight. You'll know which house is mine."

Adair bowed a third time, and when he rose, the man and the black cloud had disappeared.

PRESENT DAY

Adair woke with a start and had to shake his head hard to clear visions of the dark Venetian alley from his mind and remember that he was safe in his fortress off the coast of Sardegna. He looked down at Lanore—she was still asleep, oblivious to his alarm—and then blinked and peered around the darkened room, half expecting to see the conjurer step out of the inky blackness.

Adair hadn't thought of Cosimo Moretti, the old conjurer, for centuries. He'd actively suppressed thoughts of Cosimo (and his demise) for a very long time and could see no reason why he should think of him—even worse, *dream* of him—now. Adair couldn't help but think it had something to do with the spell he'd cast over Lanore or the Venetian book with its peacock-blue cover that she had returned to him.

Adair rose from the bed, readjusted his twisted clothing, and went downstairs to his study, tiptoeing through the silent house. He didn't want to risk waking the girls, so he didn't turn on a light until he reached his study. The book fairly glowed from across the room, from where it sat on his desk.

He pressed a hand to the cover, quite filthy by now, with centuries of grime effacing the blue linen, and he could practically feel magic emanate from it like a pulse. Cosimo's magic; he'd felt the same jangly vibrations in Cosimo's presence, just as he assumed others felt something similar when they were near him. Once a person made contact with the other world, it left its mark on him. It had made Adair into something like a portal, with the hidden, magical world a heartbeat away.

ELEVEN

Once I stepped through the door of the Moroccan hotel, I was back in the fortress, presumably in the hall on the second story. The dusty smell of the hotel in Fez lingered, however, clinging to my sweaty skin and damp cotton dress, proof that it hadn't been completely fabricated in my mind—unless the subtle mix of ginger, mint, sandalwood, and jasmine were also figments of my imagination.

The hall was still a dim and empty expanse of red carpet and dark wooden doors. No sound echoed down the long corridor, the house as quiet as a mausoleum. In the unbroken stillness, I suddenly noticed that the flames standing atop the candles in the iron wall sconces had begun to quiver, tickled by a draft coming from an unknown direction. Someone had opened a door.

I strained so hard listening for a sound that my ears started to ache. Then I heard what I'd been waiting for: a muffled thump, like a ball being dropped onto a carpet. And a second thump. Whatever it was, it sounded very solid, ominously so. The cloven hoof of a demon? I wasn't going to stay and find out. My hand closed around the nearest brass doorknob. I gave it a turn, held my breath, and slipped inside another room.

I stepped into a forest, just on the other side of the door. The forest was vast—I could tell by the vacuous silence—and a light snow was falling; only a few flakes made it through the canopy of bare branches to the ground. A fuller stand of trees stood ahead of me, mostly pine and all frosted with new snow, and behind it another stand and another. My breath misted on the cold air and my skin tingled—not from the cold but because I was home.

I knew without needing to be told that I was in St. Andrew. How did I know this? After all, I could be in a forest anywhere, but I knew. The land was as well known to me as a painting I'd looked at a thousand times. The air tasted familiar; it even *felt* familiar against my skin, though of course all of this could have been a trick of the mind. Still . . . the birdsong, the slant of light. Everything told me I was in St. Andrew.

Again, it made no sense that I should be *here*. Perhaps it had to do with the way the afterlife was configured, hardwired to the time we spent on earth. The dour, judgmental Puritan in me would like to believe that it was designed to throw me back to the place or events that were most important to me, to revisit the lesson I missed in life. That is, if there was an order to things at all, which the realist in me doubted.

I walked toward the trees, wondering where I was in the

Great North Woods, a forest famous for swallowing up people and not letting them go. The great woods went on for miles in sameness, and it was easy for even experienced wilderness guides or, in my day, axmen and surveyors on horseback, to lose their way. As I came to a thinning of trees, I heard the faint sound of running water and followed the noise until I came to the river.

Within minutes the Allagash unfurled before me. There was no mistaking it, broad and flat and calm. It might've been snowing, but it was not cold enough to cause the river to freeze over. The only strange thing I noticed about the river this day was that it was unusually dark. Black, as though a river of ink rushed over the rock bed. It must be a trick of the light, I told myself, a reflection of the overcast sky and not an ominous sign portending ill fortune.

My sense was that the village lay on the other side of the rolling water. I wondered if the river was shallow enough at that point to walk across. It looked to be, though the water was sure to be painfully cold. However, when I scanned the river's edge for its narrowest point, I suddenly saw an empty rowboat nestled in a tangle of dead vines. The boat was weathered to a silvery gray, an old and forgotten thing, crudely made. A paddle lay across the plank seat.

I climbed in, pointed its nose toward the opposite shore, and began paddling. There were stretches of the Allagash that were very gentle, and I assumed from the current that this was one of them, but was surprised nonetheless by the ease with which I reached the other side, not quite as though the boat knew what was expected of it but nearly so. It nosed onto a sloping part of the riverbank as neatly as though strong hands had pulled it ashore for me, so it was nothing to step out and onto dry land.

A path showed itself through the trees and I followed, having no better idea of which way to go, and I didn't have to walk very far before I saw someone in the distance. As I got closer, I saw that it was a woman in a long, dark coat sitting on a tree stump with what appeared to be a baby in her arms. Her straight dark hair had fallen across her face like a curtain, obscuring my view of her. I knew without question that she was waiting for me.

Despite the crunch of my shoes in the snow, she did not look up until I was practically standing next to her, confirming it was who I'd begun to suspect: Sophia Jacobs, the woman who had once been Jonathan's lover but had taken her own life—and that of her unborn baby.

I was startled—almost frightened—to see her again. When we were young women together in St. Andrew we hadn't been friends and she even had reason to hate me. I had tried to make her give up Jonathan, to hide the paternity of the baby he'd put inside her, but instead, she drowned herself in the Allagash, near this very spot. I'd thought little of her since Jonathan had absolved me of any guilt in her suicide, taking the blame on himself. And though I'd dreamed of her many years ago, when my trespass against her was still fresh, in none of those dreams had she ever been this vivid. She looked exactly as I'd last seen her in life, but seeing her this closely revealed a hundred tiny details I'd perhaps forgotten with time. Had she always been so worried and nervous? Were her eyes always this sunken, her skin ashy, her mouth hard set in a half frown? And in her arms was a bundle of swaddling that she held like a baby.

"Sophia," I said by way of greeting, puzzled as to why I'd been brought to her.

She shifted the bundle in her arms, regarding me coolly. "Well, you took long enough getting here. Come along now, you've much to see."

"What do you mean? I don't understand—why'd you bring me here?"

She was rising to her feet but froze at my words. "Bring *you* here? No, it's the other way around. I'm here because of you. Don't dawdle now. We've got to be going." She didn't wait for my reply but set off at a strong pace through the snow, the baby held tight to her chest.

Within minutes we were at the edge of town. St. Andrew looked the same as it did in my childhood memories: the long clapboards of the congregation hall; the common green in front, now covered with snow, where we spent many an afternoon in the company of our neighbors after services; the fieldstone fence that surrounded the cemetery; Parson Gilbert's house; Tinky Talbot's smith shop; the path next to the blacksmith's leading to Magda's one-room whorehouse; and farther down the muddy, choppy road, Daughtery's poor man's public house, shuttered up against the snowfall.

Faces of the people I'd known when I'd lived here as a child—my family, friends, the townspeople who ran the businesses and occupied the farms that had flanked ours—spun past my eyes, people I'd missed more dearly than I would've thought possible. "Wait, Sophia," I called to the thin figure bustling ahead of me. The top of her head and her sloping shoulders were white, as though she'd been dusted with sugar, and the hem of her long coat swept a wide path behind her.

"Can you tell me what happened to everyone? You don't know how often I've wondered . . ."

She walked on purposefully, keeping her gaze trained on the ground before her. "If you really wish to know about St. Andrew, the horrors that befell us, I'll tell you." Her tone was grimly smug, thick with schadenfreude. "The entire town was torn apart when you and Jonathan ran away." It was then I realized that for all her ghostly qualities, Sophia was not omnipotent and was unaware of the circumstances of my abrupt departure. It may have looked to outsiders that I'd returned to the village intent on stealing Jonathan's heart, but I'd come armed with Adair's elixir of life, under orders to bring Jonathan back to Boston with me. But when I returned to St. Andrew, I found the town dependent on Jonathan: he ran the logging operation, the most profitable business in town by far, and held the mortgage to nearly every farm. I had no heart to take him away from a town that needed him. Fate interceded, however, and when Jonathan was shot by a cuckolded husband, I was left with no choice but to give him the elixir and whisk him out of town to keep our secret from being discovered.

"There was a terrible row when it was discovered that you'd gone," Sophia continued with relish. "Jonathan's family was exceedingly angry with yours, taking your mother to task for raising such a wicked girl. The town divided on the matter, for and against, and you'll not be surprised to learn that very few stood with *your* family. You were called all sorts of vile names—whore, harlot, Jezebel"—she seemed particularly delighted to recall this bit of history for me—"and there was some talk of forcing your family to compensate the St. Andrews for their loss."

"That's ridiculous. Jonathan left with me of his own free will," I said even though this was not strictly true. He'd been unconscious, going through the transformation, when we'd fled from town.

"That's what your family's supporters said, and the nonsense died down. The damage was done, however. The St. Andrews were left with no one to run the business, the sisters like ninnies and Benjamin as simple as a child. If it had all gone to ruin it would be Jonathan's mother's fault for putting all her faith in her eldest son to the detriment of the others. Some said, secretly, that Ruth was getting what she deserved, for she had worshipped Jonathan and turned a blind eye to all his womanizing. To think all this trouble could've been averted if they'd just let Jonathan wed you!" I knew Jonathan wouldn't have married me, but Sophia didn't know this. As far as she knew, he'd run off with me, leaving the impression that he'd been madly in love with me.

"But God provides for his flock, doesn't he, even those as undeserving as Ruth St. Andrew and the pitiless magpies of this town," Sophia said with some spite, lifting her skirts as she stepped primly over a fallen log. "For Benjamin managed to come along a bit, enough to work with the logging foreman, and with time earned the respect of most of the town for being an honest man and not nearly as manipulative as the rest of his family." It was plain by her tone that she included Jonathan among the manipulative ones.

"Do you remember Evangeline? The wife you wronged?" Sophia asked, again delighted for being able to taunt me. "Poor thing—as though anyone needed further proof of the misfortune of being Jonathan's bride! What a miserable time she had of it when Jonathan abandoned her. She lived in a state of perpetual shame. She left the St. Andrew house and moved in with her parents to raise her daughter, much to Ruth's chagrin. She wanted that babe under her roof, she did. Benjamin made a campaign of wooing her, and at length she consented to wed him—perhaps the wisest decision she ever made. Though she waited until Ruth passed to give Benjamin her answer, for who would be eager to live under the same roof as that old witch again? But it seems your shameful deed brought about one blessing. You can thank the Lord for that kindness."

I devoured Sophia's news. Over the years, I'd speculated many times about what had happened after Jonathan and I left town. It wasn't surprising to hear that I'd been vilified, but I was saddened to learn that my family had suffered unjustly for what I'd done. It reminded me how judgmental the people of my town could be, these descendants of Puritans, hardened all the more by privation. How stifling it had been, growing up in their midst.

"So, my family was ruined?" I asked, my voice faltering.

This time, she looked over her shoulder at me, and there was a vulpine smile on her lips. "Ruined, as they deserved, for raising the likes of you. But you shall see for yourself."

After a few turns through the dark woods, we came to a cabin sitting in a clearing. I recognized the house at once as the one I had grown up in, though the land around it was not the same, and the whole vision had the distorted feeling one gets in a dream. Sophia opened the door and went inside with quiet authority, and so I followed her. The first thing I noticed was that the house had gone to ruin since my last visit. The logs in the walls had shrunk, loosening the wadding that plugged the joints and cracks, and let the wind and cold seep through. The rooms were austere, thinned of furniture. The overall impression was of a life suffered, made pinched and meager. I thought at first that the cabin was empty, but then I noticed one of my sisters crouched by a crude wooden chest. It took a minute to tell that it was Fiona, as she appeared much older than the last time I'd seen her. She continued to pack items into the chest, humming softly as she worked.

"She's leaving," I said aloud as I watched her.

Sophia nodded, shifting the baby in her arms. "Yes, she's going to Fort Kent to be married."

"For a bride, she doesn't look happy."

A vexed look crossed Sophia's face, but rather than reprimand me, she said, "She'll be joining your other sister."

"Glynnis? She lives in Fort Kent?"

"She married a farmer out that way a year ago, and she's arranged for Fiona to wed a widowed neighbor."

"And where's my mother? Is she living with Glynnis?" I asked, but I knew the answer even before the words were out of my mouth. My nose stung as I fought back tears that I didn't think would still come after all these years.

"No, Lanore. Your mother is gone. She passed last winter from pleurisy." Sophia said this flatly, taking no pleasure in delivering the bad news to me. Of course, intellectually I knew my mother had been dead and gone a long time, but standing there in the house I grew up in, where I'd always seen my mother at the hearth or bustling about, Sophia's news hit like a blow to my chest.

I shook my head, trying to shake off the sadness, and

turned my attention back to my sister. "Poor Fiona, marrying a stranger."

Sophia's face twisted again with displeasure. "We all marry strangers, Lanore. Even if it is someone you know, he won't be the same person once you are wed. Besides, none of us married for love. Everyone you knew married out of duty and in order to survive: your parents, your neighbors . . . even Jonathan. Love does not equal happiness," she said sharply.

She was right, of course, yet I couldn't help muttering, "And still, love is the greatest happiness I have known."

Sophia was surely about to say something cutting in response to my last remark when the door swung back and my brother, Nevin, stepped in. By now, I knew to expect he would look older, but I wasn't prepared for this drastic change. He was grizzled and hunched and seemed to have aged twice as fast as Fiona, his appearance ravaged by his work outdoors, regardless of the weather, looking after the cattle. His face was heavily lined and his cheeks pitted as though he'd suffered a recent bout of smallpox. He stomped his feet to knock the mud off his shoes and hung his hat on a peg, but kept his coat on.

"Are you ready to go?" he asked Fiona.

"Almost, but I need to pack a few more things. I'm afraid we'll be leaving so late that you'll need to spend the night with Glynnis and John . . ."

Nevin had begun shaking his head before she'd finished speaking. "No, you know I can't do that. Who would take care of the animals? I cannot leave the farm untended overnight. I must get back this evening."

"Nevin, I hope you'll end this stubbornness and take on a

field hand. You can't do this on your own. You'll need someone
to help you."

She had the tone of someone who already knew their words
would fall on deaf ears, however. Nevin shook his head vehemently as he stared at the tips of his shoes. "We've been over
this already, Fin"—his nickname for her—"I've no reason to
take on a boy. It'll only be another mouth to feed. The farm is
small enough that I can manage by myself."

"That's not true and you know it," she protested but softly.
"What if you get sick?"

"I won't get sick."

"Everyone gets sick. Or lonely."

"I won't be lonely, either."

Nevin was like a drowning man flailing too fiercely to be
saved, Fiona forced to row away in a lifeboat, abandoning him
to save herself. No one else in the family would blame her, but
that would be little solace when things went to ruin later. "I'll
be fine," Nevin said gruffly.

"Will you be able to return for the wedding?" Fiona asked,
lowering the chest's lid.

"You know I can't. I have the animals to see to. You don't
need me, anyway. You'll have Glynnis to attend to you."

Fiona said nothing, for it wasn't worth arguing with him
anymore.

"They'll not see each other again," Sophia leaned and whispered to me as though we were watching actors in a play. Still,
she spoke with the confidence of a prophet.

"Why—does something happen to Nevin? To either of
them?" I asked, anxious. "What happened to my family? I've
always wanted to know . . ."

She let her hollow gaze settle on the floor and not on me, mercifully, and dandled the baby high and close to her chest. "Nevin will live for another ten years. He does not take on any help for the farm and ends up dying alone one winter, his lungs filled with fluid, too weak to build a fire for himself."

I bit my lip and felt a flash of bitter pain. Stubborn Nevin.

"Your sister Fiona will die in childbirth with her first child," she said, nodding at my sister on the floor in front of us. "As for Glynnis—"

"Tell me at least one of them finds happiness," I burst out.

"She is happy enough. Her husband is a good man and they have four children together, three boys and a girl."

"Thank God," I said, and meant it. My eyes filled with tears as I watched Fiona finish her packing. Time had worn away a little of my sister's prettiness; she and Glynnis had been far prettier than I when we were girls. They had been the bright and winsome ones, quiet daughters who—unlike me—didn't break their parents' hearts and ruin their lives. It seemed cruel of fate to keep Fiona shackled to our family for so long (she was probably in her mid-twenties as she stood before me) only to have her die before she could have a family of her own. I hoped that this farmer she was to wed was a good man who appreciated her, and that he thought fondly of her for as long as he lived.

Even Nevin's future seemed especially cruel. That he would live his entire life alone wasn't so unexpected given his prickly nature, but in ten years he would only be in his forties. If we had lived farther south where the winters were not so long and brutal and life was not as demanding, he might've survived longer even though he lived on his own. There was good reason why the Puritan edict against solitary living was usually enforced in St. Andrew, for this practical consideration as well as the religious (which was so no soul would fall into ungodly behavior as there would always be a witness to steer him back on the path of goodness or turn him in, as the case may be).

It seemed absurd and cruel of fate to give me an endless expanse of time to reflect on my sins when an innocent like Fiona was made to die early. I had to guess that my family was cursed . . . and then it occurred to me that if this were the case it might be my fault, for hadn't I been singled out, too? Perhaps I was to blame, my unnaturally long life offset by their brief, unhappy ones. But that couldn't be, could it? . . . I was aghast at the thoughts that danced in my head. What strange perversion of our natures made us want to torture ourselves in this way?

For the first time, I was struck by the uniqueness of my immortality. I—and a few select others—experienced life differently from everyone else on earth. We experienced it as anyone who has taken a history class in school would expect to experience it: as a timeline, always moving forward. But as I listened to Sophia and heard the news of my family's fate, I came to see that all anyone knew of life was the brief bubble in which he or she was alive: the rest was hearsay, however well documented. Only we few immortals were able to experience more than one bubble, to witness more than one piece of it, and thus, only we immortals were really in a position to judge what was true and what was false.

I wasn't sure what to make of this trip to the underworld: Was I back in the early nineteenth century, or was this exchange with Sophia an approximation influenced by memory? It could be any number of things, really. After all, in reality I was lying on a bed on Adair's magical island. Ever since setting foot there, I'd been made acutely aware that nothing was as it appeared.

But I never questioned that I might *not* be moving forward in time, though maybe I wasn't. I remembered hearing of a theory among physicists that all of time went on simultaneously. As I stood in Sophia's company, the tug of this crazy rabbit hole distorting the periphery of my vision, I couldn't help but wonder if I was experiencing it at that very moment. It didn't seem like something you could experience consciously or rationally—and maybe that was why my brain was fighting me for all it was worth.

In any case, I wanted to be released from this unhappy scene that I was helpless to change. "Can you tell me, Sophia—do you know what you are? Are you a ghost?" It was the question I'd wanted to ask but had been afraid I would offend her.

She looked at me warily. No response, just a narrowing of her eyes.

I pressed on. "You remember dying, don't you? Going into the Allagash? Drowning?"

She turned her face away from me, but I caught a flash of red rise to her cheeks. "I remember the water . . . so cold . . . but that's all. It goes black after that. And I don't care to recall anything more, thank you."

I didn't blame her. Sophia's suicide had haunted me for years. She had killed herself because she was pregnant with Jonathan's child, proof that she was an adulteress, a serious crime at the time. The night before she took her life, I had spoken to her, pretending to be Jonathan's messenger and telling her that Jonathan wanted nothing to do with her anymore. I had been harsh with her, and the next day she disappeared. No one knew what happened to her until the search party found her half-frozen body floating in the frigid Allagash River. Although Jonathan had since absolved me of my part in her demise, I couldn't help but feel responsible.

Sophia stared at me now as though my guilt were painted on my face. "You think I drowned myself because you lied to me, don't you? You are a silly woman. It's only natural to put ourselves in the center of everything, I suppose, but still—why would I care what *you* said or thought? The only one whose opinion mattered one whit to me was Jonathan, and his position was clear enough. He would never, ever acknowledge the baby." She gazed down at the bundle in her arm. "But it wasn't my pregnancy, not really. I cannot blame this child. It was my marriage that broke my will. It was a death knell. I couldn't bear the thought of raising a child in that household, of the two us being crushed under the weight of Jeremiah's thoughtlessness and inconsideration. He wasn't an exceptionally bad man"—her eyes met mine, as though this was something every woman could understand—"but it would've been the slow death of me, to spend my entire life under his yoke. I did not end my life because I couldn't have Jonathan but because I could not escape from the choices that had been made for me."

"Have you seen Jonathan since you've been here?" I asked, hopeful that she might have information that could be of help.

At this, her stern expression crumpled a little at the edges, but after only a moment's falter, she gathered up her steely reserve again. "What's past is past—we cannot change the outcome. No matter how many times I may revisit that part of my life, the outcome will always be the same." Even in the underworld, Sophia's afterlife seemed anchored to this place as a point in time like a ball on a tether. She could travel all the way to the end of the tether or come back to the point of her origin, but she could never get away.

I looked through the window of my family's cabin into the

woods. How well I remember feeling the same as Sophia: Was I really meant to live my entire existence in these few square miles, among these same forty families? I could not accept that these two hundred people would be the only souls I would ever know. It seemed the most unbearable sentence. The next town, Fort Kent, was only thirty miles away but it might as well have been on another planet. In that small town, in St. Andrew, life's few precious milestones—birth, marriage, the birth of your children, death—were all you were given. Sophia, like me, had longed for something more.

"You could've left, Sophia. I left. What I found out there was beyond my wildest dreams." I opened my mouth to speak and tell her about the incredible existence I'd had, the places I'd traveled, the people I'd met, and of course Adair's fantastical realm, which had swallowed me whole. But then I remembered that I was speaking to someone who was chained to this time and place seemingly for eternity, who would never get to see a fraction of what I had, and I couldn't do it.

Sophia shifted the bundle she was carrying one more time, bracing it against her hip. Ah, the baby. This was something in her favor: at least she'd had her baby with her for eternity—mine had been taken away from me. I felt a pang of envy as I watched her . . . but then it occurred to me that something was wrong. I'd not heard the baby once this whole time. Not a burble, not a cry, not a sneeze. The child was very still.

"Sophia, is that your baby?" I asked carefully, my stomach tightening.

"Yes, a girl," she said but offered no name.

"May I hold her?"

She shot me a contemptuous look but, tentatively, she held

the child out to me. She was still in my arms and too heavy for her size, like a sodden bundle of wash. With trepidation, I lifted the corner of blanket covering the baby's face, steeled for something horrific. There was a neatly swaddled infant inside, but whether she was alive or dead was impossible to tell. The baby didn't seem to breathe and yet there was a whisper of animation to her, a pulse behind the eyelids, a slight tremor at the corner of her mouth. Her skin was the strangest color, a pale gray-blue as though she had stopped breathing—or because she had never breathed.

Poor Sophia. This had been her punishment for taking her life while her unborn child was still inside her: to carry the baby with her for eternity and never to see it wake up. She could not put her down, she couldn't bury her and be done with it. She was doomed to be forever hopeful that the baby might open her eyes and look at her, but to know in her heart that she never would. I thought my punishment had been horrible but it paled compared to this. This was the real lesson here, I thought as I handed the baby back to Sophia, who cooed and fussed over the lifeless child all the while in a melancholy air; this was the reason I'd been sent through that particular door out of the dozen in the hall, to be reunited with Sophia: not only to better understand my punishment, but to witness hers.

TWELVE

A dair stood at the foot of the bed, watching Lanore sleep—at least, it *seemed* as though she was sleeping—and wondering what was happening wherever she was. Was she safe? Had she found Jonathan? Perhaps she was lying in the pompous fool's arms at that moment. He pushed the thought from his mind; no, she'd promised that she was not looking to rekindle her old romance, and for some reason (perhaps the fleet look of disquietude she gave him when she'd made the promise), he was inclined to believe her. It had been several weeks since he'd cast her into this trance and honestly, he was surprised that she hadn't returned yet.

By this time, relations with Terry and Robin had deteriorated to the breaking point. Waiting on tenterhooks for Lanore's return, each minute more fraught than the last, meant that he had no patience for distractions, which included the girls' interruptions. They'd gotten the message, eventually, and now stomped sullenly about the fortress like Clydesdales, or got drunk at night and stayed up playing music, shrieking and laughing and behaving as though there were a party going on—anything to prompt a response from him, even an angry one. He refused to rise to the bait.

He blocked out as much of their noise as he could and remained with Lanore, pacing in her tiny room and watching for a sign. The only thing he *wanted* to do, however, was to hold her, aching for the reassurance of her physical presence, but he felt constrained from doing as he wished by the girls' obnoxious behavior, which undoubtedly had been their intent.

It wasn't until one night, when there had been a long silence in the dead hours, that he thought it was safe enough, and he took his chance. After bracing a chair against the door, he climbed on the bed and hugged Lanore close. He was amazed anew at how small she was, how fragile. Her toes came only to his shins. Her body was so narrow. He ran his hands over the parts of her that were exposed to him and thrilled at the rose-petal tenderness of her skin. He brought his face close to her neck, drinking in her scent, and that tiny bit of intimacy only made him want her more, made him shudder with the great physical potential inside him, like a tsunami rippling over the ocean and reaching for shore. He was seized with the desire to relieve his longing by coupling with her unconscious body. It wasn't as though Lanore would be surprised if he told her when she awakened what he'd done, he thought. Knowing him as she did, she'd probably *expect* it of him. She'd excuse his base behavior and yet . . . he knew she'd be disappointed. It would

be a bit of the old Adair resurfacing, the demon who frightened her so, proof that he hadn't been exorcised completely.

He rolled away from her, closed his eyes, and reached for
his member, already full and heavy with need. Pressed against
her on the bed was enough of a connection for what he had to
do, and he was able to bring himself to climax quickly. His relief was short-lived, however: he felt his hard-earned peace dissipate like mist, to be replaced with an aching sadness. He was,
after all, still alone, and she was still lying next to him like an
effigy on a tomb.

He went to the window and saw the entire island was in
sleep. Even the goats were huddled together under the pine
trees, their heads resting on their knees. A mist seemed to have
settled over the island, covering everything in a thick white
fog, as palpable as cotton batting.

Adair went downstairs, past the dining room, where he
found the two women passed out at the table, a number of
empty wine bottles strewn between them. He put on his greatcoat and went outdoors. It was wintertime, but aside from the
biting wind whipping in from the sea, it didn't seem like winter on the island, which was too far south in the Mediterranean
for frost or snow. As Adair stood staring at the water with his
hands thrust in his pockets, he thought that he would like it to
look like winter. What was the coldness he felt in his heart, if
not winter?

Without saying a word or even thinking about it too stren-
uously, he made the temperature fall. A frosty veil of white
started to bloom over the black rocks. Plumes of breath rose
over the sleeping goats. Where the sea met rock, a ring of ice
began to form, then spread out to the sea, until the island was

encircled by a huge disk of thick ice. Adair tried not to be surprised, because he knew that—in some way that wasn't clear to
him but was nonetheless undeniable—he'd willed this change
to happen.

Inside the house, Adair continued his vigil. He moved a chair to
the foot of the bed so that he could watch Lanore from a different angle. He brought a blanket from another room and spread it
over the first one, fearing that she might feel a chill now that the
air had gotten colder, though he suspected that she didn't feel a
thing. As he sat watching her, with a sigh he released the coldness in his heart, and as soon as he did, the temperature began
to creep upward. The goats awoke, tossing their heads to shake
off the enchantment. Before long the ice that had gripped the
shore began to groan and break apart, chunks of it drifting into
the sea.

Watching the ice break apart made Adair feel uneasy,
however. He had begun to feel a presence gathering on the
horizon. Whatever this presence was, it was malevolent. It
stalked outside his field of vision, beyond his reach, like a
wolf or jackal pacing and sniffing the air. It was testing the
outer limits of Adair's reach and would come in closer once it
felt confident. He had no idea what the presence might be, or
why he felt this strong sense of foreboding, but there it was,
just as he felt there was a connection between the girls and
the long-dead sister witches.

He worried that it could be the queen coming for him.
There was a chance that Lanore's entry to the underworld
had gotten the queen's attention and now she was amassing

her forces, preparing to capture him and drag him to hell to face the punishment he'd eluded for so long. If it weren't for Lanore, Adair would take measures of his own and leave the island. But as it was, Adair felt like a sitting duck, impatient with being helpless.

That night, Adair once again barricaded the door to Lanore's room and settled in with her. He fitted himself against her on the bed, cupping his hand over the one of hers that held the vial, and then cleared his mind so that he might drift into sleep. Darkness fell on him swiftly, and as heavily as a hammer.

VENICE, 1262

The next day, Adair could hardly wait for midnight. He'd spent the daytime hurriedly copying out as many pages as he could from the blue book, until his hand cramped and his fingers were heavily stained with ink. As much as he regretted the loss of his treasure, he hoped to get something much better in return: a mentor. Oh, of course the man he met last night might be a pretender and a charlatan, but Adair didn't think that was the case. If he was half as learned as Adair suspected, Adair had decided to try to convince him to take him on as an apprentice. At the very least, he hoped the old man would let him peruse his books on the occult. If owning even one book of secrets had made Adair this happy, he couldn't imagine what it would be like to have access to an entire collection. The sacrifice of the peacock book was a minor thing compared to the possibility of finding a knowledgeable mentor and gaining access to such an accumulation of occult knowledge.

By midnight, most of the doge's staff was asleep, even the guard at the gate in the back of the courtyard, and Adair had no difficulty sneaking out of the palazzo. Energetic with anticipation, he dashed through cobblestone alleys and over bridges until he came to the Plaza Saint Vincent. The old man had not been kidding when he said Adair would be able to pick out his house without assistance: one house alone dominated the square, and it was conspicuously well lit for the hour. Two lanterns hung in front of the massive oak doors, and chinks of light coming from deep inside the house shone through all the closed shutters.

Adair was met at the door by a footman, who led him on a trek through the palazzo and all the way to a wing at the back of the house. They finally came to a large, heavy door. The servant held the door open but only nodded at Adair, indicating that he should proceed alone, the door closing at once behind him. The room might as well have been in a deep dungeon, it was so dark and cavernous, though it was lit as well as could be by two huge candelabras standing on tall pedestals. The room obviously served as a study, two of its long walls covered with book-laden shelves. Adair had never seen so many books in his life, not at the doge's palace, nor in any of the rooms of his father's castle. For a moment, all he could do was gawk. It was like seeing his dearest wish come true. To be able to afford so many books, he figured the old man must be rich beyond measure.

It was then that Adair noticed the old man standing behind a high lectern, reading from a large book. He was slightly more modestly dressed that evening than the first time they'd met, now wearing a tunic with a full fur collar and gold embroidery at the neck and sleeves. He was using a piece of glass to magnify the words on the page, and took his time finishing what he was doing before looking up at Adair.

"You made it, I see. And you have the book?" he asked, reaching out with one massive, leathery hand. Adair took the package from under his cloak and approached the lectern, offering it up.

The old man slipped the deerskin off, then held the book up to examine it under the light from the candelabras. He flicked through the pages, pleased. At length he said to Adair, "It's a lovely book, wouldn't you agree? And a very rare one. Do you know the provenance of this tome?"

Adair shook his head.

"If you did, doubtless you would've fought harder to keep it." The old man gave him a cunning smile, pleased with himself. "It was reportedly made by a French monk who was a secret devotee of the occult arts during the Capetian reign, prior to the time of Eleanor of Aquitaine. The church has a very long and intimate relationship with the occult," he said, clearly delighting in his new possession, the way a man might extoll the virtues of a superb wine or a good spouse to whoever is within earshot.

Now happy, the old man reached into his robes and held out Adair's coin purse and proceeded to tell Adair about himself. His name was Cosimo Moretti. He was born the son of a common farmer in the principality of Naples, but over the course of many years had been able to distinguish himself as a knight in service to the prince, fighting his way out of poverty. For his entire life, however, he'd had a secret burning interest in the dark arts. For instance, on every campaign, he would seek out old crones, midwives, and herbalists, charming or paying them, whichever was necessary, to find out if there was an actual witch living in their midst. Such information was not readily shared with strangers—particularly one of the prince's men, who more likely than not would turn the witch over to the authorities—but occasionally he struck pay dirt. In this way, albeit very slowly, he accumulated a good deal of knowledge about not only the dark arts but its renowned practitioners.

Once he became too old to fight in battle anymore, he put away his sword, sold his estate, and left Naples, trekking to Venice to study with a very powerful magician. Cosimo recalled with a chuckle that he had to camp out in the courtyard in front of the magician's palazzo for three weeks before the man would even speak to him. "Can you imagine! I was quite aged at this point, a gray-bearded old relic prostrating myself in the man's doorway like a beggar! Luckily, I was plenty hardened from years living on the battlefield and the inconvenience meant little to me."

"And how long were you able to study with this mage?" Adair asked, breathless.

"A decade. He was very old by the time I met him, and it was a miracle that he lived as long as he did. As the man had no heirs, I inherited everything, including this house and the magnificent collection of books of secrets that you see here." He gestured to the towering walls of shelves, burgeoning with books of all sizes and shapes. "I've added to it steadily whenever the opportunity arises, making my own contribution to his life's work." What remained unsaid, however, was what would happen to the collection on Cosimo's death.

Adair wondered if the old warrior had a family that stood to inherit everything.

Adair imagined that Cosimo had to know what burned in his heart, that he hoped the old man would take him under his wing, just as the mage had done with Cosimo. One thing bothered Adair, however, something he needed Cosimo to clarify.

"There is one thing I wish to know, sir, and perhaps you can explain this to me. . . . You call yourself a magician, while I study the art of alchemy, and yet here we are interested in the same book of secrets. How can that be? Do you consider yourself an alchemist, too?"

Cosimo smiled, although there was little comfort in his expression, as he had the cold, reptilian smile of a lizard. "I was wondering if you might ask me this. In truth, I know little about the world of alchemy. But I *do* know that there appear to be many similarities between the two practices. I've seen what great magicians are able to do by fire and cauldron, and I have been told that alchemists employ these same means. I know the ingredients witches use, and I have been told that alchemists use the same kind. And what of the *ends* that both magicians and alchemists seek to achieve? Some would say that the things a skilled alchemist can do are no different from witchcraft, no different at all."

He came down from the lectern and clapped a hand to Adair's shoulder. "So I don't know the answer to your question, young squire. Perhaps this is what you are meant to discover on your journey." His eyebrows shot up as he spoke, and paired with the reptilian smile, he was quite a daunting sight.

The formal invitation Adair hoped for was not to come for

several more weeks, not until he'd sat by Cosimo's cauldron on a couple occasions, watching silently as the old man measured and stirred and pointed to recipes in ancient books. And it would be another month of skipping Professore Scolari's lectures in favor of long fireside talks in Cosimo's palazzo before the old man would give Adair free reign among the books of secrets, allowing him to copy out whichever recipes he chose. Adair began to spend every possible minute at the palazzo, sometimes staying the entire evening and rushing through the alleys of Venice in the minutes before dawn to return to the doge's house, so the servants wouldn't see that he was missing from his bed.

Adair thought he had his double life under control. Granted, he barely spent any time in Professore Scolari's lectures, but he had found a tutor whose teaching was more to his liking. If Zeno were to send a servant to Adair's room in the middle of the night, the jig would be up, but Adair was pretty sure that the doge had ceased to concern himself with his ward's comings and goings, if he ever had in the first place. As far as Adair was concerned, his exile to Venice was going far better than he'd ever expected.

So he was understandably surprised when he was summoned to the doge's study one Sunday afternoon. It was one of those rare times that his host was alone: usually it was impossible to see the doge except with his horde of advisers, officials, nobles, and merchants, who were all petitioning him for some favor or consideration. This afternoon, however, Adair found Zeno by himself in his study, sitting behind a desk piled high with scrolls.

Adair bowed low before him, waiting in this excruciating

position until the doge acknowledged him. Zeno wore a tight black velvet cap to warm his near-bald skull, but the cap made him look a little like an infant and spoiled his usually intimidating appearance. He looked down his large, hooked nose at his ward. "Stand up, boy, and take that chair. I need a word with you."

Adair obeyed, his nerves dancing.

The doge fixed him with a dry stare. "How long have you been living in my household, cel Rau? Refresh my memory."

"Nearly eight months, my liege."

"Your father prevailed on me to take you in because, he claimed, you had a burning desire to become a physician." Adair squirmed in his chair as Zeno rolled up the scroll he'd been looking at. "Professore Scolari tells me that you have been noticeably absent from his lectures. I wish that I could say 'of late' but he informs me that this has been the case for quite some time. Is this true, or is the professor mistaken?"

Adair hung his head. "No, my liege. The professor is not mistaken."

"Well then, perhaps you can tell me what you've been up to, if you're not attending your classes, so that I may answer your father's missives and not commit the mortal sin of bearing falsehoods?" The doge studied Adair through his steepled fingers.

"I have found a tutor of my own liking. I have been attending his lectures," Adair admitted.

Zeno raised his bushy eyebrows. "Is that so? And tell me, what is the name of this mysterious professor? Come, come, if there is a better physician to be found in the city of Venice, I should know his name. Out with it."

Adair blushed. His only desire was to get out of the doge's presence without giving up his secret studies. "Forgive me, your grace, for my attempt to deceive you. There is no other physician; the truth is that I find my interest in medicine has waned, to the point where I question whether I wish to pursue further study or not."

Zeno smirked, as though he'd known he'd been right all along. "I could not care less about your interest in medicine, I only wish to know where you have been spending your time in the evenings, if not with Scolari. Out with it: Have you been out gambling away your father's fortune, or idling your time away in a brothel somewhere?"

Adair's throat tightened. There was no lie that the doge would not be able to verify. Zeno had spies everywhere. He was left with only one option: Rossi. "The truth, then, my grace: I have been keeping company with Bishop Rossi. He made me see that my religious education has been lacking— so heavily influenced by the Eastern Orthodox Church, as it has been." That was his trump card; he knew the doge would consider it a personal victory if he could turn the near-heathen Hungarian nobleman into a proper Roman Catholic.

Zeno leaned forward in his chair. "So—been spending time with Rossi, have you? I find that surprising, cel Rau, given what your father told me about your attitude toward the church."

"*His* church, the orthodox church." Adair was surprised at how nimbly the lie sprang to his lips. "I knew almost nothing about the Roman church before coming here. There is a Roman Catholic priest in our court, but he is kept to the fringes, treated as a heretic by the other clerics, as you might imagine. I never spoke to him, and so I had no understanding of the Roman church at all. Whereas Bishop Rossi—"

"Rossi makes the Roman church seem fascinating, does he?" Zeno asked, his tone skeptical. He studied Adair shrewdly. "Well, well, well . . . as I have said, this is all very surprising. But if this is what you say has transpired, I must take you at your word. As for the matter of your medical studies, well, if you do not wish to pursue them, it makes no difference to me. However, young men are known to be changeable. Your fascination with Rossi's company may fade. For the time being, I will say nothing to your father, in case you change your mind."

Adair bowed low in acknowledgment of Zeno's consent, anxious to retreat from the room.

"Not so fast, my boy. Not so fast." Zeno sniffed. "Do not forget: it is your father I am beholden to, not *you*. You need to stop fooling around and get on with the serious business of life. You're just about out of second chances. Your father's patience will not last forever, you know." He tugged at his cap, which had come askew, so that he ended up looking a bit ridiculous at the end of his reproachful speech, like an old woman getting ready for bed.

Adair further prostrated himself before the doge. "I welcome the opportunity to please your grace."

"Please me? This has nothing to do with pleasing me, my boy. But if you truly wish to please me, you will do as your father asks. You will give up these childish distractions and apply yourself to the rank with which God has seen fit to grant you. You have been blessed with rank and title, you know. Do not make God regret he has favored you. Do not affront his beneficence." Zeno tugged the sleeves of his robe over his knuckles for warmth, signifying that the audience was over. Adair bowed so deeply that his head almost touched the stone floor before turning and stalking out of the room.

The next evening, Adair was at Cosimo's door. It wasn't one of their prearranged sessions and so the mage wasn't expecting him, but he received Adair warmly all the same.

"What is it, my boy? You seem agitated," Cosimo said once he'd closed the doors to the study behind them.

"I'm afraid I will not be able to visit you for a while," Adair said, and then laid out the situation for the old knight. To avoid Zeno's wrath, Adair would need to resume his visits with Rossi, perhaps even go so far as to return to Scolari's lecture hall again—whatever it would take to appease the doge. "The bishop is even holding a dinner in my honor in a few nights' time. I swear this is all a grand scheme: the doge is plotting with the bishop to get me engaged to the goddaughter."

"Is that all? So marry the girl," Cosimo said, and laughed.

"I'm glad *you* can speak so lightly about my future," Adair said glumly.

The mage clapped him on the back. "You're far too serious for so young a man. I swear, you are like an old man stuffed into a young man's body. Listen to someone approaching the end of his life: it would not be the worst thing in the world to take a wife. She will make your life interesting."

Adair snorted. "You haven't met Elena. I fear she would make my life *too* interesting."

"All the better," Cosimo responded. "Listen to an old man:

life is short. There is no dishonor in enjoying it a little along the way."

Bishop Rossi's party turned out to be not an overly large affair, though Adair couldn't decide if that was a good thing or not. On one hand, he wasn't being forced to repeat the same banalities over and over as he made the acquaintance of the Venetians who had come to gawk at a heathen nobleman from the wilds of Hungary. On the other, there was no getting away from Elena, whom the bishop had assigned to act as his social guide. She stood by Adair's side almost from the moment he walked through the door. She was especially pretty that night, with pearls set like stars in her dark hair, and a long strand of them circling her slender neck. Every time he looked at her, she had a simper on her face as though she were auditioning for the role of his wife. *Don't try so hard,* he wanted to tell her. Even if he were looking for a spouse, it wouldn't be the woman she was trying to be tonight. He longed for a girl with a little grit.

It didn't take him long to figure out that the dinner party was merely an excuse to make him spend time with Elena. The bishop and the doge clearly thought that taking on a wife was the cure for his alleged problems. Granted, Elena was lovely and the longer he sat next to her, the more he appreciated her charms, even if they were primarily of the decorative variety. His mind began to wander as the meal progressed, and by the time the roasts were served, he wondered what her body looked like unclothed. He pictured them rutting in a bedchamber somewhere upstairs, cupping his hands over her small breasts as he took her from behind, her white derriere jiggling as he drove into her—and broke such thoughts off, red-faced, before he created an obvious problem for himself.

Too late. Luckily, his clothing hid the evidence of his distress to a degree, but he was going to have to excuse himself to take care of the matter before it became unbearable. He headed for the pissing station outside the great hall and ducked behind the privacy of a screen. Once he was sure there were no servants nearby who might stumble across him, he unlimbered his member and, eyes closed, began to stroke himself. He was businesslike, his intention to get off and get back to the dinner party as quickly as possible. He had just gotten off to a promising start when he felt a small hand alight on his manhood. He opened his eyes in shock.

It was Elena. She must've guessed what he was up to and followed him. She had put her hand most deliberately on his cock and Adair was so surprised that speech failed him. She used that moment of weakness to kiss him. Even though it was she who threw herself against him, her mouth pressing to his, she still managed to yield softly to him. She was as tender as he imagined she would be, a hot spot of need reaching for him and melting under him simultaneously. Her hands crept to his chest, her palms pressed against the front of his tunic.

Once the kiss was over and she'd settled back to her feet, she looked into his eyes saucily. "May I help you with that, my lord?" she asked. Her hands went to work before he could even reply. Her eyes were locked on his manhood the entire time. While she obviously took pleasure from what she was doing, it was just as obvious that this was not her first time. She brought him to climax expertly, catching his seed in a handkerchief at the end. While he watched in openmouthed surprise, she tucked the handkerchief down the front of her tunic, between her breasts, and then rinsed her hands in a nearby washing bowl.

In the fog of his brain, awash with pleasure and shock, Adair suddenly understood why Elena had been sent to live away from home: the girl was an incorrigible nymphomaniac. She'd probably disgraced herself, though she was probably not so foolish as to give up her hymen to anyone, not before her wedding. She had been packed off to faraway Venice because no one would have heard of her indiscretions, and there was even a possibility that she might snare a suitable husband. Undoubtedly the bishop was trying to reform Elena while she was living under his roof, and having about as much success as the doge was having with Adair. In some respects, she was no different than he.

"Elena, we must talk—but not here," he said, leading her by the hand out into the hall. Although there was the possibility of being overheard as servants passed by with platters and pitchers to serve the partygoers in the great hall, it was less incriminating than being caught together by the piss pots. And he needed to set her straight and let her know that he had no intention of marrying her, despite her godfather and the doge's obvious attempt to pair them off.

She looked at him now with a mixture of suspicion and resignation. "Oh—I've gone and done it, haven't I? Been too eager? It's just that I wanted to see it. Your prick. I knew it would be lovely, and it is. You won't tell my godfather what I've done, will you? He'll be so disappointed."

Adair put his hands on her shoulders. "Elena, that was a

very generous courtesy you did for me just now, and while I appreciate your attentions, I must tell you—you're wasting your time with me. I have no intention of marrying. Not you, not anyone."

She drew back as though Adair had told her he had the plague. "What do you mean? Are you thinking of taking vows?"

"Becoming a priest? Oh no . . . Although, you might think my intention not so dissimilar . . ." He stood as tall as he could, trying to make himself seem older and wiser. "I'm going to become a scholar and devote myself to study of the natural world."

She sized him up cagily. "Yes, I heard you intend to become a physician."

"That's part of it, but I'm interested in more than the human body. I'm interested in all of it, everything you can touch and see. And more—I'm interested in the soul, too. The spirit."

"That *seems* very admirable," she said, but sounded tentative, as though she wasn't sure why anyone would be interested in such a strenuous undertaking. "But why does that mean you cannot wed?"

"Because I'll be traveling. I wish to meet the greatest thinkers alive. I can't remain here, in some palazzo in Venice, and expect all the wonders of the world to come to me," he explained.

She seemed to consider what he said seriously, rocking a little side to side. "And you wouldn't take your wife with you on your travels?"

He looked down on her gravely. "It wouldn't do. Besides,

a woman doesn't want to go traveling. She needs a home where she can raise her children. That's what makes a woman happy." He recalled overhearing his mother saying this to his father once, when the duke had been preparing to follow the king of Hungary into battle. It promised to be a prolonged siege and he wanted her to travel with him. She'd laughed at the notion and suggested he bring one of his favorite mistresses instead. It had saddened his father, because he had truly loved her.

"I suppose that is true," she said, giving in. "In all honesty, I cannot see myself living out of trunks. I will let my godfather know of your feelings. But you should be aware—the doge has been in on this plan from the beginning. He would like to see you wed and settled."

"I know."

"He's sent some of his men to round up your friend, do you know that, too? That's why he asked my godfather to have this dinner party for you tonight—so you would be occupied elsewhere when they went to arrest him."

His heart seized in terror. He gripped Elena by the shoulders. "Who? Who are they going to arrest?" he asked, but in his heart he already knew. Who else could it be but Cosimo?

Her eyes went wide. "I didn't hear the name. But he said the doge had you followed, to see where you disappeared to at night, and that's how they found out what you were up to."

His last visit to Cosimo—that had to be when he'd been followed, after he'd foolishly allowed himself to believe that he'd deflected the doge's suspicions. Zeno had probably dispatched a spy to shadow him from that moment forward. With a sinking heart, Adair dashed out of the hall, bellowing for his cloak and hat. As he ran from the bishop's palazzo and down the empty alleys, he began to realize that he was too late. It would be useless for him to go to Cosimo's house now: no doubt they'd arrested him already. He would be on his way to the dungeon. This was terrible and it was all his fault; he'd underestimated Zeno, thinking him an impotent old fool who didn't care what was going on right under his own roof. He'd made a ridiculous mistake, the kind of mistake made by head-strong young men, and now Cosimo would pay with his life.

Then another thought came to him, terrible in its mean-ing: the inquisitors would seize everything in Cosimo's house that could be used against him as evidence for the trial. His magnificent collection of books would be destroyed, put to the torch after the trial was over. The loss staggered him. He ran even faster, not sure what he would do when he got there.

Just as he'd expected, the arrest had already taken place. Cosimo was gone, his servants huddled out on the square in their bed clothes, crying. The front doors were thrown open to the street, flanked by a few of the doge's guards. They crossed their lances to bar Adair's way when he ran up to them.

"You will let me pass. The doge has sent me," he roared at the guards. He knew what he was doing was ill advised; he'd already gotten in enough trouble, and by declaring himself so boldly to the guards, the doge would certainly hear of it. But Adair could see no other way to gain entry to Cosimo's house, and every moment was precious. "That's right." Adair turned and shouted at the mage's servants, pretending to gloat. "It was all a trap set by the doge, and I was part of it.

It was I who led them to your master. It is incumbent upon the doge, the leader of this city, to root out evil and eliminate it from our midst. Your master is evil—truly an evil man, a priest of Satan, and so I will testify at his trial." He turned back to the guards and pushed the lances aside. "Now, out of my way. I tell you, I have been sent here by the doge himself and he will not tolerate your interference."

His theatrics worked and they let him pass. Inside, every torch and sconce in Cosimo's palazzo was lit and burning brightly. He heard the echoes of men's voices coming down the hall from the study, and his heart sank. The inquisitors were here. As he approached the doorway, he saw two men standing before the shelves, thumbing through books. The floor was covered with discarded tomes and scattered sheets of paper. The men were dressed in the black robes of the court. *Of course.* Adair realized then that soldiers had not been sent to secure the documents because soldiers wouldn't be able to read. These were two officials and they had already made two high piles of books on the floor, ostensibly to be taken away for further review.

He looked at the books thrown to the floor, and the few still clinging to the shelves like birds too frightened to come down from the trees. It seemed an unconscionable waste for all these books to be destroyed, a calamity on par—in Adair's mind—with the destruction of the library of ancient Alexandria. He felt that he had to do something, salvage whatever he could. Out of the corner of his eye, he caught sight of the peacock-blue spine of the book he'd surrendered to Cosimo. A wave of sorrow passed through him for having to lose it a second time. Surely there had to be a way to save it.

He pulled back into the shadows before the two officials could see him, and tiptoed to the kitchen. The kitchen fire blazed untended, no doubt deserted by the servants when the soldiers burst into the palazzo. There was a stack of firewood next to the hearth and a box of kindling. Platters of roasted meat stood on the table, left pooling in fat. The entire room seemed smoky and greasy and combustible, an accident waiting to happen.

It would be an extreme measure, to burn the house down. But when the officials ran outside to escape the flames and smoke, Adair thought he might have time to rescue a few of the volumes. Was it better to set fire to the house than to let the books fall into the church's possession? He wasn't sure. The church might burn them, too—but there was a chance they might be spared for further study. As long as the books were intact, there was a chance they might eventually find their way back to a practitioner, someone who would benefit from their knowledge. If they burned, they were just ash.

The thought that the church would decide the books' fate was too much for Adair to stand. To have these precious books rounded up like children and held hostage in trunks in a moldy basement at the duomo, rotting away day by day until they were nothing but mildewed pages stuck together, illegible . . . then thrown into the fires of the auto-da-fé, fuel to burn some poor luckless devil to death. No, he wouldn't let that happen. He took some kindling and dipped it in goose fat, then held it to the flame. The tender wood caught quickly. From there it was a simple thing to creep down the hall and hold the flame to the hem of a dusty drapery. . . .

The house filled with smoke in minutes as flames leapt

from wall to wall. Cries of alarm sounded from Cosimo's study and then the two officials ran out, calling for the guards to fetch water from the well. As he ducked into the study, Adair knew he had mere minutes to act—and what's more, the fire had leapt to the shelves quickly, seeming to know there were thousands of dry pages to feast on. Smoke had already engulfed the room and Adair could barely see his hand in front of his face.

Which books should he save? For a moment, he was paralyzed with indecision. It wasn't as though he had Cosimo's encyclopedic knowledge of the collection; he'd be hard-pressed to say which was the most valuable. He wanted to save them all but knowing that he couldn't, his hand went to the one book that his eye always sought first: the one with the peacock-blue cover. Holding his hand over his mouth against the smoke, his eyes tearing, he grabbed the books on either side, too, and tucked all of them under his arm. He kicked open the shutters on the nearest window and—since he didn't dare use the front entrance for fear of running into the soldiers' bucket brigade— he hurled through the open window into the alley, landing in a puddle of filth. He leapt to his feet and ran without looking back, knowing that his mentor's priceless collection was going up in flames, and by his hand.

Adair ended up hiding two books in a nearby square: all three made for too conspicuous a bundle to carry into the doge's palazzo. And as little as he wanted to, he realized that he had to return to Zeno's house. He would've tried his luck living on the street, selling his finer pieces of clothing to raise money to live on—at least he would be free—but he couldn't bear the thought of giving up all those recipes he'd copied out by hand and hidden in his bedchamber. He decided to take his chances weathering the doge's wrath. If Cosimo had been arrested for being a magician, it seemed to Adair that he had no chance of escaping the same fate. If Cosimo was going to burn, Adair stood a good chance of burning, too.

With the blue book tucked securely in a panel of his cloak, Adair cautiously approached the formidable palazzo. It was uncharacteristically brightly lit for the hour, a sure sign that something was taking place inside. Once he entered, he saw that the halls were alive with chatter and he felt as though everyone stopped to stare at him as he rushed by. He'd hoped to get to his room undetected and gather his belongings, make up a packet, and be ready for escape as early as that evening. But he had gotten ten paces into the house when one of the court officials saw him and called for the nearest guard to detain him—on the doge's orders.

He was brought to the anteroom outside the grand chamber. A flock of officials were clustered around the huge table, all in their long black robes. Old Zeno stood on the far side, his face as violent as Adair had ever seen it, frightening to behold. He could see why this man had come out on top of all the scheming and scrapping and battling among Venetian nobles and been made the doge, the ruler of the city. Bishop Rossi crouched at Zeno's side.

Adair dropped his cloak—which he had taken off and wrapped around the book to soften its edges into anonymity—and set his package onto a chair as he approached his guardian. He could see fury building in the old man's eyes as

he directed his words at the gathered crowd. "Leave us. I wish
to speak to my ward alone. No, you stay, Rossi." Zeno placed a
hand on the bishop's arm as he moved to join the others. The
clerks gave Adair baleful looks as they shuffled out, as though
they knew what fate was in store for him. He threw back his
shoulders and held his head high: he would show them how a
Magyar met his end.

Zeno waited until the heavy door had been closed before he
began thundering at him. "You! You are the very devil! Look at
the mess you have brought to my doorstep!"

Adair opened his mouth to defend himself, and then realized Zeno wasn't looking for an explanation.

"Your father warned me that you had an unhealthy interest
in the occult. But he said those days were behind you and that
you had given it all up to study medicine. If he had been up
front with me about your . . . your *obsession*, I never would have
agreed to take you in." The Venetian almost spat the words at
Adair. "You bring this occultist practically to my door. What
am I to do? I am the doge, I cannot ignore your indiscretions.
I cannot allow heretics to flourish inside our city walls! My en-
emies would jump upon such weakness and use it to topple me.
Do you understand now, boy, what a foolish, dangerous thing
you have done?"

"Where is Cosimo?" Adair demanded, finally finding his
tongue.

Zeno looked affronted. "In the dungeon, of course, where
he should be."

"He is a knight of Naples, you know. You will risk war with
Naples if you do anything to him," Adair cautioned.

Zeno dismissed the idea with a wave of his hand. "He

hasn't been a knight of Naples for a very long time. I know the prince of Naples and the prince won't care what happens to a wizard."

"What will you do to him?"

"He'll be tried and burned at the stake, of course."

Adair took a step toward the table. It was scattered with papers, and he thought he recognized a few from Cosimo's study. "Let Cosimo go and I'll do as you ask. I'll go to Scolari's lectures, I'll be his best student."

Zeno stepped around the table until he stood in front of Adair, fixing him with a steely stare, no longer the comical little man in his nightcap. "Oh, you will do that anyway, if you wish to live. That was the bargain you struck with your father. You had your chance. I am not the only one whose patience you have exhausted. Believe me, if I sent word back to your father that you had met with an untimely—but not un-expected—end, he would understand. And perhaps be a little relieved, too. He always knew you were headed for trouble.

"This mess you have made is salvageable, however. That lie you told my guards at the heretic's house—they reported it back to me, of course. And that's the story we will tell, that you agreed to be my spy and ferret out the Satanist living in our midst; that will be our explanation as to why you have been in the company of the heretic. Luckily, Moretti's servants are already spreading that story all over the city. Venetians do love a good piece of gossip," he said in an aside to the bishop.

"You can't do this to me," Adair said, in despair.

Zeno observed him coldly. "I can and I shall. It's about time you grew up, my boy. Give up and give in. We all do. You're not a child anymore; it's time to put away your childish dreams. Take your place in society, as your family wishes. Or I will crush you, and end your family's embarrassment."

"And what can I offer you in exchange for Cosimo's life?"

"There is nothing you can do for Cosimo. He must be sacrificed."

The bishop leaned over the table toward Zeno, raising a finger for the doge's attention. "Wait, your grace. There is one thing he might do. . . . I could speak to the inquisitors on Moretti's behalf if you"—he narrowed his eyes on Adair— "agree to marry Elena."

Adair's heart squeezed as though a hand closed over it. "I beg you not to ask this of me. She'll not find happiness with me. You are sentencing us both to a lifetime of misery."

Rossi was unmoved. "You heard the doge—it's time you grew up and took your medicine like everyone else. Do you think that every married couple lives in bliss? That only the well suited are allowed to wed? You make the best of it, that's what you do," Rossi said sagely as though he, an unmarried member of the clergy, had any experience in the matter.

Zeno turned away from Adair, heading back to the table. "The matter is settled. You will be engaged to the bishop's goddaughter. You will be revealed as one of my agents and responsible for the arrest of the heretic Moretti."

"You will spare Moretti?" Adair asked hopefully.

"I will consider it," Zeno answered through gritted teeth.

It was the best he could hope for under the circumstances, with the arrest still fresh. Adair backed out of the room, retrieving his cloak at the door before shoving his way through the clerks waiting on the outside, to retreat to his chamber.

He hid the book and his packet of spells with the utmost

care, moving them to another room that he could access easily should he need to make a quick getaway. He didn't think any corner of his room would be safe from search now. The next few days were spent attending Scolari's lectures, where Adair's mind wandered incessantly. How could he pay attention as the old physician droned on when Cosimo was languishing in prison? It was Adair's fault, and what's more, there seemed to be nothing he could do about it. He wondered, however, why the old Neapolitan couldn't use magic to free himself. There must've been something in one of those dusty old books that would be helpful in this situation. Surely the old man knew a vanishing spell, or a way to charm the guard into unlocking the manacles. Or perhaps he could telepathically influence the inquisitors to find him innocent. There was so much he didn't understand about magic and its reach.

He had wanted to go see Cosimo right away but knew he had to bide his time or risk pushing Zeno over the edge. He also feared he might arrive too late, turning up at the dungeon one day to find that the inquisitors' tortures had killed him. Too, Cosimo might've heard of the false rumor they'd spread about Adair being a spy and would want nothing to do with him. It pained Adair to think that Cosimo might die thinking Adair had betrayed him.

Within a few weeks, Adair received a letter from his father informing him that he'd agreed to the marriage arrangements. He even wrote a few words about the benefits of an alliance with Elena's Florentine family, but Adair knew it was all for show: with any luck, he would remain in Italy after the wedding and would, for all his family cared, cease to be their worry anymore.

Finally, after a month had passed since the arrest and Adair could stand it no longer, he went down to the dungeons very late one night. He brought coin to bribe the guard into letting him see Cosimo. By then, the old man had been let out of his manacles and put in a cell, although it was so small that he couldn't stand fully upright in it. The floor was covered with filthy straw that had probably never been changed, and the walls were damp, as though the lagoon were trying to reclaim the doge's palazzo by stealth.

Adair lifted the lantern to see the old man's face turned up to him expectantly. Cosimo was in a terrible state. His royal robes were crusted with his own blood and gore and torn to give the torturers access to his vulnerable spots. All the parts of him Adair could see—his wrists, his bare feet, his throat—were raw with evidence of torture.

Adair handed him a package of food, enough to last several days if the rats didn't get to it, and a bottle each of wine and water. Cosimo looked suspiciously at the package even as he accepted it. "Why did you bring this? To assuage your guilt for being the one responsible for my arrest—"

"I hope you know me well enough not to listen to that. It was a story I made up the night you were arrested to get entry to your house. I was trying to save the books . . ."

Cosimo's eyes glittered with life for the briefest instant. "And did you?"

He shook his head. "I could carry only a few. I hid some in a square not far from your house but I fear they've since been discovered. There is a massive witch hunt going on." He hung his head. "In the end, I was able to save only one, the blue book."

Cosimo nodded. "Of all the books in my library, that was

a good one to save. Take care of it. Don't let the inquisitors get their hands on it. Save it for the ones who come after us."

"Don't give up, Cosimo," Adair said, trying to comfort him. "I've asked the doge to release you. I've even agreed to marry Bishop Rossi's goddaughter in exchange for his support in the matter. Now it's up to Zeno."

Cosimo shook his head. "My boy, there is no way for Zeno to pardon me. He's made too much of a spectacle over my arrest. And now this witch hunt . . . The townspeople will see a Satanist behind every bush. It would be impossible for it to end any other way than with my death." He said all this with an air of detachment, as though he were talking about someone else.

Adair was shocked. "How can you say that? You mustn't give up hope."

"It is impossible."

"Then . . ." Adair thought again about using magic to help Cosimo escape. If anyone would know how it could be done, he should. "Tell me how to use the spells to get you out of here. There must be a way for magic to help you escape."

The old man seemed resigned to his fate. "I don't have the strength or the necessary equipment to do anything from inside the dungeon."

"Then tell *me* what to do, which spell to use . . ."

"No. I will not have you put yourself at risk any further by trying to help me escape. I am very old and, given that I made my living for many years as a knight, should have been dead a long time ago. I've already had more years on this earth than I deserve. I'm ready to die."

"It's my decision—"

"No." He squeezed Adair's hand one last time. "It's *my*

decision. I want you to bide your time and then make your escape. I know you to be a headstrong boy, but this one time, young squire, listen to me."

Adair left the dungeon with his heart aching. He had to find a way to save Cosimo, even if the arsenal of recipes he had to choose from was much reduced. He stayed up as late as he could that night, poring over his loose pages and the blue book, trying to find a spell that could help Cosimo. But when Adair went downstairs in the morning, he was told that the old knight had taken his life last night in his cell. He'd broken one of the bottles Adair had brought and used the glass to slice his wrists and his throat.

PRESENT DAY

The light in the room in which Adair lay with Lanore had grown dim. Outside the window, a storm tossed violently, the kind that swept up on the island without warning and battered the rock mercilessly. Adair huddled closer to Lanny for warmth, fingering a lock of her hair absentmindedly while he listened to the wind rattle the glass panes.

He was covered in sticky sweat from his recollections of Venice. He could remember those days in Zeno's palazzo with precision: the damp of the streets, the moldering smell of his bedchamber, the bottle-green silk lining of his cloak, and the long pheasant feathers fixed to his cap.

And yet he had other memories of Cosimo, impossible ones from another time, an *earlier* time. Of Cosimo not in Italy but in the Ceahlău Massif mountains where Adair had grown up, the stretch of land that had been traded over the years, back and forth, between Hungary and Romania. In these memories, Cosimo was dressed in a rough peasant's shift and coarse woolen leggings, and was not the regal figure he'd known in Venice. Adair, a boy of seven or eight, stood in a mud cottage with a thatched roof, a primitive place with pigs running in and out of the house as though it were a barn. Adair was being restrained by his father as Cosimo was dragged out of the cottage by two of his father's men. They were forcing Cosimo to kneel in the mud before the stump he used for splitting firewood, and next to the stump stood an executioner in his black leather hood, a massive broadsword in his hands.

Adair shook his head to clear it but the image lingered. How could he have two memories of the exact same incident? He couldn't have known two Cosimos; it was impossible. Just as his mind told him he was a boy in the wild, craggy mountains of Romania in the 1000s *and* a man of fifteen in Venice in 1262. It was impossible—and yet both memories were seared into his mind, unforgettable.

There was one other thing that confused him about Cosimo. The memories of those nights at the old knight's palazzo, sitting by the fireplace as Cosimo mixed potions in the cauldron, taking a handful of this and a pinch of that from his many jars and bottles to fling into the pot . . . and of copying out recipes on scraps of paper and rolling them up to hide in his sleeve so he could bring them into the doge's house undetected . . . . Did those stories not remind him of something else? Of the stories *he* told of the peasant boy whose body he'd stolen? The peasant boy who had sat at his hearth and watched him prepare potion after potion? Who had stolen his recipes and tried to escape, earning a horrific beating?

The thought made Adair's blood freeze in his veins. It was impossible to trust his mind anymore it seemed. Did this mean he was going mad, finally? It had always been his greatest fear. Man was not meant to have so many memories, the collected stories from a thousand years of existence. It was inevitable that one day the well of memory would overflow.

These conflicting memories had been coming to him since he'd set foot on the island. It was as though whatever forces were alive on this piece of rock were demagnetizing his brain, and all the little bits and fragments of his past were lifting from the shoals where memories were kept. Lifting and becoming tangled, mixing and shifting before disappearing into the ether, clouded and then lost to him forever.

He looked at the woman lying in his arms and wondered if the same thing would happen to his memories of her. Would he start to forget their time together or confuse her with someone else? As much as the possibility hurt him, there was one memory he would be happy to lose, that of her betrayal. As it was, he was doomed to live with the knowledge that she could brick him up in a wall and leave him there to face eternity, that she had it in her to be as cold-blooded as—well, *he*. Maybe he was a fool to love such a woman, but love her he did.

Too, he wondered if—seeing that he had two memories of his childhood and of Cosimo—there were two versions of his life, and if in the other version he'd never hurt Lanore. Perhaps there was a version where he'd never abused or imprisoned her, never gave her a reason to doubt that she could trust him with her love. If that were the case, he'd do anything to lift the memories she *did* have of him and replace them with this other set. What he wouldn't give to take away all her unhappy memories—her memories of that bastard Jonathan, too. He ran a hand over her brow with a heavy sigh: he would remake her entire life so that she never experienced one moment of sadness; he would make her the only human who had never been lonely or unhappy or afraid, the only one in the history of the world, if only he could.

THIRTEEN

I made some excuse to Sophia in order to take my leave, but I don't remember what I said in my desperation to get away from her. As sad as I was for her and her baby, to be perfectly honest, I was horrified by what had become of her, horrified that a person could be made to endure such a merciless penance in the afterlife. Was the next plane of existence nothing more than a prison? If that was the case, that meant the queen might be its warden, making sure the offending souls did not escape from their punishment. But if she was the warden, who was the judge who handed down the sentences? Who had put her in charge of hell?

I ran out of my old childhood home and down the dirt wagon trail. I didn't think to linger in town; no, I wanted to get out of there as soon as possible. Luckily, this St. Andrew was exactly like the St. Andrew of my past and not like a

location in a dream, where a road suddenly grows twice its
length, or where you take a turn only to find that you've ended
up somewhere else entirely, a place you'd never seen before.
This St. Andrew remained true to form and so I could find my
way back to the spot in the forest where I'd entered. I found
the door without too much difficulty, locating it in the middle
of a big, old oak tree as though that was perfectly normal.

Once on the other side, I leaned against the door huffing
and puffing from exertion and fright, trying to force the vision
of Sophia's blue-faced baby from my mind. I was relieved to
be in the quiet hall again and wondered if it would be possible
to sit for a minute and collect my thoughts. Again, I listened
for the heavy thump-thump I'd heard before, the sound I'd
been sure was an indication of a demon. Nothing. Cautiously
optimistic, I looked in both directions. The hall to the right
seemed the shorter of the two. I could almost see the end of
the hall, where it turned a corner. What waited down those
other hallways? I wondered. Perhaps this hall was *my* hall, the
doors representing different phases of my life, and the doors on
those other halls led to someone else's life, perhaps someone
close to me. Perhaps they led to Jonathan's life. It was a silly
notion, undoubtedly, but I had to try to make sense of the fan-
tastic world in which I found myself.

I trotted down the hall as noiselessly as possible and peeked
around the corner. The red runner stretched away from me,
beckoningly, down the new hallway. This hall was longer, one
of those fun house ones that seemed to go off into infinity. I tiptoed up to the first door and pressed my ear against it: there was
silence within. I gripped the doorknob, and opened the door.

It opened onto a great, whistling canyon, its walls of craggy yellow rock climbing to the pale blue sky. The canyon itself was narrow, barely wide enough for a man to pass through. I didn't recognize it at first, but as I crept along the trail, running my hands over the pebbly walls, I remembered the Hindu Kush and my adventures there with Savva during the Great Game, living among the Afghans.

What a strange place the underworld was turning out to be, not nearly as frightening as I'd feared, the episode with Sophia notwithstanding. It was like getting to live forever in your memories, reuniting with old friends over and over, revisiting the places you'd lived. Take this place, for instance: if I was in the Hindu Kush, that meant I might be about to meet up with Abdul, the wonderful tribal warlord I'd met and fallen in love with. Fate had dealt with us unfairly and we'd had only a short time together. I would be absolutely delighted for an opportunity to see him again. The thought made my heart beat excitedly, and I'd even begun to jog down the path, expecting to find him around the next corner, when I realized I was being foolishly optimistic. This was the afterlife, not a video game. I couldn't expect to dial up an old memory and relive it on the spot. I could be in the mountains of Afghanistan, or not. I could be in someone else's life. I was running toward nothing. In any case, the chances of finding Jonathan here seemed slim.

Deflated, I retraced my steps and found the door I'd entered stuck incongruously in the side of the canyon wall. Strangely, as I stepped back into the hall, in that split second suspended between the canyon and the corridor, it came to me: I suddenly knew what I had to do to find Jonathan. I had to go to the place *my dreams* had told me I would find him. I had to go to the cellar.

It wasn't a pleasant prospect. Frightening things lurked in basements, and the fortress was no exception. My knees went a little weak as I set off, but before long I managed to find a staircase. Removing a candle from one of the sconces, I descended the stairs as quietly as possible, only too aware that any noise I made would rattle and rumble down the cavernous stairwell and let anyone within earshot know I was coming. A slight draft wafted up from the bottom, which was lost in darkness. The breeze carried a bitter tang of rot and decay.

The stairs deposited me in an alcove made of stone, made of the same large granite blocks as the passageway in my dreams. The air was clammy and I could have sworn I heard a faint plop, plop of dripping water off in the distance. Holding my candle overhead, I began down the passage, wary for the slightest movement in the shadows ahead. An eternity seemed to pass before I came to the first door, and it was not the one from my nightmare. My inclination was to keep looking for *the* door, the familiar one, but that approach seemed shortsighted. I might find something of value behind one of the other doors: someone who could advise me; a clue of some kind to help me deal with the dreaded queen.

I grasped the rough iron latch and opened the door.

Standing directly in front of me were not one but *three* demons. If they were ugly individually, they were positively fearsome in multiples. They were so large that they filled the room wall to wall with reddened muscle, the tips of their long, curving horns scraping the ceiling. Their three brutish heads turned on me as soon as I'd opened the door, watery snot dripping from their black snouts, their topaz eyes gleaming. When I entered the room, I distracted them from what they were doing, and my gaze involuntarily fell downward to the locus of their activity. I saw, to my horror, that there was a man on the floor between them. They'd circled around him, had him on his hands and knees, and one of the demons was hunched over him, caught in the midst of an unspeakable act. I was aware, all at once, of their great heavy phalluses, the weightiness between their legs, their brutal animal need. Surprised by my sudden presence, they'd broken off what they were doing to the poor man, who fell to the dirt floor in a swoon.

I turned and bolted. Candle dropped, I ran in pitch blackness, bumping and crashing against the stone walls. I held back the vomit that rose in my throat, tried to push the horrific sight out of my mind, and ran. Behind me, I heard the thudding of the demons' hooves on earth, the occasional scrape of dagger-tipped horn against stone, their grunts and groans as they tried to squeeze through the narrow passageway after me. I felt the heaviness of their bodies behind me, swore I could feel their hot, damp breath on my neck, the brush of their fingers reaching for me. . . . I could swear I heard their voices calling me, *Lanny, Lanny, we're going to catch you, and when we do* . . . the threat hanging in the air. One of the voices sounded vaguely familiar . . . not that I was going to wait around and find out why.

A door suddenly popped up in front of me. It wasn't *the* door, but it was either my salvation or a trap. I had only an instant to decide. Instinct took over. I reached for the latch, threw the door back, and leapt inside.

FOURTEEN

On the island, winter weeks ceded slowly to spring. Each day, short as it was, seemed to last forever, unwinding by degrees as the sun moved across the pale blue sky. Looking through the window at his island, Adair watched the goats' coats thicken against the cold, and then bolt with the beginning of spring, leaving tufts of hair scattered on the rocks like dandelion seed. And fresh chartreuse needles appeared on pine boughs as the patch of moss grew in as thick as a blanket.

Adair stood at the foot of Lanny's bed, close to bursting with impatience. She'd been asleep for months, the vial cradled securely in her hand. He'd never guessed, when he agreed to help her, that she'd be away this long. It seemed a cruel trick and he wondered for the thousandth time if she had done it on purpose. He itched to call her back, and yet honor kept him from doing so—honor! He'd certainly never been called an honorable man before and was not oblivious to the irony. For centuries, he'd happily lived by his own code, his allegiance sworn to knowledge and discovery. Now it was Lanore's idea of honor that bound him. He thought of the things he'd done in his life that would horrify her, beyond lying and stealing and cheating. She had a notion of these deeds from his past, of course, but if she knew them *all*, really knew what he was capable of, he feared she could never love him, never trust him. He might be too corrupt to deserve love, his sins too horrible to be forgiven—this recognition of his unworthiness alone was a measure of how much he'd changed, but would it be enough ultimately to win over Lanore?

He was tired of living in suspense. *Come back to me,* he thought, rapping his knuckles impatiently against the rail at the foot of her bed. *She might come back if she knew how much I wanted her,* he thought as he closed his eyes, stoking the warm glow deep in his heart. *Surely you can feel how desperately I want you here with me.*

She might come back if everything was beautiful and at the ready for her, he decided. This idea of beauty floated over the island like pollen on the wind, and tiny seedlings began to sprout instantly where there had been only hard black rock, and from the seedlings, stems shot skyward, leaves unfurled and spread. Buds appeared—pale pink, lavender, indigo, white—then blossomed in the full light of sun. A carpet of flowers spread across the island from shore to shore, covering rock, moss, and black pebble beach. The goats attacked with hearty appetites but the flowers grew back instantaneously, undeterred. The island was covered in a riot of pastel color; vines crept up the fortress walls and soon petunias and morning glories twined around the iron bars over the windows. It was awash in scent, too, the subtle perfume of hundreds of thousands of blooms.

Wake up, he thought, climbing into bed beside her. *Can a heart that feels love this deeply and can create such beauty be entirely bad?* he wanted to ask her. *Will you believe now that I have repented for you? That you can trust me with your heart?*

Adair drifted into a light sleep and woke to the sound of music playing sweetly on the floor below. The sun had slipped over the horizon and the sky outside had turned periwinkle. It was dusk.

The sound drifting up the stairs was not the angry hip-hop and thrash metal the girls had taken to listening to before, the kind of music designed to roust him out into the open. No, this was sweet and pleasant, old Gypsy guitars, Django Reinhardt. Perhaps the forced spring had lifted their spirits—though that seemed unlikely. He'd left the girls on their own for weeks now, barely able to remember the last time he'd spoken to them. He wouldn't blame them if they had packed their bags to leave him; in fact, he rather wished they would.

Food smells accompanied the music, the rich aroma of roasted meat and caramelized onions and garlic. He guessed that the girls felt badly for behaving like petulant children and were trying to make it up to him. Weeks of grousing and slamming doors and throwing temper tantrums had failed to coax him away from Lanore's side. If they'd been upset when they saw the flowering fields—they had to know what it meant, what had caused the riot of blooms—they didn't show it. That they'd put aside their jealousy was rather touching.

Adair ran a hand through his hair roughly and decided to

go downstairs and extend the olive branch to show them that he wasn't really angry with them. At the same time, he would let them know, firmly, that it was time for them to leave. He'd enjoyed their company but it was time for him to be alone with the woman he loved.

He found them in the parlor. They'd dimmed the lights and built a roaring fire. The large, low table had been cleared of its usual assortment of clutter and had been set with platters of food, opened bottles of wine, candles. Cushions were arranged around the table for seating. Flower petals had been strewn across every surface, across the floor. Robin was stretched out on the chaise, dressed in a thin silk sarong that only served to accentuate her nakedness beneath it. Terry reclined on a low armchair, looking like the queen of a harem, fleshy and curvaceous, with her smoky kohl eyes and dark, undulating hair. They watched Adair as he descended the staircase, seeming to draw him to them with their openly desirous gazes.

Terry poured a thick liquid into a heavy crystal wineglass. "We're so glad you decided to come down and join us tonight, Adair. We've missed you."

"I can only stay for a little while," he said as he accepted the glass and lowered himself onto a pouf of brown saddle leather.

"We know," Robin said, rising from the chaise so she could take a place at his feet. She put her hand on his knee. "We understand."

He woke some time later on the floor, crumpled in a heap beside the ottoman. His hands were tied behind his back. His first instinct was panic, and he began to fight against the restraints, but one look around reassured him that he wasn't in any immediate danger. He took a few deep breaths and forced himself to calm down. He'd been trussed up while drugged unconscious twice in his lifetime, both times by women: once by Lanore, and once by the witch sisters, Penthy and Bronwyn. He'd let his guard down and written Robin and Terry off as harmless; he kicked himself now for having made that mistake a third time.

He blinked as he looked around: the candles had long since guttered and gone out. The food was cold and sat in puddles of congealed fat. The petals had turned to drops of blood in the darkness. A faint electronic buzz hummed in the background; he was fairly sure the buzz was from the stereo, left on even though the record had finished playing. He looked down for reassurance that he was still dressed. The girls were gone. The room was cold, the fire dead. Outside, dawn appeared to be breaking.

He managed to sit upright, pushing against the floor with his elbows. His head pounded sickly, as though his brain had swollen and become much too large for his skull. All he could remember was having a single glass of that heavy wine that had obviously been drugged.

From there, he clambered to his feet, headache be damned. The girls had done such a poor job of tying the ropes that he managed to get loose in only a few minutes. As the rope dropped to his feet, he stood listening for a sign of them, an indication of where they were, but he heard nothing. He dashed up the stairs, taking them two at a time, and flew to Lanore's room, his stomach knotted with dread that something had happened while he was unconscious—surely he'd been drugged for a reason.

He caught himself against the jamb, his heart sinking. The bed was empty. He bellowed for the women as he lunged for the spot where Lanore had lain. He ran his hands over the blanket, searching for a clue as to how long she'd been gone. The bed was cool to the touch. He called their names a second time, his tone unmistakable.

There was a noise behind him, the shuffling of soles on the floorboards, and he spun around. It was Terry. She tried to pretend as though she'd been asleep, clutching a silk bathrobe closed at her chest and pushing mussed curls out of her eyes, but he knew she was acting. "What is it, lover?" He flinched at her use of the word "lover." "What'dya want?"

He jumped up to confront Terry, his face nearly white with rage. "What do you mean, 'what do I want'? You *know* what I want—where is she? Where is Lanore?"

Terry shrugged, a little too broadly. "How should I know? She came to while you were passed out. She took one look at you facedown on the floor, tangled up with *us*, and that was it. She said she was feeling better and wanted to go. We radioed for a boat to fetch her."

"That's a lie," Adair said, advancing on her.

Terry scuttled backward into the hall, out of his reach. "She didn't want to wake you, especially when she saw what you'd been up to with us. . . . Don't you remember what happened last night? Really, Adair, if you didn't want her to know, you should've been more discreet . . ." she said, trying to be coquettish, trying to fool him, but he wouldn't be suckered in. Nothing had happened between them last night; he would've known, he would've felt it in the pit of his stomach.

"If what you say is true, then why did you tie me up?" he

demanded. She furrowed her brow, not seeming to follow him. It was useless, he decided; either she was deliberately trying to mislead him or she was unaware of everything she'd done last night.

Seeing his intentions written on his face, Terry turned and bolted down the hall shrieking, "You've gone mad, you have!"

"What have you done with Lanore?" he shouted back, following her into the master bedroom.

They weren't alone. Robin cowered in a corner, shaking like a scared dog. "I told you he wouldn't believe us! I told you!" she wailed to Terry.

Adair lunged for Robin, who stood stock-still, befuddled, and screamed when he grabbed her. He reeled her into him and held her in a headlock. "What have you done to Lanore?" he demanded.

She thrashed in his grasp, struggling against him, whimpering and crying. "It wasn't us, not really," she pleaded. "I wouldn't do such a thing, you know me, Adair, but it was like something came over me. . . . I didn't mean to hurt her. . . ."

"What do you mean, 'something came over you'?" Adair demanded, but she gave a frightening howl and went rigid in his arms. Something strange was happening to Terry, too. She seemed to swell, and then rise and hover above the ground. Her expression changed so drastically that she no longer looked like Terry. Gloating and proud, she looked like someone Adair had known a long time ago.

"Do you remember me, Adair, me and my sister?" the voice boomed, shrill and sharp as jagged glass. Her arm floated up and she pointed a damning finger at him. "You wronged us once, many years ago, in the wild fens wood. Took advantage of two girls on their own. Smashed up our cottage and meant to kill us. We promised we would have our revenge on you and now we have."

He'd been right all along, Adair realized. It was Penthy and Bronwyn possessing the girls somehow. "Cowards—" he growled at the apparition floating in front of him. "If you wanted revenge, you should've come after *me*, not a defenseless woman."

"This was the best way to hurt you," the brunette answered with an evil laugh. "To strike at your cold heart. Besides, we're not alone in this, Adair. We take our orders from a higher power, one that's not done with you yet."

Standing with Robin in front of the large window, without a second's hesitation, Adair smashed the glass with an elbow and then, grabbing the blonde by the throat, shoved her backward over the sill so that she was thrust halfway out and dangling over the edge of a cliff, hanging from his hand.

"Adair!" Robin gasped, wrapping both hands around his wrist.

"You wouldn't dare! Let go of my sister!" It was not quite Terry's voice that spilled over her lips.

"If you don't tell me now what you've done with Lanore, I'll throw her out the window," he threatened, "and you know I'm not one to make idle threats."

"Sister! Save me!" Robin shrieked as she stretched out her hand. Blood streamed down her arms and face from the numerous cuts she'd sustained from the broken glass. Her hair and dress billowed around her, whipped by the violent updrafts that circled the fortress, and made her look as though she were flying.

"If you hurt her, I'll never tell you where that woman is," Terry swore.

Adair addressed Robin instead. "Save yourself—tell me what you did to Lanore," he said, shaking her by the throat. When she didn't speak, he pushed her farther out the window. She kicked and clutched at his forearm.

"The sea!" she rasped finally, shuddering in his hand. "We threw her in the sea!"

He almost let go of Robin in surprise, but his senses came back to him at the last second and he tossed her to the floor instead. He bolted from the room and out the front door, and ran to the cliff closest to the house. If it hadn't happened too long ago and the tides were right, she might still be close. He looked over the edge of the cliff, but all he saw were waves crashing against the rocks and the floating dock bouncing crazily on the violent water. Not a speck of Lanny's rose-colored dress to be seen. He ran along the shore, peering over the rim, scanning the frothing water below, but there was nothing bobbing along with the waves. Finally, he came to the black pebble beach and ran into the water up to his knees. The waves wound around his legs and pulled at him like a beseeching lover. But there was nothing on the horizon, nothing.

Impossible. It was impossible that he would lose her now and for all of eternity, like this. He would not let that happen. He could call her spirit back—he was sure of it—but to where? Her spirit would return to her body, and where was her body? Adair didn't want her to regain consciousness lost on the tide or caught beneath a rock on the ocean floor. His chest heaved with despair, a great weight plummeting through him—but no, he wouldn't give up. He would move heaven and earth and *ocean* to find her. In his grief and agony, he reached out to the horizon, saying, "Bring her to me. Bring her to me now."

Suddenly, the clear spring sky turned black and clouds appeared from nowhere, thick and roiling, going from dove gray to steel to near black in minutes. The wind blew fiercely, whipping the sea into violent peaks that danced and churned like boiling water.

By then, the sisters had followed him, running out of the house and down to the water, speechless at the sight of nature turned ferocious. Waves began to pound the island on all sides, rising high as skyscrapers and then thundering down like buckets of water poured on them—offerings brought at his command. Water gushed over the edge of the cliffs and back into the sea below. The waves crashed and retreated again and again, scraping away the moss, then the pine trees, the goats, then the sisters, the latter howling and shrieking with fear. The waves threw Adair inland, onto a high peak, where he clung to a jagged boulder and watched as the sea pummeled the island.

Eventually, he saw her, a small form washed up on shore. He clambered down from the peak and scooped her up, while the wind died and waves subsided nearly as quickly as they had spun up. He cradled Lanore in his lap; how cold she was, and waterlogged, wet as a seal, her hair plastered to her head, her clothing torn by her journey on the waves, caught on who knew what in the middle of the sea. Bubbles formed at her nose and the corners of her mouth—at least she was breathing. And through this ordeal, she was still unconscious. She had drowned ten times over but she would never know it.

Adair carried her into the fortress and laid her on the floor of the great room. He quickly built a fire, and then stripped off her wet clothing. He wrapped her in a blanket and stretched her out in front of the fire, spreading her hair over the pillow that cradled her head. Then he sat back on his heels, in a puddle of seawater that had run off his own clothing and hair. He didn't have time to think about what he had done, he only wanted to cry with relief that he had not lost Lanore, not lost her body to the unknown and left her soul in limbo. She had trusted him and he had almost let her down. He vowed that he would not let it happen again.

FIFTEEN

The door rose up in front of me. Salvation. With the three demons galloping down the narrow passage after me, fast on my heels, I barreled through the door praying, *Please let there be a bolt on the other side. Please let there be a way to keep them out.*

As soon as I slipped through, however, I plunged into an entirely different world. What had been a rough, rustic wooden door on one side was smooth laminated wood on the other. There was a brushed metal lever for a handle, very modern. There was no bolt but there was no sign of the demons, either: no noise on the far side of the door, no jiggling of the doorknob, nothing. I immediately knew by the astringent smell that I was in a hospital.

It was Luke's hospital room. Every detail was as I remembered it, down to the sour stench of vomit and the odor of weak cleaning fluid hanging in the air, and the white blanket on Luke's bed, its surface pilling from many washings. Why had I been brought back to this most painful moment? Hadn't it been wretched enough the first time, watching helplessly as he declined? What more could I learn from his suffering—if, indeed, I'd been driven into this room to learn something. If I hadn't been sent here only for a dose of punishment.

I'd never cheated on Luke, but I had been in a continual state of indecision the entire time we'd lived together, unsure if I had done the right thing by returning to him after I'd been completely erased from his memory. While I'd been plagued by nightmares of Jonathan's unrest in the hereafter, it was only now that I'd seen Adair again—and seen him so changed—that I could admit, even to myself, that it was him I daydreamed of, who I longed for, who I ached for, physically. That was how I'd betrayed Luke—in my desire for Adair. It wasn't so uncommon, was it? Living with one man while your mind is on another? Being unable to stop thinking of this other man who, for one reason or another, was not the one sitting beside you. Thinking of the way his eyes lit up when he saw you, of his wicked smile and what it was like when he held you, how you responded to the touch of his hands. In solitary moments, you remembered the little intimacies, the feel of his skin against yours, the way he liked to be touched, the velvet nap of his member, the way he tasted. You thought of him even though you could never be with him. His absence nagged like an itch you could never scratch.

Some would say I should never have returned to Luke if this was how I felt about Adair, that it was wrong of me to go back to him if I had any doubts. But complete fidelity of the heart in a relationship is something that has always eluded me. I have often wondered how these people manage to live such straightforward lives, to keep their emotions so simple and tidy. Do they weed out life's complications as ruthlessly as they would weed a garden? Sometimes a weed turns into a beautiful flower or a helpful herb but you'll never know if you pull it too soon. Do they ever allow themselves regret for the things they've thrown away? I would ask these self-assured people which of us has the luxury of an iron-clad guarantee? Who can be 100 percent sure of one's choices in life? How do you know that your beloved will always remain the same, or that you'll never change your mind? Growth and change are two of the great gifts we get from time. It would be shortsighted to spurn them.

Besides, I did love Luke—I did. But he wasn't the only one I wanted, and wanting isn't the same as loving. Just as I knew I loved Luke, I wasn't sure whether I *loved* Adair. I couldn't rule out that my attraction to him wasn't an advanced case of lust, though that's not to say it was inconsequential. Only a fool would underestimate the power of lust. Kingdoms have been won and lost, men and beasts have battled to the death over it.

Now, if I had been the same girl I'd been at the start of my adventures—the same girl who had loved Jonathan so blindly—I know what choice I would've made. I would've tossed aside a good man like Luke to take my chances with Adair. And I would've been miserable before long, held hostage by Adair's precipitous temper and erratic behavior, which in my inexperience I would've accepted without so much as a whimper. I hadn't yet learned that it was okay to make demands of the people we love, that we didn't have to accept others exactly as they came to us. No one is perfect, after all.

As soon as I quieted these voices chasing each other in my head, I crept toward Luke, lying in bed. I felt queasy and anxious. God help me, I didn't want to be back in that room. I was glad to have comforted Luke when he was dying, but I didn't want to relive the experience, not so soon after it had happened. I *should've* been happy for this chance to see Luke again, but I wasn't.

An oxygen line ran under his nose. His wrists were so bony that his identification bracelets hung from them like paper manacles. His bed was set at a forty-five degree slant to help with nausea, but it made his head hang forward at a frightening angle, as though his neck had been snapped. On second thought, he didn't look as terrible as he could've; whatever power had brought Luke and me together at this moment, it had been kind enough to make Luke look healthy, not as wasted by illness and exhaustion as he'd been the last time I saw him. He even had his hair, those unruly sandy brown curls. I was thinking how much I'd like to smooth his hair back from his face—just for the excuse of touching him—when his eyes suddenly opened.

"Lanny," he said, recognition in his gaze. So he could see me, too, as Sophia had. "Is that you?"

"Of course it's me." I smiled and reached for his cheek, brushing it gently. It felt solid enough.

"Am I dreaming? Your voice . . . it sounds like you're right next to me."

"That's because I am here, Luke. This isn't a dream. You can trust your eyes."

We hugged. I couldn't bring myself to kiss him, however,

and we hung in an awkward embrace. We still had tenderness, but the passion between us was gone . . . unsurprising at
the end of a long and intense illness. Worn out by exhaustion
and fear, we naturally became numb to physical passion. After
seeing Luke ravaged by drugs and madness, I could no more
bring myself to feel attraction than he could have mustered the
energy to respond.

Lying in his hospital bed now, he didn't look all that relieved to see me; he seemed preoccupied and not entirely himself. "Where am I? What are we doing back in the hospital?"
he asked, alarmed, looking at the tangle of tubes and wires
hanging from his arms. "And what are you doing here?" His
face drained. "You haven't died, have you, Lanny? How is that
possible?"

"No," I rushed to assure him.

"Thank God." That calmed him a bit, though he was still
on edge, his gaze darting around the hospital room. "I don't
understand, though, why I'm back here. . . . Why are *you* back
here? What's going on?"

"I think maybe you and I have been brought together in
order to talk," I said slowly, trying to make sense of our circumstances. "Was there something you wanted to say to me?
Something you didn't tell me when we were together? Maybe
it will come to you if you relax," I said, taking his hand. "How
are you?"

He gave me a sideways look. "You mean how am I since I
died? How do you *think* I've been? Dying wasn't at all how I
expected it to be. Not that I was looking for a scene from the
Bible, pearly gates and Saint Peter, any of that nonsense. But
it was a little underwhelming. I had to figure everything out

for myself when I got here—I don't know, I guess I expected it to be better organized. . . . It's not like the first day on a new job, there's no woman with a clipboard from human resources welcoming you on board, no printed checklist to help you get settled in. No one tells you what to do or where to go. It just happens, whether you want it to or not."

"What do you mean, 'it just happens'?" I asked, not quite following him. "What just happens?"

"The next part. The hereafter. Eternity." Oddly, he was still wearing eyeglasses, and he pushed them up the bridge of his nose as I'd seen him do a thousand times in life. He shook his shaggy head. "Whatever comes next, it's already happening. I'm losing a bit of myself every day. My memories are fading. I don't know how else to describe it. It's like I'm breaking up and parts of me are drifting away or falling off."

He sounded so sad and desperate that, even though the prospect was terrifying, I tried to remain upbeat and cheer him up. "Well, that doesn't seem so bad. Maybe it's all part of becoming a new person, clearing out the old, making room for the new."

Luke looked at me as though I'd gone crazy. "What do you mean, it doesn't sound bad? It's the worst thing that could happen. I'm *breaking apart*. I'm ceasing to be. I suppose it means the very last bits of my consciousness are finally coming apart and all that was left of me—residual energy—is returning to wherever we come from."

He was a doctor, a man of science, so I tried to appeal to his analytical side. "If your energy is returning to the cosmos, maybe that means your consciousness is going there, too. Maybe you're about to experience the wonders of space."

The prospect seemed to depress him further. "I don't think so. I think it's all just coming undone, like a tape being demagnetized. As time goes on, I remember less and less. I *feel* less and less. Sure, it all *sounds* interesting in the abstract, but now that it's here, I'm frightened, Lanny," he said. I'd never heard him sound as scared, not even when he confronted Adair four years earlier. "This isn't what I expected. All those times I'd wondered what it would *really* be like, to be dead . . . especially after having patients die on you, being right there with them when it happened. I wasn't prepared for *this*. It's *really* going to be over. *This* is what it means to die. I've come to the end. I can't believe it. It's really going to be *over*."

He was right: this was frightening, much more frightening than the many deathbed vigils over which I'd presided. I was scared for him, and what's more, I could do nothing about it. I couldn't stop what was happening to him, I couldn't save him. As I contemplated all this, holding back tears, he snapped his head up as though he was seeing me for the first time since we'd materialized in the hospital room.

"You never did tell me . . . if you're not dead, what are you doing here?" he asked. I suppose he was suspicious, and why shouldn't he be? I was alive in the land of the dead.

I squirmed, suddenly realizing that he might be thinking that I'd come for *him,* that my presence here was all about him. That maybe I'd had second thoughts about his delirious request—*you could ask Adair to make me immortal*. I answered him truthfully. "I asked Adair to send me. I came to look for Jonathan," I confessed, trying to look as contrite as possible.

An exasperated sigh escaped from Luke and he folded his arms, awkwardly for all the wires and needles. "I should've known. I should've *guessed* that. It's always been that way with you, always Jonathan or Adair. Never Luke. Never any room for me."

It was unlike Luke to be so candid. Staring oblivion in the face probably had something to do with it; no reason to pretend anymore. Still, I was hurt and not above rebuking him. "How can you say that? I was good to you, Luke. Especially at the end. I promised I would take care of you and I did." We'd had a bargain. Four years ago, Luke had helped me escape from the police after I'd released Jonathan from his immortal bond, and in exchange I promised that he would never be alone. I would be his companion for life. I didn't realize until later that I must've made this offer to Luke because being alone was what *I* feared most. He'd taken me up on my offer, nonetheless. Maybe we're all afraid to be alone.

Here I was making good on my end of the bargain, but in a way I could never have imagined.

He seemed somewhat mollified. He looked up at me, over the rims of his eyeglasses. "I'll give you that. But—we can be honest with each other now, can't we, Lanny? Now that the end is near? Because I do have something I want to tell you." He paused and looked at me tentatively before proceeding cautiously: "If you want to know how I really feel about us . . . I feel like we never should have gotten involved. I always felt as though you never really loved me."

A sharp pain cut into my heart like a knife. "Luke, you must know I love you. I wouldn't be here now if I didn't. I know I have no right to say this to you, but it hurts me to hear you say these things. To say 'it was always Jonathan or Adair, and never any room for me.' I loved you, Luke, of course I did. If I didn't love you, I could've just walked away. It would've been a damn sight easier."

He was quiet, thinking. The monitors beeped in the background. "I suppose," he said.

"We were happy together," I insisted.

"But you never loved me the way you loved those two. You can admit it to me now. I won't hold it against you, but I'd rather die knowing the truth. Jonathan and Adair—they were always on your mind. I could tell."

My cheeks flamed. I couldn't deny it.

"I don't hold it against you, really," he continued. "I mean, I saw Jonathan with my own eyes. He was a god. One in a billion. Even in death I could see why no woman was able to resist him."

My stomach twisted, remembering the purpose of my visit to the underworld. "Luke, Jonathan's in trouble. That's why I've come here," I blurted out. "He is being held by a queen, the queen of the underworld. Have you heard of her?"

He shook his head. "It sounds like something from an old myth, doesn't it? Hades and Persephone and all that. Sorry, I can't help you, Lanny. Like I said, nothing's been explained to me. The queen of England could be here for all I know. I'm not like Jonathan or you or Adair. I'm just an ordinary guy, a speck of dust in the cosmos, and I'm going to die an ordinary death." He had the same expression I'd seen many times, a quizzical look he'd worn during the odd quiet moment. "I have a question for you, Lanny, and I want you to tell me the truth. Did you ever love me, or was I just a convenience that night when you were brought into the hospital? What was I to you? Just a gullible man who could help you escape from the police . . ."

I threw up my hands in exasperation. "Luke, I just told you five minutes ago that I love you. Wasn't I with you for the past four years?"

"You stayed out of obligation, because of your promise, not love."

"Isn't obligation a part of love?" I felt my blood rising. "I made a commitment to you, and I honored it because I love you." I squeezed his hand.

He made a sour face. "Do you know what it was like knowing that you didn't love me the way you loved the other two? That you loved them more," he said, unable to say their names at that moment.

"Does love have to be a contest? I've had a long life and it's always been that way for me: you lose one love and, if you are lucky, you find another." I tugged him closer to me, though he tried to resist. "Listen to me: I was alone for a long time, Luke. For many years, before we met, I had no one in my life. I didn't want to go through it again, you know: growing close to someone, tangling my life up in someone else's, only to lose them. I just couldn't do it—but then I met you. I couldn't remember when I'd known such a good man. I knew I was lucky. Don't tell me that I squandered the last years of your life. It would make me very sad to think that you had been unhappy."

He bumped against me. "You know that's not true. I wasn't unhappy. But I *know* what you wanted, Lanny. You wanted Jonathan to love you the way you loved him, to love you above all others, to be his one great love. I suppose that was all I wanted: to be *your* great love. That was foolish of me, since there would always be Jonathan, but . . . none of us is immune to our heart's desire."

I sensed his time was short. I was conflicted—unsure what
to say, for it was clear that he wanted to be refuted. He wanted
me to tell him that he was the great love of my life, and what
difference would it make if I lied to him as he teetered on the
brink of annihilation? Yet I couldn't bring myself to tell him
that it was Adair, not Jonathan, I loved more than anyone.
After years of chasing after Jonathan, I'd come to love him
like a brother; he was the *one* connection I had to my past, to
my family, to my home. He was the only one to whom I felt
any sort of obligation, not Luke. I was the one who'd brought
Jonathan into this mess; I had to do everything in my power
to get him out. I took a deep breath, decided which course to
take—and spoke.

"Isn't it enough to be *one* of my great loves? I'll never forget you, Luke. You were the best man I ever had in my life. A
much better man than Jonathan."

He snorted. "A better man than Jonathan? That's not much
of an accomplishment, is it? From everything you told me, he
was—a jerk, to be blunt. I don't know why you've come here
after him, Lanny."

"I have my reasons. He needs me—let's leave it at that. I
don't want to talk about it right now." Meaning I didn't want to
use up the last minutes of his life talking about Jonathan.

He blinked at me, as though fighting to see through a film.
"You know, I'm about to be sent into the great unknown and I
still don't know what I was supposed to do with my life, what
it was supposed to *mean*. I want resolution. There must be a
reason you've been sent to me, Lanny. You're the immortal one.
You must know something that isn't revealed to us ordinary
people. I want answers."

"I don't have an answer for you, Luke, other than to say you were a wonderful father and partner. Your daughters love you. You made me happy every day we were together. Maybe that's what your life was about. Isn't that enough?" I kissed his forehead. His last moments were upon us. He was dissolving, blurred in some spots, thinned in others. He looked like a ghost.

He'd closed his eyes, leaned against my cheek. "Now that we're at the point of sharing secrets, I have something to tell you. I always thought it a shame you couldn't have children. You'd have made a wonderful mother."

"Me?" I blurted out a laugh.

"You were great with the girls," he said softly, as though he were falling asleep. "Always so patient. They loved you right from the start. It made Tricia a little jealous, you know."

"Shhh," I said. His hand was getting colder in mine. The air in the room seemed thin all of a sudden, as though we were on a high mountaintop. I'd woven our fingers together tightly now, feeling the stretch as I accommodated his larger hand in mine. However, his grip was weakening by degrees and the bulk of his hand felt lighter with every second. He was fading before my eyes, drifting away piece by piece—his end *was* truly here.

I ran my fingers through his hair, but it was as though I were raking frigid air. He was almost gone; the hospital room was almost gone, too. It was freezing, as though a window had been thrown open on the coldest Maine night—no, surely colder than that—and the blinks and hisses and chirrups of the hospital room ceded to the rasp of empty, endless space. Infinity was calling. Eternity comes for us all in one form or another, and it had found Luke. We teetered at the edge of a huge abyss and I sensed that if I wasn't careful, I'd be pulled into it. This was the abyss Adair had told me about, and now that I faced it, I understood his horror. It was impossible to believe that our consciousnesses could live on in that absolute emptiness. If they did, how lonely they must be; how bereft an existence they must have in the flat black void. This was what Adair had saved me from for a great long while by making me immortal. I could not save Luke from it. This was the inescapable end.

"Good-bye," I said to Luke in a last gesture of tenderness, but he was already gone.

Within seconds, furniture and hospital equipment started disappearing all around me. Afraid of what might happen to me when the last piece vanished, I hurried to the door, cracked it open, and peered out. The passage was empty, so I crept out. It seemed positively quiet and serene here, now. I proceeded to retrace my steps, thinking that I might come across the door from my nightmares and, behind that door, Jonathan. But as I turned a corner, I came face-to-face with a demon.

My blood froze in my veins. Maybe two feet separated us. He could've reached out and snatched my arm.

But he didn't. Instead, he lowered his huge head and brought one topaz eye close, looking me over. He snorted and his brimstone breath washed over my face. He was one of those demonic creatures, yet there was something familiar about this one, something in his expression, a haughty yet wistful look I'd seen before.

The demon pulled himself up as tall as he could, given the low ceiling. He swished his tail elegantly. Again, he fixed me with his golden eye.

"Lanny."

I recognized the voice, even though it was one I hadn't heard in a long time. "Dona? Is that you?"

The demon snorted again and turned his massive head away from my curious stare, embarrassed. "It is I."

I hadn't seen Dona since we'd lived under Adair's roof in Boston, in the early 1800s. He'd been one of Adair's companions, too, a foul-tempered aristocratic Italian who'd had little use for me then. I couldn't help but think how the mighty had fallen; the always fastidious Dona couldn't be happy to have been turned into a beast. He had been a beautiful man in life. It must've galled him to be transformed into this creature.

"Dear God! Dona! I thought I'd never see you again! How long have you been here?"

"Not so long, I suppose, and yet it feels an eternity. An eternity as this monster that you see, with a tail and horns, more beast than man. . . ." His eyes were large, their expression soft and quite touching, even if they were an eerie golden color. He reached up and ran a hand distractedly down the length of one silky, long ear, perhaps a nervous habit, perhaps to confirm that he was still in this unfortunate form. It wasn't until that moment that I realized what it meant to find Dona here. As had been the case with Savva—who, it occurred to me now, would surely transform into a beast as vile as this before long—Dona could be in the underworld only if Adair had taken his life.

As if reading my thoughts through my expression, the demon flashed a look of anger. "I didn't ask to be released, you know. I was perfectly happy when Adair found me. I was at peace. I wasn't harming anyone. But Adair insisted that my time was over. It didn't matter that I begged him to spare me; he took my life and sent me here."

Shocked, I couldn't speak for a moment, and when I could, the best I could say was, "I'm sure he didn't mean it. He didn't know where he was sending you or what would happen to you."

Dona seemed unconvinced. His tail switched. "Adair always was like that, you know," Dona whispered. "A bastard. Never thinking of us as having wishes and desires of our own. Never thinking of us as anything but servants to him." The demon made a sound halfway between a bellow and a moan. "I wish for God to damn him, as we have been damned. Damn him to hell."

It didn't seem a good idea to let Dona get carried away by bitterness at that moment; I needed his help. I laid a hand on his blackened arm. "Dona, I may be crossing a line . . . I know we were never close in life, but I need your help. I am throwing myself on your mercy."

He cocked his large head, waiting.

I drew in a deep breath, preparing to be rebuffed. "You see, I came here looking for Jonathan. You remember Jonathan, don't you?"

He snorted derisively at this and rolled his eyes. "Of course I remember him. Anyone would remember Jonathan. He is impossible to forget."

"Have you seen him here, Dona? I heard he was being kept by the queen of the underworld."

At this, Dona shied back, like an animal that had been bitten and startled by some ghastly insect, his ears twitching in irritation. "Oh, why do you ask me this? There's nothing you can do for him. He is here with the queen and she will not give him up to you. Trust me on this—I am part of her retinue, you know. We demons serve the queen of the underworld. That appears to be our reward, for putting up with Adair in life. I suppose he would say that it is the price we must pay for having lived so long." He snorted again, in disgust this time.

I looked into his golden eyes. "I'm not afraid of her," I lied.

"You should be."

"Dona, can you take me to him?"

"It is hopeless."

"I just want to see him and speak with him. Please, Dona. I've come this far—don't make me go away empty-handed."

He looked from my hand, still on his arm, to my face. "All right, I will show you where he's being kept. After that, you're on your own, do you understand me? You can expect no more help from me." And with that, he turned—hooves thumping heavily on the hard-packed ground—and began to lumber down the passage, leading the way.

SIXTEEN

Somewhere along the twisty path that Dona led me on, we stopped being in a place that looked like Adair's fortress. Without my quite noticing how or when it happened, I suddenly realized that our surroundings had changed. The walls were gone. The ceiling overhead had disappeared. The world around us had shifted, broken apart and fallen away, and we were now in a place that was like the underworlds of folklore, the ones depicted by Dante and Milton, a dark, foreboding world that reeked of sorrow and regret.

We trudged through what appeared to be a cavern, though it was hard to tell as we walked through darkness with only the path in front of us lit, as though we were being followed by a spotlight. It could have been moonlight, I suppose, only there was no moon visible overhead. I heard rustlings and what sounded like whispers in the shadows to either side of the trail, but could see nothing. The tidy packed-earth floor of the passage had given way to a dirt path set on a deceptively gradual decline. I had the rather morbid sense that damned souls were hovering in the darkness just beyond sight or hearing. I could feel their gazes, desperately hungry, following us as though they wanted something we had.

"Tell me, Dona, where are we? What is this place?" I asked, growing uneasy at the changes to our surroundings. All of a sudden, I was unsure whether I could trust him.

He didn't so much as look over his shoulder to address me, but kept loping along. "Have no fears; you are safe with me," he said rather rotely.

"I feel as though we're being watched."

"We are," he acknowledged. "The souls are curious about you. They've never seen a live soul in the underworld before. They're drawn to your living energy."

I thought of the place we'd just left, with its hall of doors that led to pieces of my past. Fez and St. Andrew had been filled with souls and yet they hadn't paid me the slightest attention. This place was different. Walking through this open space with souls hovering just out of reach, I finally felt that I was in the underworld, the place of our terrors and nightmares, and I felt vulnerable.

"What is this place, Dona? Are we in hell?"

He grimaced. "Hell—what kind of question is that? There is neither heaven nor hell. There is only the underworld."

"But it must be a different part of the underworld. This is so unlike the parts I've seen already," I protested.

"Tell me what have you seen, then," he replied. So I told him all of it, how the entirety of old Fez had unfurled before me as I'd walked down the boulevard on Savva's arm, how I'd been taken back to St. Andrew of 1823 or thereabouts, exactly as I'd known it as a child, how I'd been transported to Luke's hospital room—all of these scenes set just beyond the doors inside Adair's fortress, or so it had seemed. How I'd seen old acquaintances but seemed to be invisible to everyone else.

Dona dismissed my account with a toss of his head. "It sounds as though you were brought back to a specific place in time to see those acquaintances. You were given a nice visit; don't be ungrateful."

I wasn't about to give up, though. "But how is that possible?" I asked, dogged. "That time has passed. How can we step back into it as though nothing has happened?"

"How should I know?" he snapped suddenly. "Does it look as though I have any authority here? No one tells me anything. I can't explain how it works; I only know that such things happen. That's the way things work around here, and you'll soon find out as much for yourself." Then he glanced slyly over his shoulder at me; he had his own questions he wanted answered. "So, you knew Savva in life. Is that so?"

I flushed. "Yes. It was a miracle that we met that day. It was in Fez—"

But Dona cut me off, snorting with disgust through his broad, wet snout. His horns gleamed wickedly in the wan light from overhead. "Then you know what a selfish, spoiled whelp he was. I abhorred him. He was nothing but trouble, and an impossible liar. He would say or do anything for attention. I don't know what Adair saw in him, to make him one of us . . ."

One of us? That was hardly a designation one could be proud of. We were all flawed, as was Savva. He was the same as the rest of us. Not that Dona was wrong in his estimate of Savva, not exactly. Savva was difficult at the best of times, and no one knew that better than I, but I couldn't stand to hear him spoken of that way. "You're not being fair to him. It's not his fault. He has problems, Dona, real problems."

"Don't make excuses for him. That's your problem, Lanny, you have a weakness for weak men." He seemed pleased with himself.

"You can spare me your psychoanalysis," I told him.

Dona continued, undeterred. "So, Savva is here in the underworld, is he? How does he like being a demon?"

"He's not a demon—yet," I said. "Though he told me that he is growing a tail."

"He's still in human form! He's been here how long, and he's still a human? Some people—the least deserving ones, have you ever noticed?—get all the breaks. I was put in demon form practically from the moment I arrived here. The queen took one look at me and said, 'Oh yes, you'll do nicely,' and snapped her fingers, and that was that." Dona practically shook with rage. His tail switched hotly from side to side. "I think she chose me because I was so handsome."

Though immodest, Dona *had* been handsome: tall and regal, with that famous Northern Italian beauty. A former street urchin who had been taken in by an artist, made his model and his muse—only for Dona to repay the artist by turning him in to the papal authorities for being a sodomite, in order to save his own worthless neck.

He lifted one shoulder in an insouciant half shrug. "And

now it's all gone, taken away from me. I suppose that is my punishment in the hereafter, because in life I was so proud of my looks. Now I am a hideous beast, so ugly that the spirits run away from me in fear. Let's see how Savva likes it when people run from him, when those boyish looks are gone. When those golden curls fall away and horns burst out of his skull. It hurts like hell, you know: the horns, the tail, the feet turning into hooves. Savva's good fortune is not going to last much longer."

"Do all of Adair's former companions turn into demons?" I tried not to betray my worry that this, too, would be my fate.

"The queen is punishing us for having been with Adair in life—as though we had anything to say about that decision. She's very jealous, you know," he said, lost in his own bitter thoughts, failing to explain what she was jealous *of.* . . . But before I could ask him, the terrain changed suddenly before us and the path simply disappeared. Dona and I both tumbled down the long slope toward the black gully below. Once I'd started tumbling, gravity took over. I rolled faster and faster; I couldn't stop myself. The bruising and bumping descent seemed to go on forever. Finally, my body rolled to a halt. I tilted my head back and looked up, but could see nothing; the top of the slope was shrouded in blackness.

And then I realized—the vial was gone. It had slipped from my hand when I'd fallen, probably when I'd instinctively tried to stop myself. In the dim light, I searched the dirt at my feet but found nothing. The tiny vial could be anywhere—hidden under a tussock or rock, buried in the dirt. It was lost, but it didn't matter anyway. If our signal scheme had worked, Adair would have seen it by now and I would've been pulled from this reality and sent spinning back to the earth, to the fortress, to Adair. I would've felt the swirl and tug that I'd felt at the beginning. But there was no change, nothing. I was still in the underworld.

I located Dona by the groan coming from the darkness to my left. My intuition told me that I needed to get away from him, that something was wrong. Dona didn't want to help me; he'd never helped anyone in his life. I'd wanted to believe him because I needed him, but I could pretend no longer. I scrambled to my feet. Dona was groggily lurching upright, like a horse trying to push up from the ground. He was uninjured. *Run*, every nerve in my body screamed at me. *Leave him and run for your life.*

But I had dithered too long. I had just decided to make a break from Dona while I had a chance when four demons stepped out of the shadows. A great brightness flickered overhead like a searchlight, and I saw the side of a great stone building behind them, a turret tower, a banner flying high overhead. We'd fallen into a dry moat.

Someone grabbed my elbow. It was Dona, jerking me to my feet and holding me up like a trophy he'd won. "It's the woman the queen has been looking for. *I* found her—she's *my* prisoner, and I demand to be allowed to present her personally to the queen," he said proudly.

Surrounded by a quartet of demon guards, I was marched through the castle and down a series of halls to a set of heavy oak doors. Dona, who had led our party, did not confer with the two demons that stood at the entry with spears, but went up to one of the doors and knocked on it boldly. The rapping echoed down the great empty halls. No reply. He cleared his throat, ignoring the vague restless stirring of the guards, and knocked again, even more sharply and heavily this time.

You could hear a muffled moan of irritation from within, followed by a woman's voice saying, "Oh, what is it? Must you interrupt me now? This had better be *important*." Dona threw both doors open at once, radiating with pride over my capture, and gestured to the guards to usher me in. "I have caught her, Your Majesty. I found her and caught her and brought her here for you. Just as you desired."

I was marched into a bedchamber. It was huge, a cross between the sort of royal apartment you'd see at Versailles and a neglected sepulcher. The room was vast but the furniture was clustered in the center of it, leaving the walls and corners hidden in woolly darkness. The silk wall coverings were mildewed and rotting; cobwebs hung from a giant unlit chandelier overhead. By far, the grandest thing in the room was the bed, a massive structure with posters that thrust heavenward like spires on a church. The bed curtains were great waterfalls of fabric, red velvet lined with gold satin and trimmed with braided swag. It was then, with a jolt of horror, that I realized this was the bed I'd seen in my nightmare. The coverlets were thrown back, as they'd been in my dream, revealing a woman astride a man like a succubus, their flesh tones stark against blindingly white sheets.

The queen. She was tall, almost painfully slender, and luminously white, as though lit from within. Her face was fiercely and coldly beautiful. From where I stood, all I could see of the man were his legs, protruding from under her. She rode him not with wild abandon but with prim control, her eyes closed and her face serene in concentration, pleasuring herself on him as though he were a toy, nothing more.

Dona made a low bow, his snout almost brushing the floor. "Your Majesty, I am proud to present to you the woman you have been looking for—Lanore."

At this, the queen's eyes opened and she turned her head, casting a quick gaze over her shoulder in our direction. She stopped rocking and took a deep breath, as though thinking about what she'd do next.

Finally, the man pinned underneath her acknowledged our presence by rising to his elbows. It was Jonathan, tousle-headed and slightly damp with sweat. He squinted at me and then his eyes widened in surprise. I think he would've tried to rush up to see me if it had been anyone but the queen sitting on his lap.

"Lanny!" he blurted out. "Good God, what are you doing here—"

"Silence," the queen interrupted, looking down at him imperiously.

He held her gaze. "But that's Lanny, that's my friend. And if she's here, that means she's—"

"She's not dead," the queen interrupted him again, coldly.

Jonathan didn't appear to be listening to her. He was upset and continued on. "If she's here but not dead, as you say, then how could she have gotten here except through you? It's impossible otherwise. You *must've* brought her here." Then a look of shock and recognition dawned across his face. "You *used* me, used what I told you about the tattoo, and Adair. You shouldn't have brought her here. This has nothing to do with her, she's innocent—" He spoke faster and more hotly as he got madder, and the queen's face began to curdle.

"Be careful how you speak to me," she said, seething, but remaining cool to outward appearances. "There are limits to what I will allow, even from my favorites." She swung off Jonathan as neatly as though she were dismounting a horse and snapped her fingers at the guards flanking me. "Take him away. I want to speak to this woman alone."

Jonathan rose as the guard approached him. In the instant he stood naked, I saw that he didn't look at all like the prisoner in my dreams. Jonathan was unblemished. He had no bruises, no barely healed wounds, no scars of any kind. He didn't look at all ill treated. To the contrary, he seemed perfectly fine, and it occurred to me that I might've been tricked into coming here. Not only was he not abused; if anything, he looked *better* than the last time I'd seen him—that disconcerting mix of the familiar with a beauty so exquisite and extraordinary that it was nearly painful to behold. I'd forgotten that he was perfection, so perfectly sublime that he seemed almost to shine, as brilliant and luminescent as the sun breaking through the clouds after a storm.

The demon guard, seemingly resentful of Jonathan's beauty or his favored position, grabbed Jonathan by the arm roughly to lead him away. Jonathan threw me a look over his shoulder—*don't despair, I'll see you again*, he seemed to say—and was hauled unceremoniously from the room.

Now there was only me, Dona, one guard, and the queen left in the room. She stepped down from the bed and reached for a sheer red robe as she passed by it, though it did almost nothing to hide her nakedness. She cast a sly eye downward at Dona, who bowed lowly a second time.

"What are you still doing here?" she demanded.

"A word, Your Majesty, if I may," he said, twitching nervously. He knew he was taking an awful chance speaking up at this moment, but he might not have the opportunity to address the queen again, and certainly not when she was freshly indebted to him. "It is about the value of my service to you. I wish to raise the small matter of, um, a reward, your most gracious and generous Highness. While I, your loyal and humble servant, am most happy to have been able to bring Lanore to you, I would be most gratefully, most genuinely grateful . . ." Dona was starting to falter, the queen's haughty silence beginning to unnerve him.

"A reward!" the queen squawked. She sounded insulted.

He lifted his shaggy head and looked the queen squarely in the eye. "I wish to be returned to my former body, Your Majesty. I wish to be made into the man I once was. This is what I desire. And if you do this for me, I pledge you my everlasting and undying gratitude. I shall be your faithful servant to the end of time . . ."

"Silence!" she bellowed, driving her fists to her sides as though the very sound of his voice shattered her nerves. He stopped speaking and cowered like a mouse in front of her, and the queen's cool calm returned. A wickedly false smile surfaced on her face. "So you wish to return to your human form, do you, demon?" There was something in her tone that made my hair stand on end, an undertone that reminded me of the dry, ominous shake of a rattlesnake's tail. Dona cringed before the queen in a hopeful and expectant bow, so blinded by his own desires that he could see nothing else, not even the tragedy that was about to descend on him like an eagle screaming down from the sky.

"Very well—your reward, demon," the queen said, and with that a spasm passed over Dona. A look of surprise crossed his bullish face as a ripple warped the space around him, a distortion of light and air, and then, in the next instant he was gone. And in his place was a squat, fat bullfrog—olive with black speckles, his skin glistening with slime, his bulbous eyes rolling independently of each other in his head.

The queen leaned over and glared imperiously at the frog—and there seemed to be no question but that it was Dona. For a moment, I was afraid that she was going to step on him, crushing him underfoot. Instead, she gave a voluptuously triumphant smile at what she'd done and waved him toward the door. "Impertinent demon! You dare to expect gratitude for you to do what is, after all, your duty? You expect to be rewarded for merely doing your job? Well, there is your reward! Now, off with you! And if you are wise, you will not trouble me with your presence again, or next time I will turn you into a flea or a worm," she warned. Dona did not even chirp in resignation, but hopped toward the door as he'd been commanded.

The queen then turned to me. Her icy stare sent a shiver down my back. She circled me slowly, looking me over. As she passed close by, I could make out her figure quite easily under the thin veil of her red robe. She may have been slender but she was muscular as well, and crackled with frightening energy— an energy similar to Adair's, I couldn't help but notice.

She plucked one of my curls, held it up as though she was

examining it, and then let it fall. "So you're the one he favors. For the life of me, I don't see why—there's nothing special about you."

My blood began to race. I didn't mind her insult, for it was true—there *was* nothing special about me. Even though she hadn't said who "he" was, I knew of course: she was talking about Adair. It was then I noticed that, for all her coolness, she was seething. She was hurt.

The queen placed one bare white foot in front of the other as she circled me a second time. "Yes, you're really rather plain, nothing extraordinary about you in the least. You're like a little brown wren."

I decided to put on a brave front. "It *was* you behind the dreams, wasn't it? You tricked me into coming to the underworld."

She laughed, bringing a hand to her sternum. "You accuse me of tricking you into coming here? It was no trick—you came for Jonathan, didn't you? And he's here."

"So, let me speak to him," I implored.

"In due time," she said with an airily dismissive wave. She resumed pacing around me, studying me. She even ran a hand across my shoulders, along my back, like a child taunting me. Her touch was strong and electric and made me imagine, involuntarily, what it must be like for Jonathan when they were together, what it was like to couple with her, to be inside her.

I broke away from those thoughts. "It's Adair—he's the reason you've brought me here. I know that's it, but I don't understand. . . . Why do you need *me*? If you want him, why don't you bring him here yourself?" I asked impudently. Desperation and exhaustion made me bold. After all, what more could she do to me? I assumed she needed me alive or else she would've killed me already.

She frowned, and I could swear the room dropped ten degrees instantaneously, a chill descending over it. "Indeed, the man you call Adair *is* the reason I've brought you here. Don't worry, it will all be made clear to you eventually. A little patience, my brown wren. That's all that's required of you, a little patience." She snapped her fingers at the remaining guard. "Take her away."

SEVENTEEN

M y head whirling, I was brought by the demon guard to a small room. Unlike the replica of Adair's fortress with the doors that had transported me back in time, there was nothing dreamlike or evanescent about this castle. It felt oppressively real. The room was a room and not a portal. The plaster walls were solid, withstanding the beating of my fists. The heavy wooden door looked as though it could repel a battalion. The tiny room was as neglected and run-down as the other parts of the castle that I'd seen, with the same filth accumulated in the corners and a dull, greasy film over the windows. The only piece of furniture in this room was a small wooden bench. A few old blankets had been thrown in a corner, ostensibly meant to function as a bed.

I sat on the bench and looked down at my legs. They were still smarting after the fall, and it was then that I noticed I was nicked up and bleeding. Normally, I wouldn't think twice about a cut or scrape, because within minutes I would heal as good as new. But this time, it didn't matter how long I stared: the wounds remained, the scratches looking unreal and vibrantly red against my white skin. It seemed that a different logic applied here in the underworld—for some reason, I was no longer immortal. Adair's curse had been stripped away from me.

I was hit by a sudden wave of longing for the world I had left behind. Even if my circumstances were a bit twisted, that world was familiar and normal; I knew what to expect. Here, I'd been drawn into a fairy tale, and not one of the sweet ones, either; this was one of those violent stories told to frighten children and make them behave. I was the prisoner of an evil queen who had an army of fiery demons at her command. I had been locked away in an unassailable castle surrounded by a dark, impenetrable wood that was home to evil, ravening spirits. The world I knew was a million miles away, impossible to return to—especially now that I had lost the vial Adair had implored me to hold on to as our only means of communicating in the underworld.

What I really wanted, I realized, pacing around the room with tears sprouting from my eyes as I grasped the seriousness of my situation, was Adair. I was in way over my head and he was the only person even remotely capable of dealing with this realm. By magic or sheer force of will, he could do something about this; he could make it go away. I knew in this moment that I trusted him implicitly and despaired that I couldn't tell him, that I might never get the chance to tell him.

Oh, it was weak of me to think like this, to want to be rescued, and I hated to give in to such weakness. I also knew this feeling was only temporary. I allowed myself to indulge in this momentary despair because I'd come so close—I'd made it to the underworld, I'd made my way to Jonathan—before it was snatched away from me. I was exhausted.

I was sitting on the threadbare blankets in my cell, ready to cry myself to sleep, when there was a soft knock at the door. It opened abruptly and Jonathan strode over to me quickly, cradling my face in both his hands as he kissed me on the top of my head. I must've looked cold because he slipped off the robe he was wearing and gave it to me. "Lanny, Lanny—what in the world are you doing here?"

"Believe it or not, I came for you," I said weakly, knowing how ridiculous it sounded.

He chuckled darkly. "I was afraid of that." He led me over to the plank bench and we sat, him cradling me on his lap. My cheek pressed to Jonathan's chest, I explained why I'd come after him. I told him how I'd dreamed that he was in trouble and needed me. As much as it sickened me, I told him about the dungeon, too, and how it had mimicked the basement of Adair's own fortress and how the nightmares had seemed to hound me. I told him how I'd begged Adair to send me into the underworld.

He twined our fingers like we were children. "That was brave of you, Lanny, but very foolhardy. I hope you see that. I may not be happy here, but I'm not being tortured—though even if I were, you shouldn't have risked your safety to come after me. There are limits to what anyone can do for another person."

I closed my eyes. I didn't want to believe that. There were

some people in my life for whom I would go to any lengths, and Jonathan was one of those people.

"Are you listening to me, Lanny?" he said, nudging my chin. "You needn't worry about me. I can take care of myself. And I have as good a deal as anyone could hope for in the afterlife."

"Really? This queen seems to have made you her sex slave."

His cheeks reddened and he ducked his head. "I prefer the term 'consort.' She was taken with me and insisted I remain. The day will come when she tires of me, I'm sure, and then she'll let me go. She seems to tire of things easily."

I lifted my brows. "But you don't *want* to be here, Jonathan. Do you?"

"She's the ruler of the underworld—it's not as though I have a choice," he replied. "What's the alternative? Do you know what happens to your soul after you die, Lanny? You come here to the underworld, knock around for a few days—apparently to loosen the bond to your past life—and then you are dispatched, jettisoned, into the void. Returned to the great, wide cosmos from which we came, broken down into elemental particles and energy. Recycled for parts." I thought of Luke's last moments—when he realized what was happening to him, that the finale had finally come, and how the endless void of space had opened up to receive him—and shivered.

"That's what Adair was trying to spare us by making us immortal," I said softly. "And look what I've reduced you to by taking your life—I've made you a gigolo."

Jonathan tutted and butted his forehead against mine playfully. "Have some respect. At least I'm gigolo to the gods."

Gods. I still couldn't wrap my mind around that. I leaned

in conspiratorially. "What do you know about them—the gods? Have you seen any others, besides the queen?"

He shook his head. "No. I've heard her refer to them. But no, I don't know where the others reside except 'elsewhere.' I get the feeling that once you're in the underworld, you stay here. There's no coming and going."

"So no one has escaped from the underworld? That can't be strictly true. After all, you did, once. When Adair brought you back to life."

"Right. You can't imagine the excitement *that* caused. Here, it only seemed like I was gone for an instant, because time is so much slower here. And I think they already had their antennae up because of the tattoo. But apparently I wasn't the only one to ever disappear from the underworld: I'd heard that one other soul did it a long, long time ago. They still don't know how he did it, but they caught his accomplice and put him away under lock and key," he said.

"I wonder who it was who escaped," I mused. But I knew; I felt it in the pit of my stomach. Jonathan, too; he gave me a strained look.

He wrapped both his hands around one of mine. "There's more I have to confess to you, Lanny . . . I'm afraid that your being here is all my fault. You see, I'm the one who told the queen about Adair. It's because of the tattoo. When she saw the tattoo, she wanted to know how I'd gotten it and I told her about Adair, and you. . . . She must've sent you the dreams in order to trick you into coming to the underworld, Lanny. She's been using you. I'm so sorry."

"It's hardly your fault. How were you to know?" He hugged me tighter against him, wrapping both arms around me. I continued, "What I don't understand is *why* trick me into coming to the underworld? Why not go after Adair, if he's the one she wants?"

"Because he would never come without a reason. He needed an incentive—and that's you," Jonathan pointed out.

"He'd come after me, you mean?" I started upright. "I hadn't thought of that—do you think he would do that?"

"Silly girl—what do you think?" he chided gently.

I was swamped by a wave of guilt. I hadn't thought *he* would be in danger, never. He hadn't offered to come with me to the underworld after Jonathan and it was plain that he feared the underworld more than anything he'd feared on earth. For that reason alone, I never considered that he might come after me. I thought I would be sick. "But why—why is she interested in Adair? What could he have possibly done?"

Jonathan shook his head. "I can't tell you that. I don't know. The queen has been careful not to say anything about Adair in my presence. I doubt her guards know, either. I get the sense that she plays her cards close to her vest. She's a lonely woman. Something has made her very unhappy, but she never talks about it."

Our foreheads bowed together, we contemplated this troubling mystery: the queen was unhappy and Adair had something to do with it . . . but I couldn't begin to imagine what that might be. Perhaps he'd stolen the wrong soul, the soul of someone important to her. Or perhaps it had to do with one of his companions, someone he'd wronged horribly. Then I thought of what she had done to Dona, how she didn't seem to feel compunction or sympathy for anyone. Whatever was between her and Adair, it was most likely personal.

I thought again of the vial. I could still feel its shape in my palm, a phantom, and wondered if our little trick had worked, if Adair had tried to bring me back and failed. I wished there was a way to send a message to him now—*don't come after me, don't*—but I supposed that power resided with the queen alone.

"What comes next, do you think?" I asked.

He ran a finger over my brow, brushing hair out of my eyes. "We wait for Adair to show up. I think you're safe, for now. The queen has no reason to hurt you—as far as she's concerned, you're bait and nothing else," he said, and I was just about to say that I'd never been so happy to be overlooked in my life when the door flew back, and a pair of demon guards rushed into the room—followed by the queen.

I almost felt sorry for her, to see the look on her face. She was jealous, it was plain—jealous and frustrated. I sensed no love between her and Jonathan, but the look on her face was frozen, hard, murderous—as though she could have obliterated me at that moment with a look, and yet she was holding back . . . with great effort.

She raised a hand and pointed at me, and I flinched. Then her finger started to tremble and she croaked over her shoulder at the demons: "Apparently this slattern cannot be trusted, not with any man. Take her from my sight! Take her away—and throw her in the pit."

EIGHTEEN

⟜━━━━━━━━━━━━━━━━━━━━━━━━━⟞

The island did not suffer the ill effects of the deluge for long. Adair quickly surveyed the grounds and found that the sun and brisk sea winds had gone a long way toward stripping away the excess moisture and drying things out. The floating dock had been lost and would have to be replaced. Only time would tell if the trees would grow back. The goats were gone, of course, and Adair decided he would not replace them.

Terry and Robin, too, appeared to have been swept out to sea—there was not a trace of them on the island. He was certain that those vindictive witch sisters had possessed them, and although he wished things had turned out differently, he would not beat himself up over it. What was done was done. Whether the powerful witch sisters, Penthy and Bronwyn, had been taken care of, he wasn't sure. They could be looking for another pair of vessels to take over. The whole incident made him uneasy, so Adair resolved not to think about it, not for now.

He decamped to the study, where he felt most comfortable and at his strongest. He built up a luxurious bed for Lanore directly on the floor, a feather mattress bolstered by a wall of pillows, and laid her out there, covering her in a blanket of fine cashmere, the color of moonbeams. He'd checked her hand earlier, hoping against hope that she'd managed somehow to hold on to the vial, but it was gone, undoubtedly lost to the sea.

A strange occurrence happened to him that night: he had a dream. Adair rarely dreamed. He didn't really need to sleep, and did only because it was a bodily pleasure, as enjoyable as smoking or eating. There were times, when he was upset or depressed, when he would seek the sweetness of oblivion, too, and this was why he slept now. Since sending Lanore to the underworld, Adair would hibernate around the clock if it meant time would pass more quickly and would hasten the day when she would return to him.

He hadn't dreamed any of the other nights since sending her to the underworld, but that night, he dreamed. It was one of those odd dreams, the kind that made him conspicuously aware that he was dreaming, and he had been so distracted by this very conspicuousness that he now could remember very little of it. As a matter of fact, he remembered only one crucial moment, and the vision had been so horrible that he had been thrown out of sleep and awoke sweating; he had to touch Lanore's hand to reassure himself that she was still with him, that no one had snatched her away while he was asleep.

In this dream, he'd been brought to a chamber, a squalid stone room with a dirt floor, a dank prison cell not unlike many he'd seen with his own eyes. In an odd twist for a prison cell, instead of a cot or pallet, there was a fully dressed bed in the center of the room, taking up nearly all the space. Lanore was on the bed, her hands bound, her eyes blindfolded. She struggled against her restraints. Naturally, he tried to rush to her side but was prevented by an invisible wall. He was helpless, being forced into the role of an observer. He knew, by the twisting of his gut and the terror expanding in his chest, what would happen next.

Within a minute, the door opened and a dark figure, huge and hulking, slipped into the room. Adair couldn't make out what this figure looked like until it came closer to the bed, and then he saw that it was a demon of some kind, a horrible monster worse than anything he recalled being described in mere stories. This creature was bestial, an animal with only vestigial traces of man. It was as large as an ox, with a broad, strapping back. Its muscle-bound haunches were as massive as boulders; its hocks were like pistons. Long threads of saliva dripped from its maw. It hovered over Lanore, its shadow eclipsing her, swallowing her up so that Adair could no longer see her, he could only hear her whimper in distress.

In a panic, Adair threw himself at the unseen barrier again and again, but whatever it was held as firmly as the accursed wall in the basement of the Boston mansion, the one that had held him for two hundred years. The beast put its hands on Lanore's shoulders, pinning her to the bed. He began to shift his weight over her, to climb her in preparation for mounting her, and Adair thought he would lose his mind. He tried to force himself to wake up. He couldn't watch what was about to happen.

He snapped awake on the floor next to Lanore, drenched in sweat, feeling as though his stomach had been ripped out. Now he understood why Lanore had been so desperate to go after Jonathan. No one would be able to endure such scenes, not about someone you loved. Even being fully aware that it was only a dream hadn't kept him from being completely consumed with horror. The dreams were exercises in torture, and he couldn't believe that a dream like that had come from his subconscious. He fully believed that the dream was a message.

He rose from the floor and paced around the room, trying to work out this wild, unsettled feeling inside him. He expected this feeling to dissipate like morning fog once he was fully awake, but it didn't. He thrummed with apprehension: *Do something to help Lanore, and do it now.*

It was plain what he must do: he must call her back to the land of the living. Now that she'd been stripped of the vial, she had no way of contacting him from the underworld, and her safety was obviously more important than any mission to save Jonathan. Let her be mad at him for bringing her back too soon, he decided; he didn't care. He would be doing it for her safety. Once he'd decided, he was rewarded with a huge sense of relief, like a weight lifted from his chest.

His decision made, Adair sprang into action. He knew which spell he'd use to bring her back; he'd selected it in advance and had put it aside in a special place so it would be at hand when the time came. He spent the predawn hours preparing the room: surrounding her with candles; drawing the proper magic circle on the floor, making it large enough to protect them both; anointing her with purified water and oils.

He wondered, fleetingly, as he toasted certain buds and leaves and ground them into a fine powder, if such steps were still necessary. After all, he'd been able to summon the sea to return Lanore to him with no ceremony, no trappings or incantations, nothing more than desire, and that success seemed proof enough of the power he had at his command.

Adair waited until midnight, the time when the two worlds were closest. He went through with the old steps—he lit the candles, smudged Lanore with ashes, splashed her with the potion he'd prepared. If nothing else, all that was ceremony, a way to still his mind and help him focus, not unlike any religious service. He likened it to going into an oracular trance, losing himself in the deep concentration required for the task that lay ahead. Unlike an oracle, however, he was not making himself a channel through which the gods might speak, but preparing a channel through which he could access a power on the other side. He was readying himself to wield— dare he say it?—a godlike power. But that was the feeling exactly: when he tapped into the hidden realm, he felt he was a god among men.

Tonight, as he attempted to reach the underworld, he felt at once that something wasn't right. The space between the two worlds didn't feel charged and electric, as it normally did. When he'd sent Lanore into the underworld, the void had felt alive, a living stream that he could move and shape with his two hands. Tonight it felt sluggish and unreceptive, almost as though it was actively trying to resist him. He needed to reach into that river of energy, find Lanore's soul from among the masses, and bring her back to earth. But it wasn't working out that way tonight.

Adair had thought it would be similar to bringing Jonathan back from the hereafter, which he had done one cold night in St. Andrew, Maine, at the graveside. Half of the work in a resurrection was done by the body, as the bond between body and soul was strong. A soul wanted to be with its body. This was why a soul would remain closely tethered to the earthly plane for thirty, forty days before returning to the infinite beyond, where all energy eventually returned—at least, this was how ancient religious stories had described the process. Lanore's body should be calling to her, too, but for some reason her soul wasn't responding. It made Adair think that perhaps someone was stopping her from returning; someone was actively holding on to her soul.

Adair kept trying, nonetheless. He kept searching through a murky emptiness, trying to find the presence—the thin electric feeling that connected him to his companions—that would lead him to Lanore. He wandered in the void for hours until he was exhausted, and broke off just before dawn. He woke, still kneeling beside Lanore in the study, to find the candles had guttered and the fire had long gone to ash. His head ached, and he tumbled to the floor in a swoon.

Revived, Adair sat on the floor in the cold gray light of morning, going over his options. Trying to call Lanore back was futile without the vial. Which meant there was only one way left for him to get her back, and that was to go into the underworld after her . . . which was exactly what he'd hoped to avoid. But this whole business with Lanore meant that someone was out to trap him, and his inability to recall Lanore's soul might be the final proof of this.

He looked restlessly at Lanore's still figure, pale as chalk in the silver light of early morning. What choice did he have? If it had been anyone but Lanore, he would've left her in the underworld. Adair allowed himself one last fleeting recrimination—hadn't he'd told Lanore several times that she shouldn't go? Clearly the girl couldn't think straight when it came to Jonathan—but he caught himself before his emotions got the better of him. That would be unfair to Lanore; now that he'd experienced the dreams for himself, Adair could see how frightening they were. Lanore had been enticed into going after Jonathan, just as he was being enticed into going after Lanore. Whoever was responsible for this trap was diabolical, Adair resolved.

The time for equivocation had passed, Adair decided as he clambered to his feet. If he had any reservations about descending to the underworld, it would be better to demure now. But he had no doubts, not really. His only regret was that he wasn't ready for his life to be over, but if living on meant losing Lanore, there was no choice.

He was ready to go into the underworld after Lanore—and on making this decision, Adair experienced something like a frisson at the back of his mind. It was the briefest memory, a stab of immense pain and frustration. It quickly rippled across his consciousness like a wave crossing a lake and then ebbed away. This peculiar sensation set his teeth on edge. Was his subconscious trying to tell him something, a fragment of his deep, distant past trying to come back to him?

Or perhaps, he thought wearily, he was reading too much into it. It might've been nothing more than a single memory breaking away from the shoals of the past and rising to the front of his consciousness, like a bubble breaking on the water's surface. Surely these blips of memory were to be expected. He knew exactly how he would descend into the underworld; he'd do it by force of will alone, just as he'd summoned the sea. He made only two preparations: One, with a single thought, he sealed up the fortress so no one would be able to get in, either accidently or by stealth, while he and Lanore lay helpless within. And second, he used strips of silk to bind himself to Lanore, tying one of her wrists to his, and doing the same with their feet—so that if she awakened and stirred, he might be wakened, too.

It was a risky journey. There was no one on earth he could ask to stand over him the way he'd stood over Lanore. There was no one he could petition to be the fail-safe who would bring them back. Once he'd found Lanore, if it wasn't within Adair's power to return them both, they'd be trapped in the underworld, quite possibly forever. But if that was the result, so be it, he resolved. He'd rather be with Lanore in the underworld than remain on earth without her.

Good-bye, world, he thought as he pressed next to Lanore on the pillows and took her hand in his. *Good-bye, life.* It was time for his last great adventure. On one level, he looked forward to it, for there had been a time when he liked to tempt fate and didn't worry about risking his neck. When had he gotten so concerned about his own safety? he wondered. He'd been rattling around the fortress for a long time, waiting for Lanore to return to him. It felt good to be *doing* something.

But part of him was anxious. No one could possibly *wish* to go to the underworld. It seemed, by its very definition, to be a place one went unwillingly. What's more, Adair couldn't help feeling that he'd *been this way before*, even though he knew this couldn't be true. He'd never died. Here was a question for the philosophers: Could a thing be true and untrue at the same time? He supposed he was about to find out. Without an oath, and with only a backward glance at the dark abyss that seemed to follow him always, Adair slipped away.

NINETEEN

T he demons wasted no time in fulfilling the queen's order. While one guard held Jonathan, a nasty-looking brute descended on me. They whisked me out of the chamber and hustled me down a long circular staircase that went on forever, like a corkscrew burrowing to the center of the earth.

The stairs finally petered out, dumping us into the very bowels of the castle, where we proceeded to travel down a long catacomb, skulls and bones peeking out at us from where they'd been lined up on deep shelves. We passed narrow doorways that seemed to lead to dark hollows and from which could be heard the occasional groan or moan.

At last we arrived at our destination, a low-ceilinged circular room. The mouth to the pit sat at the center, the opening perhaps eight feet in diameter and covered with a huge iron grate. I watched the demons lift the grate using brute force only, no pulleys or winches. The muscles in their arms and across their massive backs popped and strained from the effort, as they lifted it off the ground and pushed it aside to reveal a black hole. One of the demons waved his torch over the opening so we might see into it, but the light barely made any headway at all against the darkness. "You'll fall for days before you reach the bottom of this pit, sweeting," he told me matter-of-factly.

"You don't really mean to throw me in," I said in a frantic attempt to reason with him.

"No worries, love," said the other demon. "When you finally reach the bottom, you'll find you have some company. There's a right villainous fellow down there waiting for you, an enemy of the gods. He hasn't seen another soul for a thousand years. Imagine his surprise, when you drop in on him." The two demons laughed snidely.

"It won't matter if you're broken from head to toe from the fall. He hasn't had a woman in a thousand years—he's going to swive you in *two*, he is," the first demon said gleefully. He stumbled on some loose stones with his clumsy cloven hooves, and almost pitched headfirst into the pit, much to his companion's amusement. To cover up his embarrassment, he turned on me with a snarl and shoved the torch into his companion's hands, and then took me by the arm and, with one clean jerk, threw me over the edge.

I fell down, down, down through open space. Instinctively, I flailed my arms and kicked my feet, but it made no difference. I seemed to be centered in the shaft, for I fell straight down, not brushing or bouncing against the jagged walls. My flailing hands caught nothing. I tried very hard not to scream, not wanting to give the demons the satisfaction, but failed, a high, thin scream slipping past my lips.

It did indeed feel as though I fell for a very long time. It felt so long, in fact, that I was still falling when I started to recover my senses and the feeling of panic began to subside. I could think objectively about what was happening to me, as Alice in Wonderland had. And eventually my journey came to an end. As impossible as it seemed, I started to decelerate. Now descending as slowly as a feather, I saw the bottom of the pit come toward me. Oddly, it was lit with a soft, suffused glow. As I got closer, I saw someone waiting for me—an ordinary man and not a demon as I'd begun to fear. He was dressed in rags, with a cloth that wound around his neck and covered his head, like a monk's cowl, so that I couldn't see his face.

My feet touched ground. I was in a terribly vulnerable state; it would take a second for my brain to recalibrate and for the world to stop spinning. I wanted to vomit and collapse in that order, but I knew I had to be wary of this man, and sprang away from him, my back against the wall. I still couldn't see him, the cowl casting his face in deep shadow.

The man took a step toward me. "Don't come any closer," I warned.

He stopped, as I'd asked. "I won't harm you, I promise. I just want to see if the rumors I'd heard were true . . ." Rather than draw back the cowl, however, he stretched a hand toward me. "It is true, isn't it? I can *feel* him on you. I can feel his presence. You've been close to him recently."

"Feel him?" I asked, confused. "What are you talking about? Feel whom?"

"Adair, of course," the man said warmly. "He's the reason the queen brought you to the underworld. He's the reason I've been put in this hole. He is at the heart of all things."

The man finally lowered the cowl and revealed his face. He was old and rough, silver-haired all over, down to his eyebrows and whiskers. He might not have been a demon but he had their same topaz eyes, and the combination of silver and orange-gold gave him a strange, glittering appearance. He sat on a rock, and indicated that I should take a seat on one of the others. The warm golden light continued to glow dimly around us, though I couldn't tell where it came from.

"It's magic," the old man said, without my having to ask. "I may not be strong enough to levitate out of here, but I'd be a poor practitioner if I couldn't keep a little light burning." He rubbed a hand over his close-cropped hair.

"Magic," I repeated. I was still dazed from the fall and amazed to find myself in one piece. "Does that mean you're a magician, too? Is that how you knew Adair back on earth?"

He squinted at me, puzzled, thinking for a minute before he burst out in a loud laugh. "Magician? You think Adair is a magician? You don't know who he really is?"

"Magician, alchemist, take your pick." He was making me a bit irritable, being so cryptic. "He'd tell you so himself."

The old man howled in delight, rubbing his hands together. He even stamped his feet in glee, and he reminded me of that evil little troll in the fairy tale "Rumpelstiltskin." "Oh, that is too much! Too much to be hoped for, too much to be believed! For that means it worked, don't you see? What we tried to do, all those years ago—it worked, and worked to this day! Who would've thought?" His topaz eyes were gleaming at me now, as though I should understand what he was babbling about, as though we were conspirators.

"I'm sorry, but I'm not following you," I told him.

"Of course you're not," he said, cackling like an old lady. He was so delighted that it seemed he'd temporarily lost his mind. "Because if you don't know who Adair is, then you certainly don't know who I am, or why I am in this hole, or why you should be talking to me at all."

I was feeling more and more like Alice swallowed up by Wonderland. Maybe I had been hit on the head on my way down the shaft and was dreaming this. He smiled at me then the way you might smile at a curious child. "I could feel him on you—his presence," the old man explained. "He leaves his mark on all of us who serve him. Don't you know that, my dear?"

Of course I did—I carried his presence in my head, didn't I? "So you're one of his companions, too?" I asked curiously.

Everything I said seemed to delight him, and he laughed at me again. "My name is Stolas. I guess you might call me a companion, of sorts: I am Adair's first servant, his original servant." He hesitated, studying me closely. "I was his servant and his adviser, his emissary, too. And I had been with him for tens of thousands of years. Do you understand, now, what I'm telling you?"

Tens of thousands of years. The words were like a magic arrow that I watched pierce my skin and then go right through me as though I were a ghost. Of course I didn't understand what he meant; he was speaking in impossibilities—and I didn't want to believe him, I didn't want to know.

His topaz eyes fell on me kindly. "Adair is the master here. This is his kingdom, and he is the lord. You understand me now, don't you? The man you know as Adair is the king of the underworld."

It is entirely possible that I fainted. When I opened my eyes, I saw Stolas's face before mine, looking very concerned. He helped me sit up.

"You had no idea," he said, marveling at my cluelessness.

"That's an understatement," I replied drily.

Stolas did his best to explain to me how Adair had ended up in the land of the living when he was, in actuality, the king of the dead. The first thing that occurred to me was that he had lied all along, lied to me for his own dark purposes. For that was the role of the devil, wasn't it, to trick humans?

This question only drew another smile from Stolas. He lifted a finger to interrupt me. "First I must correct you for saying that the master is the devil"—Adair had become "the master" now—"because the devil is not the same thing as the king of the underworld. You are confusing the order of the cosmos with a religion. This has nothing to do with good and evil, right and wrong. The master is not in opposition to a deity. The master *is* a deity."

"Are you telling me there is no God, then?" I asked, to which Stolas only frowned, as though I was impossibly thickheaded.

"There are many gods. If you are asking if there is the one above us, a lord of lords, the answer is yes. There is a father of the gods, but the master does not oppose him. The master is bound to uphold the order of the cosmos, as is the lord of lords. As are we all," Stolas said with stiff dignity. "The master has a duty, which is to reign over the underworld. All souls pass through this way, and the process is as important as it is complicated. Equilibrium must be maintained between the lands of the living and the dead. It is a great responsibility."

"You say it's a great responsibility, and yet he gave it up," I pointed out to him. "Why did he do it? What made him want to give up being a god?"

Stolas didn't answer my question directly; as a matter of fact, he seemed intent on avoiding it. Instead, he began to tell me how this strange turn of events came about in the first place.

He confessed that he'd been quite surprised when the master came to him a thousand years ago and confessed that he wanted to leave the underworld. "No one had ever left before," Stolas said with a shake of his old head, as though dismayed that anyone would have the audacity to try. After all, it was hell, or at least purgatory, in a manner of speaking. No one wanted to be there; everyone wanted to get out. "It was designed by the father of the gods to be inescapable."

Having no idea how to leave, the master turned to his old and faithful servant Stolas, who, as it turned out, had served the father of the gods at one time. He had the answer Adair had been looking for. "It is well known that the only way out of the underworld is through the abyss," Stolas said sagely, raising a finger to make the point.

"The abyss," I echoed. It was a place I'd heard Adair

speak of, though I knew now that he had no idea why it had haunted him.

No one had ever crossed the abyss, Stolas explained. Everyone who tried had failed and been sent hurtling back into the underworld. He'd been only to the foot of the abyss, a huge cliff rising up from the edge of the underworld, and knew to scale it was an impossible task. It seemed to reach all the way to the heavens, but there was no way of knowing, as the mountain disappeared in a bank of roiling black thunderclouds. Here, lightning flashed, and the wind raged and rain fell in icy sheets, making the ascent even more treacherous.

Before the master set off, he and Stolas agreed on two precautions. First, Stolas created the story of Adair's mortal life, and used his magic to plant it in his master's head, because, as Stolas explained, "You can't carry knowledge of the underworld into the land of the living. It's one of the safeguards made to keep the two worlds separate. Even if you managed to scale the abyss and find your way to the land of the living, you would enter in a state of complete amnesia because your memory would be wiped clean as soon as you crossed over." Stolas planted new memories for Adair so he would believe he was a mortal man. It was the only way he could function on earth—and also, so he wouldn't give himself away inadvertently. He could hide from the gods because he really believed he was a mortal. He would *act* like a mortal in every respect.

"So why did you make him believe he was a magician?" I asked. It seemed a risky interest for him to have, if he was supposed to be in hiding. "Why not make him a shepherd or a blacksmith, something with no connection to the afterlife at all?"

"For two reasons," Stolas said. For one thing, even though Adair was crossing over to the world of mortals, that didn't *make* him one, too. He was still a god and was coming to earth with all the powers he'd had in the underworld. "While he was on earth, he'd be one of the most powerful forces in the universe. He could have anything he wanted. Anything he wished for would come true," Stolas said. "And if this happened, if he were to make some inexplicable thing happen, there was an explanation for it, you see: he was magician, a very good one at that. This would be his cover."

"Jonathan knew this," I said, putting the pieces together. "When Jonathan was brought back from the dead, he couldn't tell Adair much—he was prevented from remembering, just as you said—but Jonathan told Adair that he had powers. He said Adair was more powerful than he knew."

Stolas nodded. "And there was another reason, a sentimental one. You see, I planted the notion in his head that he should find a few others to make immortal so that they could be companions to him. He would be by himself in the mortal world for who knew how long, and I didn't want him to be lonely, you see."

Being the cautious sort, however, Stolas insisted that they take a second precaution, too: the tattoo. "Because the master wasn't a mortal, by all rights he shouldn't ever die. But we were in virgin territory here, you understand, and I was afraid that something might happen that we hadn't foreseen. I had to be certain that if he died and his soul was sent to the underworld, that we wouldn't lose him. I had to be able to find him, even though he was in hiding. And so we decided to use a tattoo as a secret signal. It was a gamble; no one had ever done this before—we didn't know if it would work." Stolas had never even known if the master had made it through the abyss; all he knew was that Adair had never returned.

"When Adair first disappeared, the queen was furious. She turned the underworld upside down looking for him," Stolas said. "It didn't take her long to figure out that her husband's most trusted adviser had something to do with it. She had me seized and tortured to try to get me to give up the secret, but I refused, and eventually, she had me thrown into the pit. The queen had my quarters searched, and that's how she found out about the tattoo. She found the drawing hidden away in one of my books. She's had guards at the entrance to the underworld looking for this tattoo ever since. Checking every soul that passes through. Millions upon millions of souls. She never gave up."

Jonathan. It had been Jonathan, carrying the tattoo on the inside of his right arm, who had given Adair's secret away. And it was my fault all this had happened. If I hadn't given Jonathan his release when he'd asked me four years ago in Maine, he'd never have been caught at the gates of the underworld. He'd never have been brought before the queen; she would never have known. And Adair would still be hidden from the gods, the cosmos, from himself.

"But why?" I asked finally, impatiently. "Why did he want to leave the underworld? Why fight his way through the abyss, why put this story in his head? Why did he give up being a god and make himself a man? It doesn't make sense."

"There is a reason," Stolas said with infuriating calm. "A good reason. But it is *his* secret to tell, not mine. I cannot share it with you, not without his permission. You must ask him, the next time you see him."

However, sitting where I was, at the bottom of the pit, I had no reason to believe I would ever see Adair again.

DESCENT

TWENTY

Adair opens his eyes and finds he's on his feet in a dark, misty space. At least the journey is over. It had been awful, a rocky plummet, and he had been choked with dread and, strangely, a sense of failure every inch of the way. He'd had the feeling of déjà vu the entire time, too. Impossibly, he was reminded of an experience he'd never had, clinging to a cliff somewhere, surrounded by blackness with flashes like lightning. But the descent is over now and he wants to put the journey behind him. He aches as though he has been on the losing end of a fight or locked in a trunk and thrown down a mountain.

Where has he ended up? he wonders. He seems to have touched down at a castle. He doesn't recognize it but, again, feels as though he's been here before. The sensation of déjà vu is insistent, clamoring in his head like a fire alarm, and he reacts in a basic, instinctual way. Fight or flight, his senses tell him. The urge to flee is almost irresistible.

Adair moves down the hallway slowly and carefully, listening for the sound of approaching footsteps. In a place this big, there are bound to be people: the occupants, but also guards, servants. He is diligent and checks around doorways, peeks down staircases, at a loss as to how to even begin looking for Lanore in this place. He no longer feels her presence, the thread by which they have been connected and the means by which he'd figured he'd locate her.

And he feels awful. After centuries of being perfectly healthy, of not having a day of illness—no cold or headache, or a broken bone that lasted longer than an instant—the sensation is unbearable. He is racked with pain from head to toe, as though his body is trying to turn itself inside out. He has the most powerful urge to curl over, hands on knees, and vomit. To purge himself. Something inside him is trying to get out—he is carrying something that must be expelled. Ignoring the pain, Adair presses down another hall, one that seems to take him closer to the center of the building. He doesn't know where he is, or who lives here—though he thinks he knows . . . he feels the awful truth in the pit of his stomach.

Before long, Adair realizes he is getting closer to an occupied part of the castle. He hears murmuring, distant rumblings at the end of the hall. It's an indistinct conversation being held between two people; he can hear the tone of their voices, but all the details have been washed out. Meanwhile, the pain in his head hasn't gotten any better; if anything, it's gotten worse, so sharp now that he can barely keep his thoughts together. His vision is broken up with white flashes before his eyes. His head feels as though it's going to explode, as though it would pulverize if you touched it—and there's that sense of déjà vu again, because he's felt this precise pain before. Yes, the sensation is so familiar at that moment, it's as though he felt it only yesterday—

Suddenly, Adair finds he has stumbled into the middle of a huge chamber. The ceiling stretches skyward, soaring so high that it disappears in what appear to be clouds, so that you can't tell if there's a ceiling at all. The room might actually be open to heaven. Giant columns anchor the room and they, too, reach for heaven. Through his blurred and racked vision, Adair sees there is—*my God*—the demon from his dream standing before him. The topaz eyes have definitely found him, but the beast has no reaction. In a moment of clarity, Adair notices a second demon, and a third, no—there are a lot of them, and they ring the perimeter, standing guard. Great ugly beasts they are, more frightening in life than in the flat, safe space of dreams. Each demon weighs at least a half ton if he weighs an ounce. Their glittering eyes are trained on him, each and every one. Adair's stomach drops to his knees. He expects they will seize him and take him to their queen, if he is lucky, or tear him limb from limb if he is not. He is frozen, waiting to see what they do next.

To his utter amazement, the demons do not rush toward him, snarling, with bared teeth. No, to his disbelief, they bend to one knee, each and every one of them, one demon after the other, each bending and bowing their heads to him. Adair turns in a slow circle, surveying the demons kneeling before him, and as he does so, a thunderbolt rings through his skull. Through the intense pain, he comes to a realization. He has been here before, he has lived here before. He remembers. He knows this place. His past rushes back to him, haltingly, in pieces, scenes, memories, responsibilities, duties. His time on earth, the life he has known, starts to shrink in his mind. It seems so short in comparison to what he has given to this place, to the underworld. To his home. That's what has been trying to get out of his head: false memories, the man he thought he was, the story that had been planted in his head. Stories he's believed implicitly for a thousand years, and they're all lies. It's incompatible with the truth that rushes up to him now like a happy child being reunited with its parent, embracing him, unwilling to let go of him. Recollections of his past, his *true* past, rush to fill his head.

Suddenly, the queen is standing before him. How happy she is, her sternly beautiful face lit up with joy. She walks toward him, her arms outstretched, reaching for him. She is magnificent in her way, the quintessence of a particular kind of female beauty, coldly triumphant.

Adair is dumbfounded. Unbelievably, she comes up to him, taking his hands in hers and—when he doesn't resist her—slips into an embrace with him. This embrace feels as familiar to him as breathing. Held in her arms, he knows that they have done this thousands upon thousands of times. Yet, his skin crawls when it comes in contact with hers, as though they are incompatible, as though they are two chemicals that form a corrosive acid when they mix. He wants to escape from her, but he can't. She holds him tight like the very embrace of death.

"You've come back to me," she whispers in his ear. Her voice is thick and sweet, like honey. "I knew you would come back to me, and to your kingdom. Nothing has changed; I have held it all in wait for your return. We have all waited for your return, all your faithful servants. Now that you are back, you will resume the throne as king, and as my husband, and together we will rule the underworld, as we were meant to by our father, the lord of lords." The queen is nearly crying with joy, and, trembling, she brings her lips close to his. She pauses before she kisses him. "Welcome home, my lord."

TWENTY-ONE

The room is still spinning. Adair feels as though he is in the middle of a Catherine wheel, one of the many torture devices in the Middle Ages (and one he experienced personally, he recalls with discomfort). The room revolves around him on a wild ellipse. He intuits that the bed beneath him is big, as big as a meadow, and he is sprawled across it carelessly. The queen sits beside him, running her fingers through his sweaty, matted hair, patting a cold cloth to his forehead. She cannot stop touching him, though he wishes she would—her touch makes his skin crawl.

"You cannot imagine how hard I wished for this day," she croons to him. "You are home at last. You have come home to me," she says over and over, as though convincing herself.

"Stop saying that. Stop," he says, pleading grimly. The past has caught up with him, overtaken him, and now floods him mercilessly with memories. Each memory is hard and sharp, like the whack of a bat to the back of his head. Adair remembers why he left: to escape eternal wedlock to this woman; anyone but her. He could not stomach the two of them ruling the underworld as husband and wife. When there are so few deities, there was no option but for him to be forced to wed her. And yet she is a despicable choice he cannot abide.

Have they been to bed already? His memory will not take him there. Is that why she behaves the way she does with him, why she is so stung, so hateful and resentful?

He sits up abruptly, his stomach lurching, and jerks her hand from his head, pushes it aside in disgust. She pulls back, regarding him cautiously for a moment, and then digs into a pocket and presses something small in his hand—a vial encrusted with filigree loops. Dirt clings in the cracks. "I have something for you. Do you remember this?"

He holds it up, squints at it to be sure—just as he'd feared, it is the very one he'd given to Lanore as their means of finding their way back to each other. As recognition crosses his features, she continues, "Our lord of lords, the power above us all, gave it to you when we were children. He gave one to me, too. He said it held the tears of his wife," she says, nodding at the vial.

Adair remembers the woman as perpetually sad—hence, the tears. Her tears had turned into a sticky resin and he had fed that resin, by drops, onto the tongues of mortals he wished to keep with him as fellow immortals. Adair brushes the dirt off the vial as best he can and tucks it in a pocket.

He turns to the queen. "Look, I've no desire to stretch this out any longer than is absolutely necessary. You know why I've come back. I'm here for Lanore. She is all that I want. Return her to me and I'll go. You can have the underworld all to yourself."

If his words have hurt her, she hides it well. She sits up straight and proud, her neck arched like a swan's, but her head is bowed gracefully like an obedient wife. "I don't want to rule the underworld alone," she tells him with perfect sincerity. "And I am your bride—not her."

"I'll not stay," he warns her.

"You can't go," she says. A simple statement of fact. "There is no way out."

"I escaped once," he reminds her.

"You won't cross the abyss twice, you know that. You were lucky—infinitely lucky—to cross it the first time," she says. A worried look flits across her face. "And you shouldn't press your luck a second time. If you fail, the lord of lords might not forgive you. We are not irreplaceable. You know that, too."

"I would be glad to be replaced." He knows it will make her unhappy to hear him say this, but he must be true to himself. "I'm not repudiating you. Don't take this as a rejection. It's just that—I cannot be wed to you."

Her face hardens and she turns away from him in preservation of her dignity. "How can I *not* take it as a rejection? How can it *not* be personal? You don't want me as your wife, even though we were meant to be together. This is out of our hands. It is the natural order of things. You can't fight it any more than I can."

He can't help himself; under pressure, the words blurt out like juice from a lemon. "You are not my wife. You must accept that I will never be your husband."

His declaration seems to tear something inside the queen. She leaps up from the bed and whirls on him. Her magnificence blooms when she is angry—the same as his does. They are mirrors of each other. "Do not think you can be rid of me so easily, my lord. Do not think you can be unkind to me and dismiss me. You cannot threaten me. Do you think you are my match? You're not even close—you haven't used your powers in a thousand years, whereas I have been a god for every day of those years. You are weak and in no position to oppose me."

"It doesn't matter. You can snuff the life out of me, if that's what you want. I would rather die than be with you." The words leap from his mouth. He doesn't think before he speaks; if he was impatient on earth, he is more so here, his old fury coming back on him swiftly. The queen winces; they are mean, these words, but true, and so he cannot take them back.

"It doesn't matter how you or I feel—you won't be allowed to do as you please. Order must be maintained in the heavens. Do you think the gods will let you get away with this?" she asks pointedly. She is not going to remain to be insulted and affronted, and, having said her piece, she disappears in a puff of vivid blue smoke, as though she has exploded from anger.

Adair is wandering through the labyrinthine suite of rooms in which he has found himself when he runs into Jonathan. His old friend and sometime adversary lounges on a chaise, reading what appears to be a book of poetry. He has the same inscrutable expression that he wore in life, both pleasant and yet unmistakably bored, as though nothing can possibly keep his attention. One never knew what was going on inside that handsome head. Jonathan always kept his thoughts to himself.

"Hello, old man," he calls to Adair in his usual lazily chummy way once he notices him standing in the doorway. Jonathan sits up and makes room for Adair on the chaise and the two sit next to each other, Adair sullen, Jonathan cautiously friendly. He puts the book facedown on the floor, open to his spot.

"So you are the queen's consort," Adair says, not knowing what else to say under the circumstances.

Jonathan says hastily, "Yes, though I will say in my defense that I only *recently* learned she is your wife. That fact was kept from me before." He appears to reflect for a moment on the woman who has taken him to her bed. "There's no hard feelings, right? It's not as though I had any say over the situation," Jonathan adds uneasily.

"No, of course not," Adair assures him.

Another moment passes in silence between them, each man caught up in his thoughts. At length, Jonathan continues, his tone a little more anxious this time. "So you are king of the underworld. The prince of Hades. Lord of the dead." The roll call of titles makes Adair wince. Jonathan cracks an ironic smile. "Did you *really* not know? The entire time you were on earth, you never had a glimpse of your previous existence? An inkling, a hint? I find that—extraordinary."

Adair shakes his head. "No. It was kept a mystery to me."

"Ah yes, the barrier between the two worlds. I've experienced it myself. In retrospect, it makes perfect sense. I mean, you've always had quite a *temper*, haven't you? And that cruel streak—you always were on the sadistic side. When you look at all the pieces . . ."

"I am *not* the devil." Adair feels the need to correct him. "I wasn't *born* into the position, I was chosen. It has nothing to do with personalities. I am merely the keeper of the realm." Pride flares inside him and he feels the need to educate Jonathan. "It is not a trivial position. It's not an honorary one, either. It takes a strong will to rule over the dead."

"Oh, take my word for it. I know. I've seen it firsthand," Jonathan quickly reminds him. "*Your bride* is the devil, however. I hope you don't mind me saying that," Jonathan adds. "Four years with her and it feels like four hundred—even though a year on earth is like the blink of an eye here."

Here, they are on cosmic time, the interminably slow drip, drip, drip of time. The impartial clock by which the cosmos unfolds, during which stars form and burn and finally burst, for planets to be reduced to dust and scattered to the farthest reaches of the universe. All of it just another day, for the gods. "I am the age of the cosmos," Adair says, and he feels the truth of it in his firmament, down to the electric pulse that runs through him.

Another minute passes in silence between the two. Adair wishes he had a nice whiskey to help ease the time with Jonathan. It seems like the proper gentlemanly accoutrement for the situation and, before he can even think twice, a tray appears at his feet bearing a crystal decanter and two heavy tumblers. He pours generous dollops of whiskey and hands a glass to Jonathan.

Jonathan gestures about the dingy room, whiskey sloshing onto his hand. "Now that you're back, maybe you could do something to spruce the place up. It's infernally dismal here, so dark and drab."

Adair gives Jonathan a strained look. Here he is worrying about his future happiness and Jonathan wants to talk about interior decorating. "What difference does it make how things *look*? I could give two figs for the *atmosphere*. Besides, do you think I have the slightest interest in remaining here?"

Jonathan takes a bracing swig of alcohol. "It's obvious that you're depressed. The queen is depressed, too. It couldn't hurt to brighten things up."

Adair knows there is some truth to what Jonathan says. He *is* depressed. Memories of his past existence continue to crowd into his head, stuffing his mind to bursting, and it's noisy in there, buzzing like a nest full of hornets. He doesn't want these memories back. He'd be happy to live the rest of his life without them. He wants to hold on to his memories of being Adair—he wants to *remain* Adair.

He drops his head into his hands and moans. "I don't care about all this other stuff. I don't want this kingdom or these responsibilities. I didn't ask for them."

Jonathan gives Adair a surprised look. "Why, I never thought I'd hear you talk like that, Adair. You always knew what you wanted, and that was all that mattered. You've changed." He sounds a touch disappointed.

Adair grunts. He has been stripped to his essentials, and he knows it. "I only came here for Lanore. Where is she, Jonathan? Do you have any idea where I can find her?"

"I have seen her. But the queen had her taken away, to some place she called 'the pit,' but I don't know anything more," Jonathan says.

"How am I going to find her?" Adair moans.

That self-pitying remark is the last straw for Jonathan, who gives him an annoyed look. "Dear lord, Adair, just listen to you. Stop acting like a mortal. You're a *god*, for goodness' sake. You can do *anything*—or rather, practically anything. So stop your whining and put your mind to it."

Repressing the urge to knock Jonathan across the room for his insolent remark, Adair sees the truth in it. Jonathan may be impertinent but he is right. The universe is his to command—up to a point, he knows, but finding Lanore should be within his power. He has done it twice, after all: once to find her home in Paris, and the second time on the island, when all he had to do was wish and the ocean obeyed. This is not earth or the ocean; this is the underworld, his own kingdom, for God's sake. The queen's words have made him doubt his ability to channel his power, and for a moment he hesitates. Then he pushes that doubt aside. He is in his kingdom. It should do whatever he commands.

Adair stands and starts to walk back to his chamber. The more he thinks about what it is that he wants, the more he feels the power swell and rise within him, a muscle plumping to attention. He may have been away for a millennium, but here in the underworld it has been no more than a few blinks of an eye. The slowness of cosmic time will work in his favor. His power wells up within him, coursing through his body, surging to his hands. *Bring her to me*, he thinks. *Bring Lanore to me.*

One minute, I am at the bottom of the pit, huddled on a rock and speaking to Stolas. And the next, I am levitating through the air. I'm carried along through space, up, up, up the long shaft of the pit. I can feel Adair's presence again, clear as a bell in my head. I have never been so happy to feel his presence. Once a sign of his domination and oppression, it now means something else entirely. I know he's here and I feel so many emotions at once—happiness, joy, relief—that I don't think I can contain them all. Thank God we will not go another eternity-filled minute without seeing each other again. Thank God I will have the chance to tell him that I love him. I know it now with all my heart. My prayers have been answered.

I am dropped out of the air to the floor of a room. There he is, waiting for me. I have wanted this so badly, I almost can't believe it's him. He looks different in a way I can't quite place—there's something softer about him perhaps.

We rush to each other. I have never cried so hard in my life, crying for joy, but it seems to upset him. "Don't cry," he says, trying to wipe my tears away with his thumbs.

"Forgive me for being so stupid, for dragging you here. I should've listened to you," I try to say to him, but he shushes me.

"It was inevitable, Lanore. I would've been called back to the underworld eventually, by one means or another. It is not your fault," he says. "There is nothing to forgive."

The moment when he kisses me is sublime. He cradles my head in his hands, turning my face up toward his. He slips his mouth over mine and it is all warmth, all heat and need and desire. But his need is tender now, all tenderness. It feels as though I will melt into him right there, be lost in him right there. My tears make our kiss salty, bittersweet. Bittersweet, too, because I know it can't last. He is the king of the underworld and he has a queen, a queen who will not be denied.

He sees that I am still crying. "What's the matter?" he asks, hurt and perplexed.

I tell him. "This cannot last. I know it. But I love you, Adair. I cannot give you up."

He presses a finger to my mouth. I can taste his skin, metallic and sweet. "I am a god, my love. I can have whatever I want, and what I want is for us to be together forever. It will come to pass—you can trust me on that." He wraps his arms around me and draws me to him. There is no gap between us, no space, no air. Pressed up against each other, we are aflame, so hot that I think our bodies will fuse into one. We *are* one, and yes, he is right, we will remain one. He picks me up and carries me to the bed, that beautiful bed of my dreams and my nightmares, and I know that we are going to be there for a very long time.

TWENTY-TWO

Afterward, Adair and I lie together in a tangle of sweat-dampened sheets. He holds me against him, my back against his still-moist chest, my derriere nestled in his lap. One of his hands is on my abdomen, right around my navel, and his other arm is wrapped around my rib cage under my breasts. He hugs me tightly as he kisses the back of my head. Such tenderness seems out of keeping, not for the man I know as Adair, but for the force I now know him to be.

As we lie in bed together, he sighs contentedly in my ear. "You haven't asked," he says, reluctantly. These are the first words we've said to each other since he summoned me to him.

"Asked what—if you really are a god? I haven't asked because I can see that it's true."

"There's nothing more you want to know? No questions?" he asks, sounding as though he fears it's too good to be true.

I try to turn around to face him, but he holds me in place. "Now that you mention it, yes, there is something I've been wondering about." Now is my opportunity. I tell him about Stolas and our encounter in the pit. "He explained to me how you were able to leave the underworld, but he wouldn't tell me *why* you left. He said that it was a secret and he couldn't betray it."

Adair sighs. He seems pained that I have it brought up now, and I can't bear to make things complicated when we've just been reunited, so I rush to answer my own question. I want to spare him from telling me something I probably do not want to hear, anyway. "It's obvious, isn't it?" I continue, in a rush. "You left to get away from that woman, the queen. I understand, Adair. You don't have to say anything more if you don't want to."

He stops me, releasing me from his damp arms and turning me to face him. His eyes are solemn and downcast, afraid of what he has to tell me. He holds me square to him though he still can't look at me. "There is something more I have to say to you. There is a reason I left the underworld."

Again, I try to stop him from speaking. I'm afraid of this confession, afraid that it will ruin what is between us now, which was so hard to attain. "You needn't be afraid, not of me. Who am I to question you, whatever you've done, whatever the reason—"

He gulps, hurt. "You are the woman I love. If I am not accountable to you, then who would you have me be accountable to?" He gives me a little shake, but it is a sign of his impatience with himself and not me. "You must listen, Lanore, because this is something you will hear as soon as we open that door, and you must hear this from me and not someone else." He closes his eyes and squeezes them tight. Draws a deep breath, and I watch his sternum rise and fall. When he opens his eyes again, they are racked with pain. "The queen is my sister. We are meant to rule this place together, as husband and wife."

Adair's hands go cold against my skin and he's turned away, unable to look at me. "It is a wicked, twisted tradition and yet . . . it is the way of the gods, sisters and brothers made into husbands and wives. I can make no apologies for it. It is just how it is."

I can't even feel him beside me anymore; I feel loose, like water, as though I've dissolved into a million pieces. This last revelation is too much. The accumulated weight of all that he is and has been and done threatens to crush me. I want to give in to the weakness that descends over me like a great, enveloping cloak. I wish I were able to walk away, but I can't. I love him; I cannot abandon him. It kills me to see how unhappy he is, how close to broken.

My head is swimming. I go back to the things Stolas told me, how Adair unknowingly had lived on earth under a lie, collecting his damned souls by instinct. It had been my misfortune to be caught in his net, but was it also misfortune, too, to fall in love with him? (Is it ever a misfortune to know love?) Once the attraction was there, it had been inevitable to love him, as inevitable and intractable as gravity.

When I was a young woman, I had followed my heart and had it broken, and had erroneously believed that the lesson I should take away from this was to be cautious with my heart. After this, I'd always kept a barrier between the people I chose to let into my life and my heart, even with Luke. Of course, now I can admit that my suppressed feelings for Adair probably had something to do with this. I'd been afraid of loving Adair for good reason, but now that I admit it is inescapable, it is as though something let loose inside of me and cannot be brought back in check.

I settle back into myself, slowly pulling my spirit back into my body. My throat is tight and painful; blood pounds in my ears. I press my hands to his chest for composure. "So she is your sister, Adair. I—can accept that. And it doesn't mean anything to us, not really. We love each other. We belong to each other. A union with the queen is only ceremony. It means nothing, in terms of love."

He stirs, heartened.

"I don't care if she's meant to be your queen," I go on, more vehemently. I clutch his arms and press closer to him. "That can't mean that we won't be allowed to be together. I don't need to be acknowledged as your wife. I have your love, I know I do. She can have her consorts and you can have me."

His mood brightens infinitesimally. He lifts his head. "I don't know what's possible, what will be allowed and what is forbidden," he begins, but right at that moment, we are interrupted. A wind throws back the doors to the bedchamber and sends the bed curtains and linens flapping as though we are caught in a hurricane. Our hair swirls around our heads as the room is thrown into chaos: furniture flying, ornaments spinning around the room. Glass in the windows shatters into thousands of glittering shards, suspended in midair as though possessed. Suddenly, I feel as though I'm being held in a giant hand, and I'm being crushed as the fingers tighten around my body. I can't speak, I cannot breathe. My ribs are about to crack and snap under the strain. The internal pressure is enormous and I feel as though my eyes are about to pop, as though blood will spurt out of my ears and mouth, out of my nose.

Adair is looking at me, stricken and confused, but only for a second. He knows what is happening before I do. "Stop!" he roars, his voice thunderous, shaking the rafters. Then he turns his attention to me. He doesn't need to say a word, he just looks at me and I feel the grip loosen, the horrible pressure ebb away. Once I am okay, gasping and shaking but okay, he presses me to him again, so tightly that it's almost as though he wishes to tuck me *inside* him. My cheek rests against his chest, and he strokes my head.

At that moment, a trail of cobalt smoke snakes into the room, whipping in a circle around us, as the glass and baubles and detritus seemingly are released from a trance and fall from midair, dropping to the floor. The blue smoke draws upward into a plume and then the queen materializes before us. Her arms are crossed and she glares at us, furious, her expression horrible to behold. She is angry and accusatory. The wronged one, she has caught us, the husband with his mistress in bed together, the cheater and the rival. To see with your own eyes the evidence that you are unloved and unwanted. It is clear by looking at her that war has been declared. There is about to be a battle royal and the underworld might be split apart by their fury.

"How dare you!" she hisses, brows arched. "With your mistress in your arms, here in *our* domicile! On the day of your return!" Her voice drips with pain and, having been in her place many times before, I can't help but see the situation from her point of view: I have caused her nothing but hurt. Her spouse is in love with me, and even Jonathan helped me at the risk of offending her. No wonder she threw me down the deepest pit of hell: I am the rival she has been unable to best. No wonder she wanted never to see me again.

It looks as though she wants to attack us but cannot decide which of us will be her target, me or Adair. He pulls me even closer to him to protect me, but that only elicits a howl of anguish from her. We can feel her gather strength, her unhappiness crackling the air like an electrical storm. "You will not try to hurt her again!" Adair bellows at her, holding a palm out against her. "If you do, you will answer to me."

"*She* is the interloper here, not me. You are my husband, and nothing can change that," she snaps at him.

"There is one way to change it," Adair says, brightening as a thought comes to him. "I'll abdicate."

The queen draws back, aghast. Giving up power is unimaginable to her, I suspect. She regards Adair uncertainly, as though he's just told her that gold is as common as sand and that stars are made of spun sugar. "It's not a decision you can make on your own, and you know that. The father of the gods made you king, put you in this position himself. It will be up to him. He must decide to allow it."

I can feel the tension in the air evaporate as they both back away from the brink of a fight. Adair lifts his chin when he addresses her. "Let the power above us all pronounce judgment on me in person. I want our father to tell me to my face what he would have me do. I swear I will submit to his will."

His sister sniffs at him as though it is a trick. "You want him to settle this because you've always been his favorite. But I think this time, that'll backfire on you. Being his favorite won't save you. You've tested his patience once too often. So, I agree: you shall bring your case before him, and we will *both* abide by his decision. You have my word." She doesn't wait for Adair to agree or try to get out of the bargain. Before he can say another word, she disappears again in a puff of smoke, leaving Adair and me to blink at each other, unsure of what we have just agreed to.

TWENTY-THREE

After the confrontation with his sister, Adair senses that the underworld has been placed on a kind of lockdown. The castle seems to be holding its breath, cast in a groggy half sleep like something out of a fairy tale. When he tries to push back against the frosty stillness, it resists him, and this is how he knows it's been imposed by someone more powerful than him.

He rattles down an empty hall, thinking about the challenge he threw down and all the possible ways it might go wrong. As for his sister, he's not sure where she's gone—off licking her wounds and plotting, most likely. Adair has hidden Lanore away in a secret room, which he has placed under his protection, wrapping it up with his intentions— *this space is inviolate*—like a spell, concentrating on it continuously, so that she will be safe from the queen, should she try some kind of sneak attack. But to protect Lanore like this takes up most of his energy and Adair can barely think or do anything else. He's not sure how long he can keep this up.

Everyone has disappeared—the demons, the various servants—and Adair wonders if his sister has taken them away with her or if they've made themselves scarce, like animals anticipating a tornado. Even Jonathan has disappeared, though Adair figures he is with the queen. Adair suddenly wishes for Stolas's company, remembering the old man's canniness. He is a good tactician. But Adair knows he cannot pull Stolas from the pit without reducing his ability to protect Lanore, who is helpless without him. She waits in her hidden room like Rapunzel in the tower, dependent on her prince to figure a way out of this dilemma. Stolas must remain where he is for now.

Continuing on his solitary watch, Adair turns the corner to see an old man sitting on a marble bench. He's familiar looking but Adair cannot put his finger on where he saw him last. (Ever since Adair returned to the underworld, he's found that it's like this with everything, the name of every sight, sound, and scent dancing just out of his reach.) The old man watches Adair as he approaches, smiling only at the last minute.

He wears toga-like robes as if he were an Olympian god and looks vaguely Greek or Roman. He has a beard and long hair, gray with streaks of white, and he wears it tied back in a loose ponytail, the way Adair often likes to wear his. Watching Adair approach, the old man doesn't seem unkindly—nor does he seem to be anyone's fool—he has a no-nonsense aspect about him.

When Adair draws close, the old man stands up and claps his arms around him. "Look who's back. The prodigal son."

Adair jerks in the old man's embrace. The state of familial relationships on this plane has always been murky. The old man has been known to share his favors rather freely, and there has always been reluctance to spell out things like paternity. Adair remembers his long-suffering mother, remembers cherishing his relationship with that woman. The reserve he feels toward the old man probably has something to do with this. If the time has come that the old man wants to treat him as his son, then so be it, Adair decides.

The old man releases him and inclines his head toward Adair. By his weary reserve, Adair can tell that he felt Adair stiffen in his arms. He squints at Adair, sighs, and hooks his arm over Adair's. As soon as the old man touches his arm, Adair feels an indescribable surge of power radiating through every cell of his being merely at the touch of his hand. "Come—walk with me," the old man says.

They start down one of the dim, cavernous halls, the old man tut-tutting at the filth accumulated in the corners, the lack of light, the ugliness of it all. Still, he's not presumptuous enough to change it with a wave of his hand, which he most definitely could. He could make it go away or replace it with trees and fountains, a park, or a ballroom complete with a brilliant white chandelier. "When was the last time you were here?" Adair asks as they walk.

The old man doesn't need to think about his answer at all. "It was the day you left—or rather, disappeared. Your sister was very upset, you know." He cocks an eyebrow at Adair, as if measuring his guilt.

Adair knows he should feel more sympathy for his sister. They were close once, confiding in each other, watching each other's back. It never occurred to him that they might be paired together as mates, though there had been examples all around him, aunts and uncles, cousins who were part of the pack of young gods that ran around together. They did everything together: hunting, wrestling, playing, having fun. Then suddenly individuals would be culled from the herd only to reappear together as a pair and vaulted to the ranks of adults, put in charge of a realm, given attendant responsibilities. It was all very mysterious until the day the old man had come to him, clapped him on the back (not unlike what he was doing at this very moment), and told Adair he was going to become the king of the underworld, and that he'd have to take his sister as his queen.

"But why is it even necessary to have a king and a queen in the underworld? Why can't I rule it alone?" Adair asks as they stroll slowly down the hall.

The old man turns up his palms, as if to say *be reasonable*. "Well, it's a tremendous job, isn't it? And one of the most important, too. We can't have any mistakes made on this end, can we? It would lead to chaos. Must keep things moving in their proper order. Must keep the souls moving, sending energy back out to the cosmos. We can't have someone too tenderhearted, mucking up the system. And because it's all so important and so complicated, there has to be a backup, a deputy, in case anything happens." Here, the old man gives Adair a fishy look, as though he suspects the ruler of Hades has stopped listening to him and is, instead, piling up more arguments in his mind.

"Then why *can't* it be a deputy, or a lieutenant, just as you said? A second in command, instead of a mate. It could be run more like the military, or a business, rather than a royal kingdom. Why does it have to be a spouse?" Adair argues.

The old man lays his arm across Adair's shoulders. "Being the king of the underworld is a very lonely position, my son. You've experienced that for yourself already. We've found that this way is best, having the pair work in tandem, closely. That way there's almost no chance of something coming between them."

A dark frown creases Adair's face, his brow. "Why, then, I tell you, your system is already spoiled. I can never be close to her again, never. We will always be at each other's throats."

"Oh, don't be so unreasonable. You've always been so dramatic—but then, I guess it is your nature. That's the reason you were chosen for this position, you know. You were tailor-made for it, given to impatience. We knew you'd be perfect for it—your sister, too—and that you were made to rule together. Who else could we pair you with, anyway? You were both so troublesome, so argumentative. No one else would have you, either of you." The old man chortled to himself, amused by his memories. "Anyway, as I was saying, it doesn't matter if you can't stand each other. Few of us can, you know. Husbands and wives—it just works out that way. Think of the old fellow, the one who ruled the underworld before you. Hades and his wife, Persephone. She couldn't stand the sight of him. Eventually, she came around—enough to tolerate him, anyway. And they ruled a good long time. It'll happen that way for you, too. You'll see."

Adair feels despair fill his chest. He'd promised to obey the old man's decision and yet he knows he won't be able to bear it.

"No, it won't be all right. I'm telling you, it won't work out. You see, I've fallen in love."

Now it is the old man's turn to go dark. His expression is as frightening as a thundercloud. "So I've heard. A human? They are sweet diversions, my son, but you know that never works. Not in the long run."

"She's extraordinary. She's changed my nature. I'm not the same soul I once was. I'm not all hellfire and damnation. To be honest, I don't think I can do it anymore." Adair gives him an imploring look. "If you're afraid that someone too tender-hearted will mess things up—well, that's me. I've become empathetic."

The old man laughs and lifts an eyebrow. "You're joking, aren't you? She's tamed you, you say?" He looks Adair over. "She sounds extraordinary," the old man says finally.

Adair claps a hand to his shoulder. His mind goes to the room where he's put Lanore, and he lets the protections unwrap and slide away, like a dust cover falling to the floor, so the hidden room can be seen, so that it becomes real. "She is. I would be honored if you would meet her for yourself."

The place where Adair has left me is lonely. It looks like an ordinary room. It has four walls, a ceiling, a floor, and furniture. It even has a door. But I know that it's different. For one thing, it feels like an elevator, like a small, finite space shut up on itself. It feels disembodied, as though it's floating in space. I can only imagine what his sister might do to me if she was able to catch me—still, I pleaded with Adair to stay. "Don't leave me," I said as he was preparing to go. I even grabbed at his shirt, but he pried my fingers gently from the fabric. He explained to me that I would be safe, that he would be able to wrap me in spells and protections so that no one, not even she, would be able to find me. "I have to see the god above us all." He tried his best not to seem worried in front of me. "I don't know what sort of mood he'll be in. I defied him when I chose to leave. He doesn't usually stand for that sort of thing, and he's not the forgiving type." He kissed my hand and then walked out the door.

What he meant to tell me, in so many words, is that the outlook for us is not good. The odds are that this deity will not decide in our favor. I suppose under a relatively benign outcome, Adair would remain here and resume his reign. If things go really badly, I imagine Adair could be punished for disobeying the god in charge, sentenced to something really horrible and long-lived like the fate of Prometheus, who had his liver torn out every day by eagles as punishment for sharing fire with humans. I pass the time pacing in circles, trying not to surrender to worry, but I'm so nervous that my teeth are chattering.

I'm startled when there's someone at the door. It's Adair, and he gives me a faintly encouraging smile before stepping aside to hold the door open for a tall old man.

"I wasn't expecting company," I say to them, though I'm so unnerved that I'm surprised I can joke.

Instinctively I know who this man is—God. There's no mistaking him: he's dressed the part in luxuriant robes the exact color of the moon, but even if he weren't outfitted like this, even if he didn't have long hair and the beard, there would be no mistaking him. He projects a certain air, calm and all-knowing, though he has a hint of a darker nature (vengeful, wrathful), too, a side that is reflected in Adair.

"Lanore, come here," Adair says. He takes my hand when he sees that I'm unable to move, my feet frozen to the floor. "There's someone I want you to meet." The only way I can become unstuck is by telling myself that this man isn't God but Adair's father, that I'm not meeting the force behind all of creation but a member of Adair's family—as though that on its own isn't frightening enough. The air is absolutely electric, like the seconds before the break of a huge, juddering thunderstorm. Imagine a thunderstorm stuffed into a space as small as your drawing room. Yet the three of us go on pretending that nothing's out of the ordinary.

I don't know what to say, what to do, if I should take his hand or drop to my knees in worship. Instinct kicks in and I start to ask if he'd like something to drink before I realize I have nothing to offer, and have no idea what kind of refreshment to offer God, anyway. I become completely self-conscious, remembering that he most likely knows all the terrible, stupid things I've done, which causes me to flush with embarrassment and regret. I'm literally meeting my maker and it is every bit as awful as you might think it would be.

"He's told me so much about you," the old man says as he gestures to Adair, then settles onto the couch, arranging his robes around him.

I want to say something witty back—believe me, when you're in the presence of God, you want to impress him—but I can think of nothing to say. Nothing. My mind goes blank, as though someone has pulled a plug at the back of my skull and let all of my intelligence drain away. My mouth struggles to form a word: nothing. Adair, patient, takes my hand to steady me.

Finally, I blurt out, "He's told me nothing about you." Well, it's true.

Nonplussed, he just nods his head. I suppose he's used to people saying stupid things when they first meet him. He pats the spot on the couch next to him, indicating that I should join him.

God works hard to put me at ease. He tells me about the origin of things: how he got the idea for cellular structure and waveforms and black holes, then goes on to explain why the giraffe has its long neck and the dodo went extinct. "It's all connected, you see. It all comes out of one calculation, like one gigantic formula," he says of his greatest creation, the universe. "That's the beauty of it. Once you set it in motion, there's no stopping it. Each step is inevitable; it all must play itself out," he finishes, and looks expectantly at me, as though he thinks that I understand his grand plan. As if—just like that—I am able to absorb the secret of creation and life, mysteries that have eluded the greatest minds since the dawn of civilization. God has just told me the thread on which all of life hangs— and I've forgotten it. In my panic, I've lost it.

Both Adair and God know that this is all beyond me. I'm blowing it, this audience with God, and the truly frightening part is that Adair's and my future happiness might depend on it. What if God is judging right now whether to grant Adair his freedom based on my reactions? What if God condemns Adair to the underworld for eternity because I am not good enough or smart enough for him, because I don't know how to behave or what to say?

They are staring at me, waiting for me to say something. I take a deep breath to steady my nerves and press my palms against my legs. Exhale. *Try not to think of him as God,* I tell myself. *Think of him as Adair's father.* A smile comes naturally to my lips and I turn to him. "Tell me what Adair was like as a little boy," I say. "If he ever was a little boy. I want to know everything about him."

There is a hint of delight in God's smile, as though he has been waiting a long time for someone to ask him this very question.

By the time God rises from the couch to bid us farewell, we have drunk our way through a tray of tea that magically appeared, and I've heard a half dozen stories of things Adair did in an earlier time, and it is quite apparent that God is very fond of Adair. As a matter of fact, Adair might be one of God's favorites. "A pleasure," God says to me as we part at the door. Adair gestures for me to wait a minute and then slips out the door behind him.

Adair spent the entire audience watching Lanore proudly. She would make a good queen—fair, kind, empathetic—but not, perhaps, of the underworld. He remembers some of the things he was forced to do as the king of the dead, judgments handed down, punishments meted out to obstinate souls who swore on their innocence even as they were sucked into the cold black maw of the cosmos or consigned to roast in eternal fire, or were sent to another, equally heartless fate. As one who is guilty of bending or breaking rules in order to survive on earth, Lanore is too forgiving to be queen. As one who has committed thousands of heartless acts during his time on earth, Adair flinches at the thought of returning to his throne and passing judgments on others. He's not hypocritical enough to think he has any right to condemn his fellow sinners. Perhaps there's a good reason why only a god sits on the throne here. You can't have been mortal and do this job.

In fact, Adair cannot even see Lanore choosing to *remain* in the underworld, let alone be queen. He remembers Persephone, the last queen: she may have reconciled herself to living in the underworld, but she was never happy. A strange deal had been worked out with the old man, where Persephone was allowed to leave her husband and return to the world for six months of every year. If she didn't have those months to look forward to, she probably would've willed herself to die, Adair thinks. It just goes to show that the old man isn't heartless. There might still be a way. He wouldn't want Adair, his favorite, to die of unhappiness.

Which happens. Even gods don't live forever, and they know it. The most determined ones will last a long time, for as long as a giant red sun, even longer. But the sad ones and the unhappy ones, they find a way to short-circuit their lives. Or disappear from the ranks suddenly, no explanations given, a replacement dug up from somewhere, a hasty appointment made.

Out in the hall, once the visit is over, the old man throws his arm around Adair's shoulders affectionately. "You're right—she's a lovely woman. I can see why you want to keep her."

Adair tugs on his thin beard. "I want more than to keep her," he says shyly. "I want to have children with her. . . . I will die without her."

"How human you have become," the old man says—and he doesn't mean it in a good way. The gods think themselves above men. To be human is to be weak and concerned only about one's self.

"I served you well in this position for a time, and you know it," Adair reminds him. He has to be careful; he can't risk making the old man mad at him. He needs the power above them all to release both him and Lanore from the underworld, as he's the only one who can. Adair knows they would not make the journey through the abyss.

He needs the old man, but at the same time, his famously short temper is burning up like a lit fuse. "You've always said that this is the hardest job in all the heavens. I've done my share: now is your chance to prove your generosity by granting my release."

"And what about your sister?" the old man counters wearily. "One could argue that she's served me more faithfully than you. *She* never ran away. *She* held down the fort while you shirked your responsibilities. Why shouldn't she be the one to get what she wants?"

"You're right; I left my post, but I did so out of principle. I could not wed my sister. And now I have fallen in love. Haven't you always said that love is your most perfect creation? That of all the things you made for man, love was your crowning gift? Why should only men be allowed to fall in love? Why should your greatest gift be reserved for men and not shared with the gods? You cannot fault me for falling in love. My sister is good and acting out of duty, but she isn't in love with me. Give her the chance to fall in love, too."

Exasperated, the old man throws up his hands. "I should

have made you the god of oratory and not the underworld. Tell me, what would you have me do?"

"Let us go," Adair implores. "Send us back. We'll live out our lives quietly among the mortals. You'll never hear from us again."

"And your sister?" he asks gruffly. "What about her? Is that really fair to her?"

Adair hangs his head. For that, he has no answer except that unfairness comes to all of us. For a god, she is young and her story isn't finished being told.

Changing his tactics, Adair asks, "Do you know what the difference is between man and god?" The old man shakes his head. Adair continues, "If it is within their power, most men will make the most humane choice every time. Not the ideal choice, perhaps, but the one that results in the greatest kindness. Whereas a god will not be swayed by humanity. An entire village will be wiped out by a tsunami, an entire race eradicated by disease or pestilence, if that is what fate demands. The gods are bound to uphold fate. We are *slaves* to fate." He knows the old man has made plenty of decisions like these, and even though he is a god, such inhumanity takes its toll. "For once in your life," he begs, "make the *humane* choice. Show compassion."

The old man shakes his head at Adair, dismayed. "*You* never would've shown compassion, in the past. You were the epitome of a god, my boy. Unswayable."

"And I was wrong."

The old man scratches the back of his head, shoulders rounded in a shrug. "You're putting me in a very bad spot."

Adair embraces him one last time, their whiskery cheeks

brushing. "I put our fate in your hands. I trust you will do the right thing." After all, what are gods for if not miracles?

"Is that it?" I ask Adair when he returns to the magically suspended room a few minutes later. "How will we know what he's decided? When will we know that he's made his decision?"

He is much calmer than I imagine possible and I want to interpret this as good news. Adair wraps an arm around my shoulders and squeezes me tight to him. "I have to believe that he's already made his decision, or otherwise—take it from me—things would've gone much more *badly*."

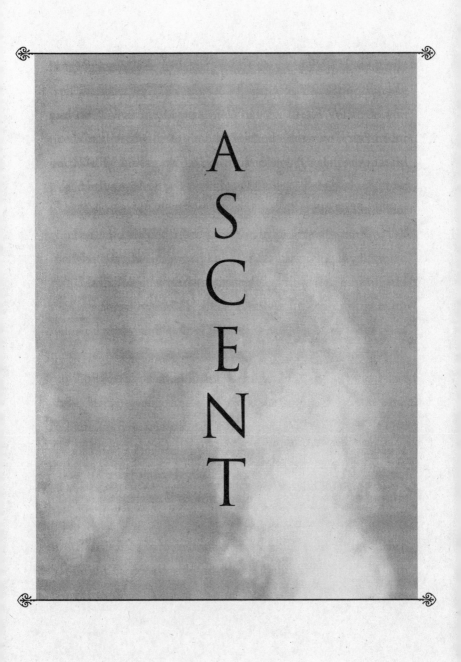

ASCENT

TWENTY-FOUR

I woke up in the fortress, back on the island, lying on a low bed made of cushions on the floor of Adair's study. Gulls called from out over the sea. It was daylight outside, and the bright white ocean light bouncing through the window lit up the entire room.

I sat bolt upright. My head sloshed as though I had a hangover. For no reason I could think of, I had the taste of seawater in my mouth.

Adair was lying on the floor next to me. He was very still. Dear God—I grabbed his arm: he felt cold and heavy. I shook him, jostling harder and harder when there was no response. *Wake up. You must wake up.*

His eyes popped open. I burst into tears.

He was up, comforting me in an instant. "Why are you

crying?" he said, trying to soothe me. "There is no reason to be sad. We've been returned. It's a miracle. We are the luckiest people in the history of the world."

He was right, of course. We were lucky. I threw my arms around his neck and blotted my tears on his collar. "I can't believe we're back, that's why I'm crying. He listened to you. He gave you what you asked for," I said.

"He isn't without a heart. I was just able to move him to use it."

"I don't understand. . . . These memories . . . how are we able to remember what happened in the underworld?"

"A gift, I imagine. I'm sure he wants for us to know exactly how generous he has been to us."

"And the queen—I suppose this means she'll rule alone?" I asked.

Adair gave me a sheepish look. "Not alone, not exactly. She has Jonathan with her, remember. I may have persuaded the old man to see Jonathan in a new light. You see, gods are made when a lucky confluence of conditions come together at the moment of creation. I think you could say that Jonathan was the product of one such lucky confluence: take his extraordinary beauty. I think that, under other circumstances, he might've been intended to be a god, perhaps even Eros, the god of desire. But waste not, want not; he was there in the underworld already—why not give him a try?"

"You persuaded the old man to make Jonathan your replacement? To be king of the underworld?" I said doubtfully. Adair had always teasingly called Jonathan "the Sun God." Maybe he'd had a sixth sense about it.

"You have to admit, there is a poetic justice to it," Adair said with a little smile. "He's been given tremendous privileges throughout his life, but for the first time, he will have to work hard for it."

We lay back on the bower of cushions and the cashmere blanket, shoulder to shoulder, in a square of strong white sunlight. It was a delicious moment of respite, a curiously normal moment of calm, and I think Adair and I came to the same conclusion at the same time: we were back on earth in the house where everything had started, but how did we know that anything had changed? We'd been returned to the land of the living, but beyond that, how did we know that we weren't exactly the same as we'd been before the journey?

"I want to see for myself," Adair said, determined. He sat up and reached to his desk and began searching with his fingertips for something on the desktop. After a moment of groping and cursing under his breath, he found it: a penknife. The tiny blade, with its ivory handle, seemed an anachronism, a device from another time.

He pressed the blade to the tip of an index finger until it pierced the skin. A corona of red welled to the spot. We held our breath and waited. A minute passed and the wound hadn't healed over yet. After another minute, a drop of blood rolled down his finger. The wound remained doggedly open.

"My God," he said, raising it to his mouth to suck on the wound. With a burst of alarm, I realized that Adair could be made to hurt now, to suffer, to feel the burr of pain from a headache, a broken bone, or a tumor. Now wasn't the time to turn my thoughts to the fragility of life, not when anything could press down and rupture our delicate human bodies, crush us like eggs, but I saw that I could lose Adair still. He could be taken away from me as swiftly as Luke had been.

I stared into his face and I knew that it had changed, almost unperceivably, but it had changed. I knew that soon time would be etched there, recorded in small lines near his eyes and mouth. It would come to me, too. We would see proof of time's progress on each other and would be forever reminded of the bargain we struck today.

He'd given up so much for me that it was nearly incomprehensible to grasp the scope of it. Who would give up everything for love? Give up infinite power, all of time? And in exchange for the precariousness of the human condition, illness and decay, never knowing which day would be your last. Still, he'd agreed to this because of me. Me. It was humbling. I felt grateful that Adair could love me so much.

Then it struck me, the tremendous responsibility that came with love. He'd traded the entirety of the cosmos for this world, the infinitely small and yet complete world that contained just him and me. Together, we would experience everything that world had to offer. We would have children and raise them together; we would grow old together, and one day we would die. We would experience a common, everyday life, and that was the true miracle of love, I saw. That two people could be the world to each other. We had only the days of one lifetime to dedicate to the task, and suddenly—after two centuries of living as though life would never end—that timeline felt ridiculously short, as though we'd been cheated. Would the days of one lifetime be enough? They would have to be.

Again, Adair seemed to read my mind. He took my hands and looked into my eyes. "We have a set number of days together now—and who knows how many—so we must always remember that our forever is the rest of our two lives, our two lives together. Are you ready to do this, to spend the rest of our lives together, Lanny my love?"

My love. Those words had never sounded better. I leaned into him. "Yes," I said, holding tightly to his arm as we lay back together on the cushions, bonded together for the rest of our lives. "Yes, I am."

ACKNOWLEDGMENTS

I'd like to thank the folks who brought The Taker Trilogy to life. First and foremost, my thanks to the family and friends who have been so supportive during the whole adventure. Special thanks once again to Eileen McGervey, and Terry and Lelia Nebeker from One More Page Books; fellow Washington-area authors Allison Leotta, Rebecca Coleman, Kathleen McCleary, and Rebecca York for reading pages and generally keeping my spirits up; Janet Cadsawan for her sage advice; and all the wonderful, enthusiastic book bloggers—especially Jennifer Lawrence and Swapna Krishna Lovin—who have been behind the books from day one.

Thank you to my fearless editor at Gallery, Tricia Boczkowski. To Louise Burke and Jen Bergstrom, my gratitude for their commitment to The Taker Trilogy. My thanks to everyone at Gallery for taking care of these books every step of the way: Alexandra Lewis, Mary McCue, Natalie Ebel, and Elana Cohen. Thanks also to Liz Perl, Jennifer Robinson, Wendy Sheanin, and Stuart Smith at Simon & Schuster for their incredible support.

Thanks to Anna Jean Hughes and now Georgina Hawtrey-Woore for seeing The Taker Trilogy through at Century/Random House UK. My sincere thanks to Giuseppe Strazzeri, Fabrizio Cocco, Valentina Fortichiari, and Tommaso Gobi at Longanesi for the wonderful time in Milan for the launch of *Immortal* (*The Taker*). Thanks to Milla Baracchini, Ana Prado, and Julian Cunha of Novo Conceito for the spectacular rollout of *Ladrão de Almas* (*The Taker*) in Brazil. I am grateful, as always, for Intercontinental Literary Agency work on my behalf, especially that of Nicki Kennedy, Sam Edenborough, and Katherine West, and to Gray Tan of the Grayhawk Agency.

And as always, I thank my husband, Bruce, for his love and support.

THE
DESCENT

ALMA KATSU

INTRODUCTION

For Lanore McIlvrae, immortality has been more of a curse than a blessing. It has distanced her from the rest of humanity and left her lonely and unhappy. Too, she has been haunted by guilt for the things she's done in order to survive. She's especially haunted by what she did to Jonathan, the first man she ever loved.

After being desired, scorned, and widowed throughout the hundreds of years of her life, the one thing she desires more than anything—to feel loved—has eluded her. In the conclusion to The Taker Trilogy, Lanore sets out on an epic mission to release Jonathan from the prison of the underworld. Just like immortality, the mission turns out to be more than she bargained for, and the powers of darkness threaten to snuff out her chances for true love once and for all.

TOPICS & QUESTIONS FOR DISCUSSION

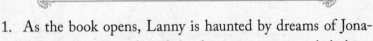

1. As the book opens, Lanny is haunted by dreams of Jonathan being tortured, and she determines to go to help him. Given the history of their relationship, what do you think compelled Lanny to pursue this mission? Would you have been willing to make the same choice?

2. Lanny convinces the captain of the boat she's hired to leave her on an island off the coast of Sardegna (Sardinia) where she hopes to find Adair. What does this decision reveal about Lanny and how she feels toward Adair? What did you feel as she got out of the boat and signaled the captain to leave? Would you want to be left on a seemingly barren island without any plan for an exit? Why or why not?

3. Why do you think Adair allowed Terry and Robin to stay on the island with him in spite of his suspicions about them? What role do they play in the story? What does it say about Adair that he was willing to risk their companionship?

4. In part, *The Descent* is an exploration of one of the great mysteries of life: what happens when we die? On page 37, Lanore describes the process of being with Luke during his final days. How did she respond to his imminent death? Have you been with someone at the moment of death? Do you agree with Lanny's observation that "they're afraid of what's coming, afraid and confused"? How do you feel about death? Have you contemplated your own mortality?

5. Lanny confesses that "Immortality had made me less human" and "robbed me of the ability to feel real emotion in the face of death." How do you feel about this tradeoff? Would you be willing to trade being fully human for the "gift" of immortality? Why or why not? Do you think people would behave differently if they knew they would never die?

6. At the point where Lanny asks Adair for his help to accomplish her mission of going to Jonathan, she realized that "Adair had truly changed." Do you agree? Describe. Had Lanny changed? Describe.

7. How does Adair's island home foreshadow his identity? What role does the weather on the island play in the story?

8. When Lanny arrives in the underworld, she initially is transported to various experiences and relationships from her past. What purpose did these travels serve in her journey? If you could travel to a prior time and place, what would it be and why?

9. During Savva's visit with Lanny, he says about Adair: "We're rarely attracted for the reasons we think. . . . There was something in him that we were looking for, each of us in our way." What do you think Lanny was looking for in her relationship with Adair? Did she find it?

10. Describe some of the qualities of Adair during his youth in Venice studying under the bishop and ultimately Cosimo. What was the main desire that fueled his hunger to learn alchemy? How was the profession of alchemy ultimately a cover for his true identity?

11. During Lanny's reunion with Luke in the underworld, she reflects that "being alone was what *I* feared most." Why do you think someone who was immortal would be afraid of being alone? What was her strategy to avoid aloneness? Is fear of being alone universal? Do you resonate with this fear? If so, what is your strategy to avoid it?

12. When Lanny finally meets Jonathan in the underworld, how is their reunion different from what she imagined? How does her journey to help him turn out to be ironic?

13. Do you think Lanny and Adair are capable of true love and fidelity to each other? Why or why not?

14. What was your response to the end of the story? How did it compare or contrast with your imagined ending?

15. What was your favorite scene or chapter in the book? Explain.

ENHANCE YOUR BOOK CLUB

1. Visit www.AlmaKatsu.com to learn more about the author and listen to an interview with her.

2. The author calls The Taker series "anti-romance" in that it reveals the dark side of love. Make a list of examples from the book that connect various characters' evil/dark actions to a corresponding desire to be loved. Discuss your lists at your next book club meeting. What do you learn or observe from this exercise about the human heart? How do the experiences of the characters in the story compare and contrast with your own experiences with love, or the experiences of people you know?

3. *The Descent* describes Eternity as a breaking apart and disintegration into absolute emptiness. Is this view of man's place in the cosmos similar to, or different from, that of religions with which you are familiar? Read *The Universe Next Door* by James Sire and contrast the various views of eternity presented. Which view most closely resembles your own? Discuss.

4. Make a list of the things you would do, risks you would take, places you would visit if you knew you were immortal. How is this list similar to or different from your actual bucket list?